Prai

"Suspenseful and well-written, *The Lonely Mile* shows how far a father will go to save his child."

—Debbi Mack, New York Times bestselling author of *Identity Crisis* and *Least Wanted*

"Written with edge-of-your-seat suspense and precise detail…The successor to Michael Crichton has landed. And his name is Allan Leverone."

—Vincent Zandri, Amazon bestselling author of *The Innocent* and *The Remains*

"Allan Leverone delivers a taut crime drama full of twists and conspiracy. A serial killer thriller with a heart."

—Scott Nicholson, Amazon bestselling author of *Liquid Fear*

"Allan Leverone raises the stakes with every turn of the page…"

—Sophie Littlefield, Anthony Award-winning author of *A Bad Day for Sorry*

"Thriller fans will enjoy Allan Leverone's new book, *The Lonely Mile*, which will carry readers along as a daughter is stolen by a vengeful serial killer."

—Dave Zeltserman, author of *Pariah* and *Monster*

"A dark and creepy chiller!"

—Ron Malfi, Bram Stoker Award-nominated author of *Floating Staircase*

"Fast-paced and eerily seductive, *Darkness Falls* is a well-told and atmospheric tale of loss and obsession, of madness and revenge. Allan Leverone is a terrific writer with a bright future…"

—Mark Edward Hall, author of *Apocalypse Island* and *The Lost Village*

"I was floored by the great writing…this book is a steal for anyone that is a fan of a good crime thriller."

—Book Sake

"…a chillingly realistic suspense thriller that will have you holding on for the ride of your life."

—Life in Review

"…this story drew me in, grabbed my attention and would let go until the very surprising and climactic ending…one hell of a roller coaster ride…"

—Café of Dreams Book Reviews

"...the suspense never stops...an intense thriller..."

—Martha's Bookshelf

"From page one to the end you will be breathless with suspense...simply an entertaining and enjoyable and intense story...This is one of the things that I love about book blogging—finding new authors from smaller presses that are true gems."

—My Reading Room

"...a must have for anyone looking for a great page turner with mystery and mayhem"

—Community Bookstop

"If you enjoy thrillers...this is a great option. It's a fast-moving storyline...and you'll find you care about the main characters..."

—My Book Retreat

"...feels like I'm watching an episode of 24. There is not a dull moment, and absolutely no lag time...The characters are well developed, and I find the plot easily believable and very easy to get absorbed in."

—Southern Fiber Reads

"…a high suspense thrill ride…"

—Derry (NH) News

"…keeps you on the edge of your seat, reading pages as fast as you can…I highly recommend that you read this book…you will not be disappointed."

—Two Ends of the Pen

"…absolutely fantastic…The story moves along at a good pace, dripping with atmosphere…The frights come at you hard and fast…A great story, believable characters, tension, atmosphere, frights galore, blood, and a nice twist at the end…"

—Literary Mayhem

"…the storyline was haunting and creepy…I would recommend *Darkness Falls* to anyone who enjoys a really nightmarish tale."

—Horrornews.net Book Reviews

Books by Allan Leverone

Final Vector

The Lonely Mile

Paskagankee

Novellas by Allan Leverone

Darkness Falls

Heartless

The Becoming

Short Story Collection

Postcards from the Apocalypse

REVENANT

ALLAN LEVERONE

With friendship + best wishes!

Allan Leverone

A PASKAGANKEE NOVEL

Copyright ©2012 by Allan Leverone

All rights reserved as permitted under the U.S. Copyright Act of 1976. No part of this publication may be used, reproduced, distributed or transmitted in any form or by any means, electronic or mechanical, including photocopying, recording, or by any information storage or retrieval system, without the written permission of the author, except where permitted by law, or in the case of brief quotations embodied in critical articles and reviews.

This is a work of fiction. Names, characters, places, and incidents either are the product of the author's imagination or are used fictitiously. Any resemblance to actual events, locales, or persons, living or dead, is unintended and entirely coincidental.

First edition: 2012 by Rock Bottom Books

Cover art by Neil Jackson

Print edition formatting by Robert Shane Wilson

No one exists on an island, but everyone needs a rock. My rock is my family: My wife, Sue, twenty-eight years and counting. My children, Stefanie, Kristin and Craig, three wonderful young adults who represent a legacy far better than any I could ever have dreamed of leaving. And my granddaughter, Arianna, for whom the future is limitless.

PROLOGUE
THREE MONTHS AGO

Don Running Bear's brakes screeched out a complaint as he pulled to a stop at the end of his dusty driveway. He shut down the engine and his ancient Chevy pickup kicked and bucked like a temperamental stallion, eventually giving up the ghost and wheezing into silence.

He sat in the cab and mopped his face with a well-worn handkerchief. Faded renderings of sacred Navajo animals covered the light cotton, dulled by the passage of time from white to a sickly greyish-brown. The hankie had been a gift from his grandfather and was now threadbare and clearly past the end of its useful life. Don knew he should take some action to preserve it, maybe store it between the pages of a book or something, but he had used the damn thing for as long as he could remember and could not imagine going through even a single day without being able to touch the only remaining link to the man he so admired.

The temperature outside the pickup had soared to well over one hundred degrees, which meant inside the truck it was probably close to one-forty, but Don was in no hurry to get into his house, despite the fact the air conditioning would provide a welcome respite from this blast-furnace heat. Don needed to think, and to do that he had to be alone. So he sat in his truck, barely noticing the sweat running down his weathered copper face.

Don Running Bear was worried. He hadn't been sleeping well, being assaulted nightly by dreams filled with violence and bloodshed, nightmares which were clearly meant as a sign. And worse, the problem was not that he didn't understand the significance of his terrible dreams, but rather that he feared he did. In these visions, all of them disturbingly similar, a beautiful young Navajo girl wrought death and destruction, murdering strangers and cracking open their cold corpses, plunging her tiny hand inside their chests, ripping out the hearts of her victims, then turning to dust and disappearing.

In these horrifying dreams, the identity of the young girl refused to reveal itself to Don, although she seemed strangely familiar and he knew he should recognize her. Each morning he awoke trembling, drenched in sweat, certain that with just a little extra effort he might be able to identify the girl, and maybe then begin to decipher the meaning of the nightmares. But so far, her face had remained elusive.

Don wished he could turn back time and salvage a few hours with his grandfather. Niyol Running Bear had died more than a decade ago, and with his passing, so too had many of the mystical secrets of the tribal medicine man been lost. Niyol had adamantly refused to share his wisdom and knowledge with his son, Nastas—Don's father—saying only that the knowledge was explosive and dangerous and he would not involve his family in any more of it than necessary.

Nastas had died young, killed in a horrific car crash driving drunk at a high rate of speed on the reservation, leaving only Don and his grandfather, and when Niyol had become seriously ill, he had reluctantly entrusted a very valuable relic—a stone—to Don, telling him only that it was to be hidden and protected at all costs, that it was sacred, imbued with ungodly power, magical and fearsome and terrible.

Don had been thinking a lot recently of both his grandfather and the stone. He wondered if the nightmares he had begun experiencing were somehow related to one or both of them. He suspected they were, but since his grandfather had never gone into specifics regarding the danger the stone represented or its awesome power, Don could do no more than guess. But the very fact he associated his dreams with the stone after Niyol had been gone a decade illustrated the impression the old man had made.

Don Running Bear sighed and stepped out of his truck. Dwelling on the dreams and their possible relation to the sacred stone, long tucked securely away, was pointless without further information, and he had no way of acquiring that information. He vowed to let it go, to forget about the damned stone, but he had made that vow hundreds of times, probably thousands, and knew he would never be able to follow through on it. The hot, dry wind which seemed to blow endlessly across the plains raised little eddies of dust around his shoes as he trudged across the front yard.

He stepped through the front door into the cool stillness of his small home, distracted and upset. He made it two full steps inside the house and then froze in confusion and fear. Seated directly across the room, facing the door so there was no way Don could miss the sight of them, were his wife and teenage daughter. They had been fastened to matching kitchen chairs placed side by side, immobilized by thick strips of shiny silver duct tape wound around their wrists and ankles. Don regarded his family in surprise and they stared back in terror, eyes bulging, utterly silent despite the fact they had not been gagged.

Behind the two women, looming over them in a stool taken from the breakfast bar in the kitchen, was a middle-aged man Don had never seen before. The silver haired intruder displayed a long, curved knife, holding it above Eagle Wing's and Kai's heads, turning it slowly in the air so that the sunlight pouring through the window winked and glittered off the polished blade's surface. If the man was trying to get Don's attention, his efforts had been terrifyingly successful.

For a long moment no one moved. Time seemed to stretch into infinity. The stranger lowered the knife blade so that its razor-sharp point pressed against the soft skin of his younger captive's throat.

Eagle Wing gasped softly and Don finally spoke. "What's going on here?" He worked hard to keep his voice strong and calm, fearing he knew the answer to the question but asking it anyway. Sometimes life's little dramas must play out according to a script written by fate. He forced himself to direct his full attention at the man, not because he wanted to, but because he suspected that to do otherwise would be consigning his family to death.

"It's very simple," the stranger said, maintaining a steady pressure with the knife-blade at Eagle Wing's throat. "An item of great value was entrusted to your care many years ago. You're going to give it to me."

Don had an instant to decide how to respond. What were the odds the man with the knife was talking about anything other than the sacred Navajo stone? Essentially nil. But for the heavy weight of responsibility his grandfather had laid on his shoulders, Don Running Bear was an ordinary Native American man living an ordinary life. He was the proprietor of the reservation's General Store, a nearly invisible forty year old man who owned nothing of monetary value, certainly nothing worth breaking into his home and threatening murder to get.

Nothing except the stone.

And it was imperative the stone never see the light of day.

"I don't know what you're talking about," he said evenly, and as he did, the man's lips hardened into a thin bloodless line and he flicked his right wrist, drawing the tip of the knife-blade half an inch across Eagle Wing's throat. Blood welled sluggishly out of a tiny gash. Eagle Wing drew in a breath, a short, panicked gasp, but seemed to realize instinctively that to scream, or even to move, would be to risk suffering much greater damage, perhaps even death.

Kai Running Bear knew no such thing. Don's wife let loose a roar of rage and fear, thrashing helplessly in her chair in a desperate attempt to launch herself at the silver-haired man harming her child. The man rotated his left arm at the elbow, still holding the knife to Eagle Wing's throat, and drove his fist into Kai's face. The crack of her cheekbone shattering was followed by a dull thud as the chair and its suddenly unconscious occupant smashed backward onto the living room floor.

Don rushed forward instinctively, stopping only when the man with the knife leapt from the stool and screamed, "Come any closer and she dies!" and Don knew he meant what he said. The stranger's eyes were black and determined and devoid of any shred of compassion or empathy. He might as well have been a Diamondback coiled under a rock in the desert, alert and lurking, prepared to strike.

For one second, then two, the men faced each other, locked in a silent standoff. Kai lay motionless on the floor, duct-taped to her toppled chair, her face already beginning to swell hideously. Eagle Wing panted, the point of the knife pressed into her throat, her body shaking as it reacted to the stress and the pain of the knife wound, as well as the sight of her unconscious and badly injured mother.

"Now," the man said almost conversationally, "the next few seconds will determine the fate of your entire family. Do not make the mistake of assuming I won't simply murder all three of you. I know that the object I seek is here somewhere; you would never risk storing it anywhere else. If necessary, I will kill you all and then conduct my own search at my leisure. So I ask one final time: Where is it?"

Don wondered what his grandfather would have done. The danger the stone represented was monumental; he could not allow it to fall into this man's hands. But he *would* not allow his family to be butchered, either. In the end it was an easy decision; it was no decision at all.

Don held his hands in front of his face, palms out, willing the stranger to relax. He could see the knife blade bobbing in a steady rhythm against the soft skin of Eagle Wing's throat, keeping time with her elevated pulse. "You win. I'll do as you wish," he said quietly. He began sliding sideways across the room, moving on the balls of his feet, hands still suspended in front of his face, never taking his eyes off the man with the knife.

At the far end of the room he stopped in front of a flat-screen television placed atop an imitation wood-grain TV table. The table supporting the television was mounted on casters and Don bent at the waist, wrapped his arms around the table, and rolled it heavily to the side. The intruder watched from behind Eagle Wing's chair, his face expressionless, his reptilian eyes taking it all in. On the floor, Kai moaned and shuddered and then once again fell still.

Don knelt down on the spot formerly occupied by the TV table and hooked his fingers under what appeared at first glance to be a knot in the oak flooring. He lifted his hand and a hidden two-foot by two-foot hinged wooden square rose noiselessly, appearing as if out of nowhere. Bolted to the support beams beneath the floor with a pair of heavy iron bands was a personal safe, installed so that the safe's door opened upward into the room upon removal of the trap door.

Don hesitated, still searching for a way out of this predicament that didn't involve releasing the sacred stone to this stranger. He could think of only one. He glanced up at the man, sighed, and punched a series of numbers into a small alphanumeric keypad built into the safe's door. Then he twisted a heavy handle and the lock gave way with an authoritative *clunk* that Don knew would be audible all the way across the room in the heavy silence.

He pulled open the door and reached inside. The safe's contents were mostly obscured by shadows but it didn't matter. The heavy steel box contained only two items and Don knew the positions of both in the darkness of the safe like he knew the back of his hand. He bent down, maneuvering his body so that its bulk formed a barrier between the stranger and the safe. At least he hoped it did, or else he was condemning his beloved daughter, his only child, to a sudden and painful death.

Don withdrew the two items simultaneously. One was a perfectly square wooden box, roughly ten inches by ten inches. It could have been a cigar box on steroids. Intricate Native American carvings of Southwestern animals decorated all sides of the box, similar in style and rendering to the ones adorning Don's treasured bandanna. He lifted that item slowly and carefully with his left hand, while slipping the other item into the right front pocket of his cargo pants, praying the movement would go unnoticed. Then he stood and turned.

The man removed his knife from Eagle Wing's throat for a moment and flicked his wrist, much as he had done moments ago when he nicked her, only this time he waved the knife in the air, indicating Don should bring him the box. He said nothing.

Don trudged across the room while the man returned the knife to its previous location, nestling it just under his daughter's jawline. Don noted with relief that the cut the man had made was mostly for show; it had nearly stopped bleeding already. But there was little doubt he could end her life at any moment if he so desired.

Don stopped directly in front of Eagle Wing's chair. Her eyes were closed and she was making an obvious effort to breathe normally. He was filled with pride for his sixteen year old child's demonstration of composure and inner strength. He knew his grandfather would have been proud of her as well.

"Open it," the man commanded.

Slowly, with extreme reluctance, as if by drawing the moment out he might somehow be able to prevent it from happening, Don lifted the hinged lid.

Inside the box was a stone, larger than a baseball but only slightly. The stone was perfectly round and smooth, as though it had been lovingly polished by its owner until it gleamed, although it had not been. He was aware of no more than a small portion of the stone's history, but the knowledge he had was enough to give Don Running Bear a healthy respect for its fearsome power. He had opened the box only rarely, and never for more than a few minutes at a time, since Eagle Wing was a very young girl.

The man's cold eyes flicked from the contents of the box to Don's face and back again. "Is that it? It just looks like a rock."

"You think I would keep an ordinary rock locked up in a hidden safe?"

The man gazed at Don, taking stock. Don stood impassively, the box held out in front of him, waiting. "You understand what will happen to your family if I am being misled." It was not a question.

Don shook his head in frustration. "You're not being misled, I told you that already."

"Do you understand what will happen to your family if I am being misled?"

"Yes, yes, I understand! Please, if the stone is what you're after, just take it and go, so I can tend to my wife and child. They need me."

The stranger's eyes bored into Don's and for a long time neither man spoke. Nobody moved. Eagle Wing sat still under the knife blade, although her eyes were now open. They were trusting and guileless as she watched her father. Don loved those eyes. On the floor, Kai groaned and twitched, pulling against her bindings. She was still unconscious but would be coming around shortly and would need medical attention for the shattered bones in her face.

At last the man seemed satisfied. "Put the box over there," he said, indicating a small butcher-block end table adorned with only a lamp. The table was located between the couch and the front door. Don eased the box's lid closed, relieved not to have to look at its contents any longer, and turned his back, walking slowly toward the couch and placing the box next to the lamp as instructed.

"Now, go back to the safe. Close it and lock it and lower the trap door." After Don had complied, the man said, "Roll the TV table back where it belongs," and he did that, too.

"Now, stand in the corner." Don moved to the point in the room opposite the front door. He hoped the stranger would not force him to turn around and face the wall. If he did, all would be lost. He arrived in the corner and stood facing the man, who said nothing about turning around.

The man withdrew the knife from Eagle Wing's throat and Don breathed a sigh of relief. He had feared the intruder would try to kill them all before leaving with the box, but it seemed the man realized he would be in for the fight of his life if he murdered Don's daughter in front of his eyes, and it appeared he wanted simply to take the box and make his escape.

The stranger slid off the stool, knife held chest-level between his body and Eagle Wing's. He sidled around her chair and then began backing toward the door, never taking his eyes off Don Running Bear.

Don waited, not moving, forcing himself to maintain his impassive appearance, wondering how the hell he was managing to do it when his heart was hammering in his chest like a freight train pounding across the desert floor. At some point, the man with the knife was going to have to turn slightly to open the door, and Don had decided that was when he would make his move.

The stranger arrived at the end table, moving slowly and cautiously. He bent and hefted the wooden box containing the mystical stone. "It's lighter than I would have expected," he announced to Don, who said nothing in return. Then the man swiveled his head to the right, reaching for the knob to open the front door.

The moment the man turned his head, Don snaked his right hand into his pocket and grasped the Colt .38 revolver he had removed from the safe. His plan, if you could call it that, was to rip his grandfather's gun out of his pocket and fire in one smooth motion, hopefully putting the man down. Even if he missed with the first shot, Don reasoned, the suddenness of the attack should catch the man by surprise, giving him the opportunity to fire again before the man could move in and either gut him with the knife or slice Eagle Wing's throat open. Not a perfect plan, not by a long shot, but it was the best he could come up with.

And it might even have worked.

Except the gun's hammer snagged on the metal ring holding the General Store's keys. The ring hung from his belt loop and as Don pulled the big pistol out of his pocket, the hammer caught on it for an instant, not a long time at all, maybe half a second, but it was enough to twist the barrel toward the floor where Kai lay taped to her chair.

Don cursed, yanking the gun up toward its target and squeezing the trigger. Against all odds, he hit the exact spot he was aiming for, too, but the man with the knife was no longer there. He had dived toward the floor and into the middle of the room the moment he saw the Colt appear. His reflexes were razor-sharp. The wooden box fell off the table and the stone rolled out of it, spinning on the floor like a top.

A loud *Boom!* shook the tiny house on its foundation and the acrid smell of smoke filled the air. A ragged, splintered hole appeared in the front door where until a split second ago the man had been standing. Don cursed again without realizing he was doing it and adjusted his aim, preparing to fire a second shot, knowing everything was going to hell, knowing he was already too late.

The man rolled onto his back, less than a foot behind the injured Kai Running Bear. He flipped the knife in his hand, grabbing it by the blade without even looking at it, and with one smooth, easy motion, fired it at Don, who tried to flinch out of the way but didn't stand a chance. The knife rocketed through the air with stunning speed, striking Don in the middle of the chest.

Pain blasted through his rib cage and he felt his arm

go numb as he toppled to the floor. He heard the big Colt clatter to the floor as well, sliding across the polished oak and coming to rest in the corner.

The stranger rose and stepped calmly over Kai, whose eyelids were fluttering and who appeared to be on the verge of regaining consciousness just as her husband lost it. Don watched helplessly as the man stopped above him. The stranger stared for a moment, a contemptuous sneer on his hard face, then reached down and pulled the knife out of Don's chest, twisting it viciously as he did so. Don screamed in pain and saw blood spurt frighteningly from the wound. Somewhere in the background he could hear Eagle Wing screaming as well, like they were performing some crazy duet from hell.

The man wiped the knife blade on Don's shirt, which was already becoming soaked with his own blood. He retraced his path, stepping over Kai again, and picked up the stone. He replaced it in the ornate wooden box and secured the lid. Then he calmly looked the room over one more time and stepped through the front door.

The last thing Don Running Bear heard before losing consciousness was the rumble of an engine starting up and a car driving slowly away.

1

PRESENT DAY

Hank Williams—senior, not junior; the *real* Hank Williams—blasted through the ancient speakers of the Ridge Runner, warbling about love and loss and liquor, not necessarily in that order, his vocal stylings floating through the tavern like a little slice of down-home heaven. Earl Manning held down his usual stool and drained the last of a Budweiser, simultaneously signaling for another with his left hand as he slammed the empty mug down on the table with his right. The smoke of a dozen lit cigarettes hung thick and heavy in the unmoving stale air. Smoking in bars and restaurants was against the law in Maine, but nobody cared about such minor details inside the Ridge Runner.

Earl had lost track a couple of hours ago of how many beers he had drunk, not that it mattered. He would continue drinking until one of two things happened: He ran out of money or the bar closed. Right now the two outcomes were running neck and neck, although drinking through all his money seemed to be pulling ahead in a race that would likely come down to the wire.

Earl had been a regular at the Ridge Runner for so long no one dared consider sitting in his spot, even when he wasn't there. Far end of the bar, wobbly two-person table kitty-corner across the room from the entrance. Close to the john, far enough from the door to be out of the firing line of the almost lethal gusts of frigid air that swept into the room any time a patron entered or exited from late October through late April, day or night. Winter was by far the longest of the four seasons in Paskagankee, Maine.

Bartender and longtime Ridge Runner owner Bo Pellerin slopped a fresh beer on the table as Billy Ray Cyrus—the *real* Cyrus, not wannabe rock-star daughter Miley—whined and complained about his achy-breaky heart, whatever the hell that meant. Earl Manning considered himself something of an expert in the field of achy-breaky hearts, as his last trip to the doctor, roughly three years ago, had resulted in a stern warning from the old quack to slow his drinking pace. Earl didn't think that was what Billy Ray was talking about.

Actually, "Stop drinking entirely," was what the quack doctor had said, "before all that alcohol kills you." The guy spun some bullshit about mitral and tricuspid valve deficiencies and plaque buildup in the arteries— apparently Earl's achy-breaky heart had less to do with love and loss than a weakening muscle critical to the body's continued operation, at least if he believed the quack, which he didn't—just before hitting him with almost a three hundred dollar charge. Earl had ignored the outrageous bill just as he had ignored the diagnosis, vowing at that time never to return to the fucking quack's office.

That was three years ago, and look at him, still sitting at his table just beyond the far end of the bar, still drinking—more, if anything, not less—and still very much alive. Sure, he suffered from the shakes some mornings (most mornings if he was being honest with himself); and sure, there were those disconcerting moments when he had trouble catching his breath climbing a normal flight of stairs and was forced to stop and rest halfway, but that sure as hell wasn't due to heart trouble. After all, Earl reasoned, he was only in his late twenties, and achy-breaky hearts were for geezers, Billy Ray Cyrus's opinion on the matter notwithstanding.

The front entrance swung open and then slammed closed. Earl barely noticed. It was almost midnight and the Runner was hopping, so the damned door seemed to be on a swivel, anyway. Plus it was early summer, meaning the cold air that normally accompanied the arrival of a new patron had gone on vacation for a few months. It would be back soon enough, but for now, the only things that might have entered the bar were a new customer and a few mosquitoes, and Earl couldn't care less about either one. As long as he could still get Bo's attention when his thirst demanded another beer, he didn't give a damn if Billy Ray Cyrus himself had just walked in.

His disinterest didn't last long, though. He glanced

up, bleary-eyed, and discovered it was a woman who had entered, a woman he did not recognize, and a beautiful one at that. Aside from Blanche Raskiewicz, who had been frequenting the Runner longer than Earl and whose skin was so weathered and dried out it looked like her face had been patched together out of strips of old leather, the "fairer sex" tended to stay away from the Ridge Runner. It was not an establishment that saw many female faces.

Especially female faces like this one.

The woman was young and beautiful. Long jet-black hair cascaded in waves halfway down her back, terminating in lazy ringlets a few inches north of her butt, which was accentuated in skin-tight faded jeans with no visible panty lines. Earl knew because it was the first thing he checked. His eyes might be red-rimmed from all the Budweiser and he might almost have reached the point where he would soon begin seeing double, but he was as much an expert in panty lines as he was in achy-breaky hearts, and he would have bet his miserable life this chick wasn't wearing any.

The face framed by that black hair could fairly be described as angelic, with flawless copper skin, a delicate, slightly upturned nose and the most intense green eyes Earl had ever seen. Her mouth was a slash of vivid red as she pursed her lips in concentration, walking slowly through the crowd, clearly searching for someone specific. Ridge Runner patrons parted before the beautiful young woman like the Red Sea before Moses. She didn't seem to notice. She was probably used to it.

She meandered through the bar and the raucous cacophony of drunken voices dimmed, eventually fading away entirely. Even the music seemed to have stopped for the time being. An occasional cough and the shuffling of boots on the dirty floor were the only sounds. Earl wondered who the lucky bastard was that she was looking for and, more importantly, why. He knew pretty much everyone in here, and all of these dumb fucks put together didn't have the class this babe had in her little finger. That much was obvious.

Earl didn't care how classy she was, though. He had a prime view of this chick's pantiless ass and that was good enough for him. She had made a hard right turn after entering the bar and was moving steadily counterclockwise around the outside of the room, still searching, peering left and right as she walked. Soon she would pass directly in front of Earl's mesmerized face and shortly after that would be right back at the front door where she started.

Obviously, the guy she was looking for wasn't here, which was hard to believe. Earl figured if *he* was the lucky son of a bitch who had made plans to meet up with this hot piece of ass at the Ridge Runner, he would camp out a couple of days in advance, just to be sure he didn't miss her. Although, in his case, that wouldn't have meant doing much of anything different than usual. His waking hours more or less coincided with the Runner's hours of operation, anyway.

The girl reached Earl's rickety table and instead of continuing past as he assumed she would, she took a seat, easing onto the empty chair next to him and fixing him with a stare from those curiously green eyes. They were spellbinding, and it took a few seconds for Earl's brain to process the fact that she had just spoken to him. "Uh . . . 'scuse me?"

A knowing smile flitted across her face, as if she had this effect on men all the time. Probably she did. "I said hello," she repeated. "How are you doing tonight?"

"Just great. Getting better all the time, in fact." It finally occurred to a stunned Earl Manning that *he* was the one she had been searching out, as hard as that was to believe.

"Buy you a drink?" Earl asked, frantically attempting some basic math in his alcohol-addled brain. He wasn't sure he had enough cash left to buy anything for this gorgeous specimen, but didn't really care, either. If he couldn't pay that asshole Bo Pellerin at closing time he would worry about it then.

"White wine would be lovely," she said, still smiling, her eyes locked onto Earl's. God, but they were captivating.

Earl signaled Bo and the bartender approached with a look of incredulous disbelief written all over his face. Earl figured the same look was probably on his own face. "White wine for my friend, please," he said, wondering if anyone had ever ordered wine before inside the Ridge Runner.

For just a moment he thought Pellerin was going to make some sort of wise-ass remark. The bar's owner didn't, though. Instead he turned without a word and walked back behind the bar. Bo grabbed a dusty bottle Earl had never noticed before off one of the mirrored shelves and poured the contents into what Earl guessed was a wine glass. Who the hell knew? Hopefully the damned thing was at least clean, although the prospect seemed unlikely.

Bo placed the glass in front of the chick and walked

away and Earl realized he had no idea what to say next. He wracked his slow-moving brain as panic threatened to overwhelm him. This was the most stunningly beautiful girl he had ever had a shot with. The only other one who even came close was that bitch Sharon Dupont, and that had been a long, long time ago, back when she was still a high school kid, years before she had kicked her drinking habit and become a cop, of all things.

His mind snapped back to the present, and to the awful knowledge that if he didn't say something soon, preferably something suave or at the very least semi-coherent, this gorgeous babe was going to think he was mute and maybe mentally deficient, too. The only thing he could think of was, "Do you come here often?" which was pointless. For one thing he already knew the answer to that particular question, and for another he realized, even in his present state of drunkenness and rising panic, it was the most clichéd pickup line in the book.

She saved him.

"So, do you come here often?" she asked, and coming from her it sounded like the wittiest conversation-starter ever. Bo Pellerin dropped the wine bottle down on the bar with a thud and walked away, shaking his head as he went. The girl continued gazing at him, smiling softly, acting like he was Jake Freaking Gyllenhall or something, rather than what he was: a twenty-nine year old rail-thin raging alcoholic with bad skin and a balky heart sitting in a dive bar in the middle of God-forsaken nowhere, a rifle shot from the Canadian border.

"Yes, as a matter of fact, I do," he answered, surprising himself by speaking clearly and not slurring his words. He wondered how long he could keep up *that* little bit of verbal gymnastics. "But I know you don't; I would definitely have remembered you." Earl had no idea what the hell was going down here, but he was determined to ride this train all the way to the station, and felt like he was doing a pretty damned good job so far, even if all he really was doing was hanging on for dear life and waiting to see what would happen next.

She sipped her wine and Earl gulped his beer. "I've been looking all over for you," she said, as if they were a couple, rather than total strangers, as if it was perfectly normal for a model-beautiful young woman to be sitting here in the Ridge Runner chatting up a loser like Earl Manning. He was acutely aware that every man in the place—*every single one*—was watching them like some practical joke was being played and they didn't want to look away because they were afraid they might miss the punch line. For just a second Earl wondered if that might be the case.

"Is that right?" he finally ventured. "Well, now that you've found me, what are you going to do with me?"

"Everything." She smiled suggestively, placing her hand lightly on his arm. Earl thought briefly he might lose it right then and there, and wouldn't that be hilarious?

"Wh-whass your name?" he asked, his diction finally betrayed by the combination of nerves and drunkenness. He was a little surprised it had taken this long.

"Raven," she said, acting as though she didn't notice his little slip-up, although it had to have been obvious. The young woman finally dragged her gaze away from Earl's face and glanced disinterestedly around the bar, only now seeming to realize that they weren't alone. Earl thought it might be the strangest thing he had ever seen. Of course, this whole bizarre episode would probably qualify.

Raven leaned over, supporting herself by placing one delicate hand in Earl's lap, instantly bringing him dangerously close to losing it again. She whispered into his ear, "What do you say we get out of here and get started? I don't think I can wait much longer." Her voice was soft and girlish and Earl would have sworn her breath shuddered a little with anticipation. Or maybe that was his.

"Okay," he agreed, rising unsteadily to his feet and reaching into his pocket. He pulled out all of his money and tossed it onto the table, not counting it, not even looking at it. He didn't care how much was there. If it was more than he owed for this night of drinking then that asshole Pellerin could treat himself to a nice, undeserved tip.

Raven looped her arm through his and began walking toward the front door, leading Earl through the crowd of disbelieving drinkers. Again they parted at her approach and again she seemed unaware. Earl took the opportunity to slip his left hand into the left rear pocket of her jeans. They were so tight he had to work to slide it in, but he figured it was well worth the effort.

The rickety wooden screen door slammed closed as they walked into the gravel parking lot, Raven moving confidently and Earl half-stumbling along behind, hand jammed into her back pocket, feeling like a guy who has just found out he won the lottery even though he didn't buy a ticket. The buzz of excited conversation swelled behind them and then faded with the closing of the door.

The darkness became more pronounced as the pair moved away from the dirty lighting of the tavern. Bo

Pellerin had once confided in Earl that he didn't see the need for exterior lighting in the Ridge Runner's lot—not many women came here and most of the ones who did, well, Bo seemed to feel were better-looking in the dark, anyway. Dudes could damn well find their own way to their vehicles. Plus, floodlights were too fucking expensive to maintain.

Most of the time Earl didn't even notice the darkness as he made his way to his fifteen-year-old Ford pickup. Hell, by closing time he was almost always blind drunk anyway, so what difference would lights make? Tonight, though, maybe as a reaction to the strange turn of events, he felt a shiver of fear worm its way into his gut. Anything could be out here. Anything.

Raven tugged insistently on his arm and, seeming to sense his trepidation, whispered, "Please lover-boy, don't make me wait. Stop teasing me!" And just like that, Earl Manning forgot all about the darkness and what it may or may not contain.

The beautiful girl pulled him right past his truck, continuing on to a candy-apple red Porsche 911 parked at the outer edge of the lot next to the massive, looming northern Maine forest. She unlocked the passenger side door with a button on her key fob and dumped Earl into the leather bucket seat, then somehow managed to squeeze in too, falling into his lap and giving him a hard kiss, pressing her body into his.

Then she was up and gone, moving around the little car and sliding into the driver's seat with the speed and grace of a feline. "Where are we going?" Earl asked, more out of a desire to make conversation than because he really gave a shit.

Raven smiled but didn't immediately respond. She pressed a finger to his lips. "You'll see soon enough, lover-boy. And I promise, this will be a night you will never forget."

She turned the key and the engine started with a purr and the young woman gunned the Porsche out of the lot, spraying gravel, peppering the vehicles—mostly pickup trucks—clustered outside the bar. Earl Manning's last thought before he fell asleep was that this whole bizarre episode was like some teenager's wet dream.

2

"Help me with him, for crying out loud," Raven grumbled. "He might look like a bag of bones but he's still heavy!"

Max Acton ignored the petulance in her tone and strolled out the front door of the crumbling, two-story Victorian home. He had watched from the living room window as she leapt from the driver's seat of the Porsche with her peculiar, cat-like grace and crossed in front of the car to the passenger's side. Now he smiled in amusement at the sight of the tiny young woman grabbing their sleeping target by both shoulders and shaking him awake, tugging on his arms insistently, trying to pull him out of the vehicle.

It had taken exhaustive research followed by months of surveillance to narrow the list of potential subjects down to Earl Manning. Paskagankee was a small and isolated community, but even in a town this small, dozens of men fit the profile Acton was looking for, and selecting the proper target was not a decision to be rushed into or taken lightly.

In the end, though, it had come down to Manning. The loser in this particular sweepstake was relatively young and in apparently decent physical condition, despite years of heavy drinking. He was single, a loner with no wife or girlfriend, no steady job, and only a broken-down alcoholic mother to raise the alarm when he suddenly vanished. Max knew the cops would pay little attention to her.

The only real cause for concern regarding Earl Manning's suitability as a test subject was his past relationship with a female Paskagankee police officer, a beautiful young woman named Sharon Dupont. The last thing Max Acton needed was some ex-lover cop digging into Manning's disappearance, unearthing—Max smiled to himself at the pun—things that were best left undisturbed.

The more research Max conducted, though, the clearer it became that this Dupont bitch would be a non-factor. The relationship—such as it was—between the cop and Max's chosen test subject had taken place years before, while the girl was still in high school, and had been based more upon a shared passion for alcohol and getting high than on any kind of mutual love or respect. Dupont had gone on to straighten her life out, eventually attending the FBI Academy before eventually returning to Paskagankee to care for her terminally ill father.

Now, all indications were that Officer Sharon Dupont had become involved with the Paskagankee Chief of Police, Mike McMahon, leaving little doubt she had left her tenuous connection with Earl Manning behind forever. Of course, Max knew that if he was wrong, he would be inviting trouble of the worst sort, but the fact of the matter was that eventual police involvement was inevitable. There was no way around it. Even if they avoided arousing suspicion with Manning's disappearance, when Max began putting his plan in motion an investigation would definitely be launched.

The goal was simply to avoid the appearance that anything was amiss for as long as possible, and to leave nothing tying Max Acton to the fallout when the authorities did become involved. Earl Manning seemed to be the subject who would best allow him to accomplish this goal, so Earl Manning it was, despite his long-ago ties to a member of the Paskagankee Police Department.

In a way, Max was comforted by his discovery of Sharon Dupont's alcoholic past. He had seen Officer Dupont around town, and her beauty was truly breathtaking. She was perhaps the equal of Raven in the looks department and it was a rare woman who could make that claim. The connection between a pretty go-getter like Sharon Dupont and an alcoholic loser like Earl Manning had initially mystified Max. There was no accounting for taste, though, as the old saying went, and his discovery of Dupont's alcoholism explained a lot. Addicts liked to hang together.

Max stood back a couple of paces and watched Raven struggle to remove Manning from the Porsche. The subject had been roused from his torpor but still seemed logy. Manning peered around confusedly, clearly attempting to get his bearings but just as clearly unable to do so. Max wasn't surprised. He had leased a home in one of the most out-of-the-way, obscure little corners of an out-of-the-way, obscure little town. It was entirely possible, likely even, that Earl Manning had never seen the house or even visited this area despite being a life-long resident of Paskagankee.

Raven grabbed Manning by the elbow, yanking, pulling the drunk out of the car with surprising strength for such a delicate-looking woman. The drunken man scrabbled for purchase as he exited, trying to get his feet underneath his body, standing too soon and smacking his head against the car's frame with a loud *clunk*.

"Come on baby, slow down," he protested, rubbing one hand vigorously over what was going to be a good-sized bruise on his forehead. "We'll get started soon enough, don't you worry, I'm gonna—" He froze when he saw Max in the shadows and began backing up, shrugging out of Raven's grasp. Only now did he seem to suspect that his anticipated night of passion was never going to happen. But now, of course, was much too late for this potentially life-saving insight to make any difference.

Max moved forward quickly and flanked Manning on the left, leaving Raven to steady his right elbow, and together they began escorting their guest across the driveway in front of the Porsche and up the cracked flagstone walkway toward the front door.

"What's this all about?" the drunk sputtered, turning his attention to Raven and in the process spraying her with spittle. She grimaced and wiped a palm over her face and didn't answer.

He looked to his left. "Who are you?" he asked Max, who didn't have to wipe any saliva off his face but who didn't answer, either. They were moving quickly, taking advantage of the surprise factor to hustle their guest into the house. He would be joining them inside now no matter what—that particular die had been cast the moment Manning joined the seductive Raven in the Porsche—but the farther they could move things along before he got truly frightened rather than just angry and confused, the easier and more painless the whole process would be.

At least for them.

They bum-rushed their stumbling, complaining guest up the three rotting front steps, through the door and into the house and as they did, Max withdrew a heavy plastic bag from the back pocket of his sharply creased dress pants. He moved methodically, taking his time. It would not do to drop the damned thing now that they were so close to completing the first step in the plan.

Raven continued to shepherd Manning into the living room and Max hung back after pulling the front door closed. With their guest safely inside the house, there was no need for haste. Their victim's fate was now sealed.

3

Earl Manning stepped reluctantly through the front door and into the living room of the creepy old home. He supposed when the house was new the room would have been considered a parlor—that was what his grandmother would have called it, and they were probably from the same era—but as a guy who did his growing up in the 1980's and 1990's, it was a living room. The space was wide-open but stuffy, as if whoever lived here hadn't opened a window in decades.

And it was empty. Not one piece of furniture had been set up. No TV, no couch, no rugs or carpets; nothing. Just a cavernous shell of a room.

Under different circumstances Earl might have found the emptiness unsettling, but not tonight. Tonight Earl

Manning was suffering the early stages of a monster hangover, and smacking his head on the side of the Porsche hadn't helped. Plus—and here was the worst part—Earl had no idea where the hell he was or what the hell he was doing here, although he had pretty much concluded by now that he wasn't going to get laid by one of the most beautiful, sexy women he had ever seen inside the boundaries of Paskagankee, Maine. Or anywhere else, for that matter.

In fact, although he didn't know what was about to happen, Earl guessed it wasn't going to be good. He reached for his cell phone. It was gone. That traitorous bitch Raven must have appropriated it while he was passed out in the car. Or maybe he had left it at the Ridge Runner; he couldn't remember. *Damn, it's hard to think when you're halfway between drunk and sober.*

But Earl knew one thing: he had had enough. He came here thinking he would be alone with Raven, and instead the shadowy-looking man had forced him inside this house. Looking at it now, he concluded that allowing the guy to push him around had been a mistake. He should have stood up for himself immediately.

Well, it wasn't too late. He could still fix their wagon. He would simply refuse to move another inch until the shadowy man or, preferably, Raven explained to his satisfaction just what the hell they thought they were doing. Not one inch.

Earl walked roughly six feet into the living room that might have been called a parlor by his grandmother and stopped, turning to voice his objection to this whole charade, to complain about being treated like a sap by that little black-haired bitch. He spread his feet and set his shoulders, wobbling thanks to all the alcohol coursing through his system. He turned, ready to demand some answers, to know just what in the *holy hell* this was all about, and as he did, the shadowy man stepped up close, too close, violating his personal space.

The man whipped his right hand over his head in a circular motion like Pete Townshend making his guitar scream during the concert by The Who Earl had seen down in Portland in '96, only instead of holding a guitar pick in his hand like Townshend he held a large plastic bag. The bag fluttered through the air and down over Earl's head and Earl immediately had two thoughts: 1) It really is true that alcohol dulls your reflexes, and 2) It appeared *he* would be doing the screaming instead of a guitar.

A heavy length of twine, almost but not quite a rope, had been threaded through the mouth of the plastic bag, and after yanking the bag over Earl's head, the man pulled the ends apart like a garrote. The bag closed neatly around Earl's neck just under his jawline. In his panic Earl drew in a deep breath to scream, knowing somewhere inside his Budweiser-addled brain that he was making a mistake, that it was the absolute *worst* thing he could do, but he did it anyway. He couldn't help himself.

The bag sucked into his open mouth and Earl gagged and coughed it back out. He shook his head violently back and forth as if registering extreme dissatisfaction with this turn of events, which, in a way, was exactly what he *was* doing. He struck out with his fists, not punching as much as flailing wildly, and felt a millisecond of satisfaction when he connected solidly with some part of the man's body, although which part he hit, he had no idea and didn't much care.

After that tiny victory, though, things went downhill fast. Earl stopped flailing and grabbed with both hands at the twine/rope being pulled with steadily increasing pressure around his neck, cutting off his air supply and digging into the soft skin, but it was useless. The shadowy man had all of the leverage, plus he was younger, stronger and presumably sober to boot.

It ain't a fair fight, thought Earl, realizing immediately it would be a stretch to call it a fight at all. Then all conscious thought departed. He thrashed and grunted and sucked the bag into his mouth again, coughing it out again, his lungs screaming for oxygen, his body weakening by the second, his panicked reaction growing even less effective.

He felt his extremities tingling, he was losing feeling in his hands and feet. All of a sudden he could feel his bladder release. Urine, hot and wet and humiliating, soaked his jeans at the exact moment he began falling toward the dingy hardwood floor.

His head struck the floor and he heard something crack and was surprised to discover he didn't feel any pain. Didn't feel anything at all, in fact, other than a warm, sort of fuzzy ambivalence. Turned out dying was a lot like getting drunk. Earl thought that in some ways it was a damned shame you could only do it once.

Panic subsided and serene acceptance took its place and Earl's last thought before the blackness descended like a shroud was that he would never have imagined in a million years that he would die on a stranger's parlor floor.

4

Max turned to Raven, whose gaze was glued to the prone body of Earl Manning. She was moaning and breathing heavily and a shudder wracked her body as she licked her bright red lips. Max smiled. He enjoyed watching Raven's reaction to violent death almost as much as he enjoyed the actual killing. It was always the same and yet it never lost its appeal.

He stared until she turned her attention from the unmoving victim to him. A sheen of sweat coated her angelic face and her eyes were glazed. She swallowed heavily and Max said, "Shall we celebrate?"

5

Mike McMahon lifted his hat and raked his hand through his thick brown hair, shaking his head in frustration. He slid into a booth at the Katahdin Diner and placed the hat on the seat next to him before glancing across the table at Sharon Dupont. "I don't know how many times we need to have this conversation," he said. "Listen closely: You are a valuable member of this police force and I need you on it."

The sun shone through the window next to the table and waitresses hurried back and forth carrying trays piled high with silverware, food and coffee, somehow managing to avoid running each other down. This was the breakfast rush, the Katahdin's busiest time of the day.

Sharon shrugged. "You need me on the force? That's bullshit. The truth of the matter is I'm more trouble than

I'm worth, and you know it. I'm a double-whammy: a low-time officer with little practical law enforcement experience who is sleeping with her superior. The first half of that equation is an annoyance, but the second half will get you fired once the Town Council gets off their asses and decides to take action. They've looked the other way about us seeing each other to this point only because they wanted a steady hand to guide the department after last fall and the whole fiasco with Chief Court supposedly murdering all those people.

"I still can't believe anyone in this town bought that load of crap, especially after everything Walter Court did for Paskagankee. The idea that he single-handedly ripped a bunch of people apart with his bare hands is simply ludicrous. But the point is, sooner or later the public fascination with the murders will die down—I think we're just about there—and when it does, the council will decide our living arrangements are unacceptable, and they'll move to terminate you."

Mike sighed and placed his hand gently over Sharon's arm. "I know you were close to Wally Court, and there's no question his reputation took a beating in the official investigation, but what choice did the State Police have, really? Would anyone, anywhere have believed the truth—that the aggrieved spirit of a dead Abenaki mother had been reawakened and was wreaking havoc as vengeance for her baby's murder more than three centuries ago? Hell, I was *there*, I saw the thing with my own eyes, fought with it, and sometimes I still have a hard time believing it."

"But, still—"

"—And don't forget," Mike interrupted, "Chief Court is dead and gone, so he can't defend himself. Add to that the fact he didn't have any close living relatives to demand answers to all the unexplained questions, and the result is that he's going to remain the scapegoat, no matter how either of us feels about it."

"Until Melissa Manheim's book comes out, that is."

Mike snorted, half in amusement and half in frustration. "Okay, Manheim the Maneater knows exactly what happened in that cabin out in the woods, but my question remains the same—who's going to believe it? Her book is going to be viewed as the hysterical ranting of an attention-grabbing reporter trying to make a name for herself—"

"—which she is," they said simultaneously, and laughed.

"But that doesn't change the truthfulness of her account," Sharon pointed out.

"Truth? The truth is whatever people want to believe," Mike answered. "And most people aren't going to buy the whole reanimated spirit angle that Manheim the Maneater is selling, whether she's a star reporter for the Portland Journal or not. And whether it's the truth or not."

A young waitress cleared her throat and the pair looked up at her in startled surprise. It was clear from the confused half-smile on the waitress's face that she had heard at least some of their conversation and had no idea how to react to it. "Are you ready to order?" she asked hesitantly.

Mike deferred to Sharon, who ordered a half-grapefruit with apple juice and coffee, and then Mike added, "A Lumberjack Special with a large black coffee for me, please." The waitress wrote it all down on a small pad and walked away, clearly relieved to be hearing words that made sense again.

"Anyway," Mike continued, "my point—which I don't believe I made before we got sidetracked with talk about Wally Court and Melissa Manheim—was that I don't give a rat's ass about the Town Council. I think you know me well enough by now to understand that. And as far as being a 'low-time officer with little practical law enforcement experience,' how the hell do you think you *get* experience? You work the job! I was a 'low-time officer with little practical experience' at one point, too, but I worked the job, day after day, and you know what happened? Eventually I gained the experience and wasn't viewed as a rookie anymore."

He shot her an earnest look and she shook her head glumly. She appeared ready to say something then stopped and stared at the table as the waitress reappeared, her tray piled high. No one said a word as the young woman unloaded their meals and then walked away.

Mike blew on his coffee, sending tendrils of steam dancing away on an invisible air current. "Don't quit the force on me," he continued. "You're going to be a damned fine police officer some day; you're already much better than you give yourself credit for. Plus, I need somebody to watch my back around here. It may not seem like it with all that's happened since I took this job, but I'm still the new guy in town, and I have no real idea who's going to back me up in this department—besides you, that is—and who will throw my ass to the wolves the first chance they get. Don't quit," he said again.

"I'm not talking about quitting the force," she replied quietly. "I'm passionate about law enforcement, I have been since my very first day at the FBI Academy, and I know some day I can be a good officer. I *want* to be a good officer. I want to be an officer like you," she said simply. She looked everywhere but at Mike and he began to feel uneasy.

"Then what are we talking about? I thought you were worried about the Town Council. If you're not thinking about quitting the force, then . . ." Mike grew silent as the impact of what she wasn't saying began to dawn on him. "You don't mean . . ."

Sharon nodded miserably. "Yes," she whispered. "I think we should stop seeing each other. It's the only solution that makes sense." She raised her gaze from the plate on the table to look up at Mike. Her eyes were red-rimmed and moist.

"Shari, we can work this out, there's got to be another way."

"This town needs you, and it's going to need you even more when Manheim's damned book comes out and when filming begins on the movie being made out of the book. Once those things happen, every kook in the northeastern United States is going to trek to Paskagankee, Maine to see the place where the cursed spirit butchered a half-dozen people. We need someone in charge who understands what really went down and who has a good, strong head on his shoulders. That person is you."

"Shari, let's slow down a little, okay? Why don't we wait until the Town Council makes a move and then try to figure out the best way to respond?" He saw the pretty young officer shaking her head, her short black hair framing her face in the way he loved, and stopped.

"No," she insisted. "We can't wait. If we wait for the Town Council to make the first move it will be too late.

Once they fire you they'll never reconsider. We have to head off that possibility now. Besides, the uncertainty is too painful. I can't live this way, knowing that at any moment you could lose your job because of me."

Mike sat unmoving, his hand hanging in the air halfway to his coffee cup. Things had seemed almost normal this morning as they dressed for work. Sure, Sharon had been quiet, but he assumed she was simply suffering one of the lingering headaches that had plagued her off and on since her emergency brain surgery last fall.

"Besides," Sharon added, trying to smile but failing, wiping away a tear with the back of her hand. "I'll still get to see you at work, right? We'll still see each other pretty much every day. We'll still have that." A sob wrenched her tiny frame and she stood, jostling the table in her haste and sloshing her juice into her grapefruit. "I'm sorry," she said. "I have to go." She grabbed her hat and rushed out of the diner.

Mike watched her leave, stunned by the suddenness of this development, and then pushed his plate away, no longer hungry. Outside he could hear the door to Sharon's cruiser slam shut and then the rumbling of the engine as she backed out of her space and exited the parking lot. The engine noise faded away and then Mike was alone.

6

The basement was dank and forbidding, even under normal circumstances, although it seemed more terrifying than usual now, Max thought. But maybe that was just because of what was about to happen here.

Two portable work lamps had been set up on sturdy metal tripod legs to augment the dim lighting, one mounted on the north side of the basement and one on the south. The lamps faced each other at an angle, splashing their light across roughly an eight foot gap, focusing the glare onto a heavy-duty tarp which had been spread out on the concrete floor.

Max and Raven stood side by side next to the tarp, dressed in identical denim coveralls, their hair stuffed under baseball caps. Latex medical gloves adorned their hands and disposable paper booties covered their feet. It was probably overkill—*pun definitely intended,* Max thought with a smile—but he didn't care. There was no point risking contact with dead human tissue and bodily fluids when a few simple precautions could more or less eliminate the possibility.

"Ready?" he asked, and Raven nodded. Together they walked to the corner of the basement where an industrial grade floor freezer had been set up against the east wall. The freezer was constructed of shiny stainless steel and its interior measured more than six feet in length and two-and-a-half feet in width, roughly the size of a casket, making it perfect for their needs. It had set him back nearly twenty-five hundred bucks. He considered the price a bargain.

Max raised the lid and gazed down at Earl Manning, now almost five days dead, his body a solid block at the bottom of the freezer. The corpse was naked from the waist up. Removing the plastic bag from their victim's head had been messy and difficult; Max had pulled the sturdy cord so tight during their brief but deadly struggle that it had disappeared into the delicate tissue, leaving a narrow furrow running under the victim's jawline. It resembled a ghastly necklace.

Manning's lifeless eyes stared fixedly at the ceiling. The expression of fear, helplessness and confusion frozen onto his face made it seem as though the corpse was accusing them of his murder. *Perfectly understandable, under the circumstances,* Max thought. *Not that it will do him any good. He's still dead. For now.*

Max looped an arm around Raven's waist and pulled her into him. He could feel her body trembling like a tiny bird's as she stared at the dead man. "Let's do this," he

REVENANT

said, and walked to the north side of the freezer. Together they reached to the bottom. Max hooked one large hand under each of Manning's armpits, feeling his fingers immediately begin to stiffen from the intense cold despite being encased in the gloves. Raven placed her own, more delicate hands under the dead man's ankles.

Max counted to three and they hauled the body up and out of the freezer. It rose with surprising ease, with their victim's weight distributed relatively evenly along his nearly six foot frame. It was similar to lifting a heavy wooden plank. They began walking the corpse slowly across the basement floor.

They worked in silence, the only sound an occasional grunt from Raven as she struggled to balance the dead man's lower half. When they reached the tarp, they bent and set the cadaver on its back in the middle, then stopped back to catch their breath. Manning had been a perfect fit inside the industrial freezer, filling it lengthwise, his shoulders clearing the side walls with a couple of inches to spare, almost as if he had been measured for it.

Now, however, the body looked small and lost, positioned in the middle of the mostly empty basement atop the oversized tarp. Its empty eyes stared steadfastly upward as if beseeching God—or anyone else who might be paying attention—to explain what was going on here. If God had an answer, though, he kept it to himself.

A thin layer of sparkling frost which had built up over Manning's body now began to melt, giving him the appearance of a sweating athlete, which Max found amusing. Earl Manning's days of heavy physical exertion—if there had ever been any—were long past, a fact demonstrated by his thin arms and generally scrawny build.

Max picked up a Black and Decker cordless rechargeable drill, which he had placed in a line of tools on the floor next to the tarp. He squeezed the trigger, listening to the satisfying whine of the motor. The drill was fully charged and ready for use. He straddled the slab of frozen flesh, one knee on either side of the subject's waist, and placed the tip of the drill bit in the center of the chest, just below the sternum.

He squeezed the trigger again, exerting a steady downward pressure, and in a matter of seconds had punched a small hole through the mass of unyielding bone and tissue. Backing the drill out of the hole, Acton set it aside and reached for the next tool, a cordless rechargeable jigsaw, also fully powered and ready to use. Raven crouched on her knees next to Max, watching quietly, obsessive fascination glittering in her emerald-green eyes.

Max smiled at her, then slid the jigsaw's blade into the hole in Earl Manning's chest and began cutting. He sliced the flesh in a straight line to the top of the rib cage, the saw's motor screaming in protest, almost as if speaking for the dead man who could not. The frozen tissue gave way grudgingly but steadily, and after a few moments, Acton withdrew the saw, placing it on the floor next to the drill. He had begun to sweat from the exertion, despite being seated astride what was essentially a six foot long ice cube.

After a moment to catch his breath, Max picked up a rib spreader, a frightening-looking contraption consisting of a pair of heavy metal bars placed side by side, each one widening out to a flat surface with a curved lip. The two bars were connected at their base by a third bar, adjustable along a corrugated track by a large thumbscrew. Max rested on his haunches atop the lifeless Earl Manning, holding the spreader in his right hand. He smiled again at Raven. "Having fun?" he asked. She smiled back tremulously and said nothing.

Squinting in concentration, Max leaned down and placed the twin bars of the rib spreader into his crude incision, positioning each lip snugly against the dead man's ribs. Then he began turning the oversized thumbscrew, literally spreading Manning's ribs apart inside his frozen chest.

It was hard work, made even more difficult by the body's frozen state. Max began to breathe heavily and Raven asked, "Why did we have to freeze him? Wouldn't this have gone much smoother with a normal body?"

Max wiped the back of one gloved hand across his forehead. "Sure, it would have been easier. But I froze him for two reasons. Doing it this way is not as messy; there are no nasty bodily fluids running all over the place. It makes clean-up a lot easier. That is the secondary benefit."

Raven nodded. "What's the primary benefit, then?"

"The main reason we froze him, sweetheart, is because I want to delay the inevitable decomposition of our friend Mr. Manning for absolutely as long as possible. We are only going to have a finite amount of time to accomplish what needs to be done, and every minute counts. So by freezing him, we are left with a body in as close to its original state as possible."

"But won't the freezing and thawing cause damage to his body?"

"He's dead, remember? Who cares?"

"Of course I remember he's dead, I just wondered if the tissue damage would cause problems for us down the line."

"I hope not, but who really knows? This is uncharted territory, my dear." Max pursed his lips and resumed cranking, moving the metal arms steadily apart, spreading the corpse's ribs wider and wider. A *Crack!* split the air and Raven jumped. Max chuckled and continued cranking, breaking more ribs, one after the other, until the opening in Manning's chest was wide enough to serve his purpose.

He reached inside and grasped his victim's frozen heart firmly with his left hand. With his right he picked up a surgeon's scalpel and began slicing muscle tissue, arteries and blood vessels. He started with the pulmonary veins and arteries, making clean incisions with a steady hand. Then he raised the scalpel, sliced through the thicker inferior vena cava, and finished with the superior vena cava at the top.

The victim's heart was now separated completely from his body. Max lifted it out of the frozen chest and held it up for Raven's inspection. She showed no reaction. He shrugged and stood, holding the muscle carefully in both hands, and walked to a small table set up along the wall near the industrial freezer.

A box adorned with beautiful, intricate animal carvings had been placed squarely in the center of the table. It was the prize Max had gone to so much trouble to procure three months ago in Arizona. Next to it was a similar box, although much plainer. Both lids were standing open. Inside the fancy box was the strange, perfectly smooth grey stone recently liberated from Don Running Bear, and inside the plain box was a sealable quart-sized plastic freezer bag.

Max slid the heart inside the bag and zipped it tightly shut, then placed the bagged heart into the plain box. He closed both lids and secured the latches.

"What do we do now?" Raven asked, glancing at the frozen body of Earl Manning, prone atop the tarp, chest gaping open like it had suffered an explosion from within.

"Now we wait."

7

The geography of Paskagankee, Maine was deceiving. For a town with such a small population, the landscape encompassed a very wide area, featuring wild, rugged terrain, most of which was heavily wooded and virtually impassable even in the best of weather conditions. Such a large area to patrol made being the chief of the tiny police force a challenge, but was one of the many things Mike McMahon loved about the job.

He had spent the first fifteen years of his career as a patrol officer in the city of Revere, Massachusetts, a blue-collar, hardscrabble city immediately north of Boston, dealing with issues on a daily basis which were often very different than those he faced now. He had left Revere for the chief's job in Paskagankee after the tragic shooting of a little girl during a hostage standoff on a steamy July evening, determined to make a fresh start and expecting the job to be a relatively easy; a nice change of pace.

What he inherited instead, almost immediately upon his arrival, was a horrific killing spree like nothing he had ever encountered, victims being murdered and their bodies savagely torn apart. Looking back on it now, the nightmare seemed somehow surreal, as if he had imagined the whole thing, but Mike recalled with perfect clarity how he and Sharon Dupont had nearly been killed themselves before being saved by Ken Dye, Professor of Native American Folklore at the nearby University of Maine. Dye had identified the murderer to be not a townsperson, not even a person at all, but rather the remorseless spirit of a Native American mother butchered three centuries earlier. The professor ended the bloodshed only at the cost of his own life, validating his life's work as he sacrificed himself to the vengeful spirit.

As that nightmare scenario unfolded, Mike and Sharon had bonded like true soul mates, two flawed individuals overcoming their own weaknesses—Mike's self-flagellation at the accidental killing of seven year old Sarah Melendez during the Revere hostage standoff, Sharon's life-long problem with substance abuse—to team up with the professor and save the town, literally at the last possible moment.

Mike opened his broken heart to Sharon Dupont despite their nearly fifteen year age difference in a way he had not done with anyone since his divorce shortly after the Revere shooting. It hadn't been easy; he had sworn he would never expose himself to the pain of lost love again. But when he recognized in her a vulnerability so similar to his own, he found himself drawn irresistibly to her.

And her striking beauty didn't hurt, either. Without fully realizing what was happening until it was too late, Mike McMahon had fallen for the young officer, regardless of her position as his subordinate on the Paskagankee Police Force.

To Mike their status as a couple was a non-issue. He was quite capable of separating their working relationship from their personal relationship, and he knew Sharon could do the same. Whether it would eventually become an issue for the Town Council he did not know, but had assumed all along it was something they would deal with together, as a couple, if and when the circumstance arose.

Now he thought about the bombshell Sharon had dropped as he drove along the nearly deserted rural blacktop, the Paskagankee Police Ford Explorer sure-footedly handling the gradual rise of the terrain as the road burrowed deeper and deeper into the wilderness. Maybe, after more than six months as a couple, Sharon had come to view the difference in their ages as more of a detriment than she had initially thought it would be.

Their relationship had certainly been an eventful one, between the grisly events of last November and the rehabilitation, both physical and mental, they had both been forced to endure. Perhaps Mike had been nothing more than a stepping stone for Sharon, a way to remain grounded as she progressed through the recovery process. Perhaps now that she was more or less back to normal it only made sense that she would take a step back and reconsider her feelings for him.

If so, Mike certainly understood. In fact, he was happy to have been able to help Sharon regain her bearings, even if that meant now she was ready to be on her own.

Understanding didn't make it any easier to bear, though. His attraction to the rookie officer had grown stronger over time even as he had expected it to wane.

And now, apparently, he was alone again, the second time in barely three years a woman he loved had cast him aside. He felt like there was a hole in his chest where his heart should have been. He shook his head at his own foolishness, forcing his thoughts back to the present, to the reason he was making this drive into the Paskagankee hills on a bright, warm June morning.

As chief of the Paskagankee Police Department, Mike McMahon was expected on occasion to perform the sorts of duties he would have scoffed at as a patrol officer back in Revere—ceremonial appearances, community meetings and the like. Today was one of those occasions, and he pushed his thoughts of Sharon—and their accompanying heartache—to the back of his mind, for the time being at least, concentrating on the task at hand.

He muscled the SUV onto a dirt trail so well concealed by the surrounding vegetation he nearly missed it. The vehicle bumped slowly over the rutted track. The forest loomed, centuries-old trees effectively screening the road from sight of his rear view mirror before the vehicle had traveled twenty feet.

Mike grunted as the Explorer lurched into a massive hole hidden by the natural ground clutter of the forest floor, the truck nearly bottoming out before exiting the other side. Holy shit. He had heard of rich people building out-of-the-way shelters to maintain their privacy, but this was ridiculous. He asked Sharon last night—when they were still officially a couple, he thought ruefully—whether she was familiar with this address and she had just looked at him blankly. And this was a kid who had grown up in Paskagankee and spent virtually her entire life here.

Finally, as Mike turned a corner and crested a small hill, a massive log home rose into his field of vision, materializing as if by magic. The house was clearly new but had been designed and constructed to look old. Mike wondered how much the architect who designed it had been paid. The place was magnificent. Built low to the ground, the log home—there was no way anyone could call this a "cabin"—practically melted into the forest, meshing with the surrounding vegetation and the ancient North Woods so completely he wouldn't have thought it possible if he hadn't seen it with his own eyes.

The home was all one story, but easily comprised four thousand square feet of rambling living space. The exterior logs had been stained a dark brown, their monotony broken up by banks of large, gleaming windows. A gigantic fieldstone chimney ran up one side of the house, soaring toward the sky, making Mike wonder how big the damned fireplace on the other side of the wall must be. An oversized farmer's porch ran the length of the home, disappearing around the corners on both sides. For all Mike knew, the porch might encircle the entire place. It certainly looked like it did.

He whistled in appreciation, his problems with Sharon momentarily forgotten. He wondered what this show place had cost to build, then remembered who he was scheduled to meet today and realized cost would, literally, have been no object. Still, for a shelter that was probably only going to be inhabited a couple of months a year, even a guy as rich as Brett Parker must have had to think long and hard before committing the kind of money to the project he obviously had.

The dirt road widened into an approximation of a driveway as it wound closer to the house, and Mike pulled to the side, shutting the Explorer down next to a massive black Lincoln Navigator. Brett Parker's luxurious vehicle shared the same family tree as the Paskagankee Police Explorer, but that was where the comparisons ended. Mike wondered whether Parker was planning on storing his car here year-round, then decided he must be. Even a big-time software developer like Parker likely wouldn't want to pay what it would cost to ship the SUV back and forth across the country.

Mike grabbed his hat off the seat, easing out of the Explorer and starting across the driveway toward the log home. As he did, the front door swung noiselessly open and a blocky-looking man with a sullen demeanor stepped onto the farmer's porch. The man watched impassively as Mike approached, hands jammed into his pockets, saying nothing until Mike had almost reached the front steps.

"Hello, Chief," he finally ventured.

Mike stuck his hand out. "Mike McMahon."

The stocky man fished a hand reluctantly out of his pocket and grabbed Mike's with one huge, fleshy paw. He shook once and then released his grip. "Josh Parmalee," he grunted. "Security for Mr. Parker."

"Formerly Seattle PD, correct?"

"Once upon a time," Parmalee answered. "I retired almost ten years ago to work for Mr. Parker. Best move I ever made, too."

Mike wondered about that. Parmalee appeared to be a good forty pounds overweight, a big man who had once probably been an impressive physical specimen but who had, over time, let himself go until now he carried more flab than muscle on his frame. Mike wondered if that kind of gradual decline was what the future held in store for him and whether perhaps Sharon had considered that possibility, too, and decided his was a future she wasn't particularly interested in sharing.

He forced his thoughts back to the present, annoyed with himself. There would be plenty of time to brood later, but for now he had a job to do, even if it was largely ceremonial—meeting the visiting dignitary and reviewing security procedures. Clearly Parmalee wasn't losing any sleep over his employer's safety; he looked as though he had just awoken from a long nap.

"This is quite an impressive home," Mike said.

Parmalee ignored the comment and said, "Come on, let's take you to meet Mr. Parker." He turned his back on Mike and walked into the house, leading the way through a sitting room which was larger than Mike's entire apartment. From there they threaded their way through a formal dining room complete with a massive cut crystal chandelier hanging over a sturdy oak slab dining table set for two. Mike wondered who Brett Parker might be entertaining later. He guessed it wasn't Josh Parmalee.

At the far end of the dining room was a hallway which appeared to run the length of the house. The pair walked wordlessly. At the end of the hallway, Parmalee rapped twice with his knuckles on a closed door, then opened it without waiting for an invitation to enter.

Seated at a desk inside the small study was a man Mike assumed must be Brett Parker, although he had seen few pictures of the media-shy mogul who was one of the twenty richest people in America. Parker was slight of frame, with thinning sandy hair and gold wire-rimmed glasses perched at the end of his nose. Dressed casually in khaki pants and a baby blue dress shirt with the sleeves rolled up to the elbows, Parker smiled and stood to greet his guest.

"Chief McMahon," he said. "I'm Brett Parker. It's a pleasure to meet you." He spoke softly but firmly and seemed much more interested in social niceties than his security man had been.

They shook hands and Mike tried again. "You have a beautiful home," he said, and Parker smiled. "Thank you. The builders just finished. This is the first time I've ever seen it. I wanted to check it out before bringing my family for an extended vacation next month." Mike recalled reading that Parker was married with one child, an eight year old daughter.

"It's perfect for our needs," he continued. "I wanted a place where my family and I could disappear; a place we would be out of the glare of the public eye for as long as we wished."

"You certainly got that," Parmalee interrupted with the air of someone who would rather be anyplace else in the world.

Parker chuckled. "Anyway, it's a pleasure meeting you, Chief. I'll let you continue your tour with Mr. Parmalee; I'm sure you have plenty more important things to do than spend all day chatting with me."

He sat back down at his desk and the two men eased out of the office, pulling the door closed and continuing down the hall. "The construction is finished," Parmalee said, "but the alarm system has yet to be activated. The house is fully wired and will be protected by a hard-wired system with a battery backup, connected directly to your police station, as you know. Additionally there will be a full perimeter warning system which will alert us if anyone steps inside the boundary of Mr. Parker's ten acres of property."

Mike nodded. "Pretty heavy security," he said.

Parmalee grunted. "You don't get to the position Mr. Parker has in the world of computer software without making a few enemies along the way. It's a fiercely competitive industry, complete with enough corporate espionage and dirty tricks to fuel a hundred Hollywood movies. I know he looks like an easygoing guy, but Brett Parker is a shark in his world. There are plenty of people who would like nothing better than to harm the man or even get him out of the way entirely."

"You're not concerned having him here for the weekend with the security system still offline?"

Parmalee shrugged. "It's only for a couple of days," he said. "Just a quick scouting trip, in and out. Almost no one knows he is even out of Seattle. Beside, I'll have him in my sights the entire time. Anyone wanting to get to Mr. Parker will have to go through me."

Mike bit his tongue. There was no point alienating Parker's head of security, but he had little difficulty picturing a determined intruder getting past Parmalee. Despite the man's impressive size, he had gone somewhat to seed and struck Mike as less than the best the Seattle Police had had to offer even in his better days.

And as far as no one knowing Parker's whereabouts, Mike had a fair amount of experience dealing with VIP movements from his days in Revere, a good-sized city just outside Boston, and he knew that leaks were inevitable where a VIP's schedule was concerned. Anyone with an interest in determining the founder of Parker Software's schedule could do so with relative ease. There was always a secretary or travel agent or even a member of the VIP's own security team more than willing to part with schedule or travel information for the right price.

By now the two men had circled the house and stood just inside the front door. Parmalee strode outside and across the porch to the driveway, moving with a spring in his step he had not shown to this point. Mike wondered what Brett Parker would say if he knew just how perfunctory his head of security's "tour" had been. It was plain Parmalee wanted nothing more than to get rid of the local yokel from the Paskagankee Police Department and get back to whatever had been occupying his time before their meeting.

And that was fine with Mike. His job was to come and make nice with the billionaire's head of security and he had done exactly that. The fact that the security itself appeared sloppy and substandard was none of his concern. Besides, whatever he thought of Parmalee, the man was probably right about one thing—Parker's visit was just a quick two-day in-and-out. What was the likelihood anything would go wrong?

8

In the corner of the dark basement, the industrial-sized floor freezer hummed monotonously, its motor powering a compressor, the compressor flooding the inside of the container with ice-cold air, cooling . . . nothing. The freezer's former occupant lay unmoving in the middle of the floor, a gaping hole in his chest, severed veins and arteries framing the location where Earl Manning's heart used to reside.

The corpse's extremities, which had previously been stiff and unyielding after being frozen through and through, now rested limply on the tarp separating the body from the concrete floor. A soupy mix of bodily fluids had gradually thawed, following the irresistible pull of gravity as they did so, and had collected on the tarp, molding around the dead body like the world's most disgusting bath water.

Manning's skin was dark grey, devoid of any of the color provided by a beating heart pumping blood through a living body. His eyelids remained open, dead eyes staring unseeingly at the ceiling, a thin, milky caul covering each one.

The stairs creaked and groaned as Max Acton and Raven descended them. The pair turned at the bottom and stood at Manning's bare feet. Max examined the corpse with a critical eye, his lips compressing into a thin line as he concentrated. He glanced at his watch and did a little quick figuring. Then he smiled. "I think we're ready to proceed," he told Raven, who nodded once and looked away.

They were dressed in fresh jumpsuits and booties. Latex medical gloves once again covered their hands. Raven stepped to the side and watched closely as Max wheeled a five-gallon wet-dry vac across the floor, easing it to a stop next to the corpse and flipping a switch. A high-pitched whine filled the room and the two of them grimaced as Max maneuvered a plastic tube fitted to the end of a rubber hose around the body, sucking the fluids off the tarp and into the vacuum.

He flipped the switch again and the motor died, the whine fading away, leaving a ringing in Max's ears and, he assumed, in two of the four other ears currently occupying the basement. Fresh fluids immediately began collecting on the tarp, trickling slowly out of the body, replacing what had just been cleared away.

Max sighed and knelt on the floor. He reached over Manning's chest and rapidly turned the thumbscrew on the rib spreader, drawing the metal arms toward each other, allowing the broken ribs to collapse into the chest cavity. A wet sucking sound accompanied the movement of the bones; to Max it sounded like a drumstick being pulled off a well-done roast chicken.

After a few moments, the resistance of the bones on the rib spreader had been eliminated and Max pulled the metal contraption up and out of Manning's body. It was slick with watery-looking blood and some kind of residual yellowish pus-like substance. Max examined the mess with distaste and set the rib spreader aside. He placed one hand on either side of the large incision he had made yesterday, then pulled the dead man's slack skin back together with his palms. It felt thin and rubbery and it sagged in the middle of Manning's body, where there was no longer the support structure of a functioning rib cage to hold it in place.

Max turned and nodded to Raven and she opened a small plastic box, setting it on the floor next to Max. Then she backed up and resumed watching. She was clearly on edge and for a moment Max thought about shouting "Boo!" and watching her piss her pants, then he decided just to get on with the business at hand. He reached into the box and selected a suture needle and surgical thread, then went to work, leaning over the corpse and efficiently if not artfully stitching the two sides of the corpse's chest back together.

When he had finished, he leaned back on his heels and examined his handiwork. The chest was caved in at the center, the result of the broken rib bones and, of course, the missing heart muscle, but under the circumstances looked relatively passable. Despite the delicate appearance of the mottled grey skin tissue, it appeared the stitches would hold for as long as Max needed them to.

He smiled up at Raven. "Looks pretty good, don't you think? I'd say this might even be an improvement over what you dragged out of that bar last week."

"Well, it would be hard to get any worse," she said wryly.

"I'll have to give you that one," Max said as he rose to his feet, brushing the knees of his jumpsuit and stretching his back. He strolled toward the small table next to the freezer, upon which lay the two wooden boxes, one ornate, adorned with the intricate Navajo carvings, and the other simple and plain.

Raven followed a couple of paces behind. "Is this really going to work?" she asked nervously.

Max stopped and turned, scowling at Raven. Her face blanched and she took a step back. "You're the one that turned me on to this whole deal," he said. "You're the Navajo squaw with the background in all this Native American mumbo-jumbo. It goddamn well better work after all the time and effort I've invested in this project. I don't think I need to remind you what will happen to us if we don't deliver the goods to the North Koreans. Not only will we not get paid, no one will ever find our bodies again."

"I know, I know, don't get upset, baby." Raven held her hands up in a placating gesture. "You're right, I *do* know it will work, it's just hard not to be a little nervous, that's all. I can't believe you're not nervous, too!"

"Why would I be? If what you've told me about this special rock is true, we have nothing to worry about. Right?"

Raven said nothing.

"Right?"

She finally nodded.

Max thought he had never seen a less-convincing emotion. He continued staring until she dropped her gaze to the floor and left it there. Then he reached over and unlatched the boxes, lifting both lids. Inside the plain box was the zip-locked plastic bag containing Earl Manning's heart, now completely thawed and looking exactly like what it was—an unmoving lump of dead muscle tissue.

Inside the more ornate box decorated with the intricate Navajo carvings was the baseball-sized stone Max had stolen from Don Running Bear three months ago in the Arizona desert. The stone looked almost ordinary but just a little . . . *off,* somehow. Max gazed at it almost as if expecting something mystical to happen. Nothing did. The stone sat in the middle of the box, ancient and inanimate.

After a moment Max reached inside and rolled the stone to the edge of the box. He needed to free up space inside the small area for its new roommate. He then picked up the sealed plastic bag containing Earl Manning's heart and lifted it out of the plain box, placing it next to the Navajo stone in the ornate box. Then he stepped back and waited expectantly.

And he waited.

And he waited.

And nothing happened.

Max turned slowly, his face reddening. He glanced pointedly from the wooden box to Raven's face and back again, saying nothing. She backed up another step, her mouth working overtime but managing nothing more than a tiny squeak of barely controlled fear.

"Why is nothing happening?" Max said softly, the

words more menacing for their lack of volume than if he had screamed them.

"I...I...it's..."

Max took a step toward her and her pretty green eyes widened in terror. But she was no longer looking at his face. She was peering intently over his shoulder.

He stopped and turned.

Walked back to the table.

Looked in the box.

Inside the clear plastic bag, Earl Manning's severed heart was beating, slowly and steadily.

9

Sharon Dupont had never been so miserable in her life, and she was not without considerable experience against which to compare and measure her present pain. She had grown up essentially on her own, her father retreating into a beer bottle after the death of her mother when Sharon was twelve. She had followed his path, becoming an addict as well, eventually trading sexual favors for drugs and booze as a high school student, convinced she would never escape the tiny town of her birth.

She had eventually been saved from the cycle of destruction by none other than former Paskagankee Police Chief Wally Court, who took her under his wing her senior year of high school, giving her something she had been missing for most of her formative years—a reliable and responsible role model. It was because of Chief Court that Sharon had decided to dedicate her life to law enforcement, attending the FBI Academy in Herndon, Virginia before being forced to return to Paskagankee to care for her terminally ill father.

Then had come the serial murders last fall, the horror reaching its peak during the town's annual pre-Thanksgiving bonfire, when the vengeful spirit had taken Sharon, nearly killing her in the process. She had been saved—barely—by Mike McMahon and in the days and weeks following the chaos, had cherished her growing attraction to him, but had been forced to watch helplessly as her mentor and hero, Walter Court, was vilified, the dead ex-police chief blamed for the killing spree.

So Sharon was well-acquainted with misery. But what she was experiencing right now was worse than anything she had gone through. Ever. To hurt Mike like she did, to tell him she was no longer interested in him, to watch his reaction—the pain and confusion evident on his handsome features—was worse than the most hopeless morning she had ever faced as a frightened and confused high school drug addict, worse even than waking up injured and helpless last fall at the mercy of a centuries-old spirit.

She wheeled her cruiser around the corner of Main Street and Route 24, turning right at the Baptist Church, theoretically patrolling for speeders but in reality just passing the time, lost in her thoughts. What choice had she had than to let go of Mike? She knew this town much better than he—she had been born here, she grew up here, had raised hell here, and then had left, certain she would never return. But she *had* returned, after just a few months away, meaning almost her entire twenty-six year lifespan had been spent right here in Paskagankee.

As a life-long resident, Sharon knew how closed-minded the town's elders could be, how intractable and bull-headed they were regarding the decisions they made in what they believed to the town's welfare. And it was only a matter of time, and probably not very much of it, before they came to the conclusion, if they hadn't already, that the chief of police living with one of his officers was not a suitable arrangement.

Her only other option would have been to quit the force. Realistically, that was probably what she should do. Resign from the Paskagankee Police Department and leave town; look for work elsewhere. Her parents were both dead, there was nothing holding her in Paskagankee anymore.

Nothing except Mike McMahon.

If she left now, she knew she would never see him again, and that scenario was unacceptable. So she did the only thing she could do, and that was break off their relationship. But the pain was raw and throbbing and the last thing she wanted to do after work was face Mike. She decided she would go for a drive after work and give him an opportunity to get all his things together in private and move them from her house back into his old apartment. The place was still available and she knew he would have no problem renting it again. It wasn't like people were flocking to this remote village and demanding housing.

The police radio squawked. "Unit Two, come in."

Sharon lifted the handset and keyed the mike "This is Unit Two, go ahead Gordie."

"Yeah, Sharon, we just got a call about a missing person. We need you to go out to Old Mill Road and take the complaint."

"I'm on it. What's the name and address of the complainant?"

"Address is Forty-Seven Old Mill Road."

Sharon's heart skipped a beat. Forty-Seven Old Mill Road. That was an address she knew from a lifetime ago, when her entire being revolved around drugs and alcohol and sexual favors. Her stomach seized and she thought she might be sick.

The dispatcher continued. "The complainant is the victim's mother. Name of the victim is Earl Manning."

***

Sharon rolled the cruiser to a stop in the dusty driveway outside a run-down mobile home that had probably not seen any significant maintenance in forty years. Threadbare roofing shingles covered a home tilting precariously to one side, as if the concrete foundation was simply crumbling away, which was probably exactly what was happening. Ancient aluminum siding, warped and cracked and weathered, covered the exterior walls, and the windows appeared not to have been washed since the Nixon Administration.

An old Ford F-150 pickup was parked next to the home; a vehicle Sharon remembered all too well from her high school days. It had been creaky and rust-dotted and ready for the junkyard back then and she could hardly believe the thing was even safe to drive now. Based on her memories of its owner, that wouldn't have stopped him. She sat staring at the truck, stomach churning, until it occurred to her that it might look odd to be seen sitting motionless inside her cruiser staring in horror at a rusted hunk of metal.

She sighed nervously and exited the car, glancing in all directions as she approached the broken-down trailer. The area seemed deserted, which was unsurprising since this address was remote even by Paskagankee standards. Sharon rapped once with her knuckles on the flimsy door and it swung open before she had a chance to knock a second time. It was obvious the trailer's occupant had been waiting for her to approach and she wondered briefly if her reluctance to exit her cruiser had been observed.

Standing in the door was a fleshy woman who might have been fifty or eighty or anywhere in between. The woman didn't strike Sharon as grossly overweight; she was just *large*. Her arms hung from her sides like they had been tacked on after the rest of her body was sculpted from a chunk of Maine granite. Deep crevasses lined her haggard face and sagging jowls made it look as though she might be storing food in her mouth for her next meal.

"'Bout time," the woman said by way of greeting.

"Hello, Mrs.Manning. You called about a missing person?"

"That's right. My boy's disappeared. Someone goes missing and the best the cops can do is send a tiny little girl?" The woman gave a snort that sounded like the air being let out of a balloon and threw the door open the rest of the way, retreating into the trailer's tiny kitchen. "Come on in, then."

Sharon pulled a small notebook and a pen out of her breast pocket. "This is about Earl?"

The woman dropped onto a tubular aluminum chair with a padded seat covered in garish orange vinyl that had to have been manufactured in the 1950's and swiveled her head, looking up at Sharon suspiciously. "You know my boy?"

"Uh . . . yes. We . . . uh, we went to school together, Mrs. Manning. Earl was a couple of years ahead of me but I . . . uh, knew him." She knew she sounded like the village idiot and mentally kicked herself. She was here to take a missing person's report, not to review her long history of poor life choices.

"How long has Earl been missing?" she asked, determined to rebound from her poor first impression.

"Well, let's see," the woman answered, placing her massive chin into one cupped palm. "I'd say it's been over a week now."

"Your son has been missing a week and you're just getting around to reporting it now?"

Anger flashed in the woman's eyes and she gazed at Sharon with contempt. "That's right, missy. I'm just reporting it now. You're quite the sharp detective, ain't you? Sometimes Earl goes away for a few days; stays with friends and such. Better he stay put if he's on a bender than to be driving around this God-forsaken town trying to get home, don't you think?"

Sharon mentally kicked herself again. She hoped her brain didn't start to bruise inside her head from all the kicking going on. "I wasn't passing judgment, Mrs. Manning, just trying to pin down exactly how long Earl has been gone. When was the last time you saw him, exactly?"

"Guess it woulda been a week ago yesterday. Friday night, I believe, before he went down to the Ridge Runner like normal."

"And he didn't come home last Friday night?"

"Already told ya that. I ain't seen him since." The woman started to cry, one large teardrop rolling down her face, zig-zagging from one crevasse to another until it arrived at her chin and dropped onto the kitchen table where she angrily wiped it away with the sleeve of her housedress. "Earl's stayed away a few days every now and then, but never for this long. Something's happened to him, I'm sure of it."

"Did Earl seem upset or preoccupied at all before he disappeared?"

"No more'n usual," his mother replied. "Earl ain't never been what you'd call a fountain of optimism, even on his best days. What would he have to be happy about? No job, no money, alcohol problems, always getting harassed by *you* people." She gestured vaguely in Sharon's direction.

She felt the woman's attention wandering and tried to refocus her. "So in the days before his disappearance, Earl seemed to be acting normally."

"You catch right on, don't ya?"

"Mrs. Manning, I'm trying to help here. Is it possible Earl took a trip without telling you?"

"A trip. And how would he get where he was going on this 'trip' when his truck is right out front? What'd he do, walk? No," she said, finally answering the question. "Earl didn't go on any trip. He don't know anyone outside this town, anyway. He ain't got no reason to go nowhere."

"You said he went to the Ridge Runner last Friday night. How did he get there if his truck is parked here?"

Mrs. Manning nodded and a smile tugged at the edges of her mouth. She pulled it down before continuing.

"Maybe you ain't quite as hopeless as you look, little missy. Good question. The answer is, *I* went and picked up Earl's truck. When Monday come around and it was still sitting in the Ridge Runner lot, Ol' Bo Pellerin called me and told me he ain't seen Earl in a few days and if he didn't want his truck towed, he better come get it. So I called my sister and she come and took me down there and I picked it up and drove it home. That was Monday afternoon. The truck ain't moved from here since."

"We'll get right on this, Mrs. Manning, I promise," Sharon said, closing her notebook and ignoring the woman's snort of derision. "If you think of anything else that might be helpful, anything at all, please call."

"Yeah, call, right. Sure."

Sharon retreated out the front door of the trailer and struggled to close it behind her. The sagging structure had pulled the aluminum door frame out of square and the damned thing didn't want to click shut. Finally she heard it catch and she hurried to her cruiser, glad to be out of there. She backed out of the dirt driveway in a cloud of dust and turned toward Paskagankee proper.

10

Max Acton stared at Earl Manning's heart, severed from Manning's dead body and sealed inside a plastic bag next to the mystical Navajo stone. The heart was beating softly, throbbing roughly once per second, steadily regaining color as Max watched despite the fact it was connected to nothing—no blood supply, no oxygen, nothing. The detached veins and arteries jiggled slightly with each beat.

The scene was terrifying and awe-inspiring. Max had fully expected their plan to work; he was a believer in much that was non-traditional. In fact, he had barely batted an eye when Raven—one of his followers back in the Arizona co-op that was really a cult—came to him with the story of a mystical Navajo stone with the power to reanimate the dead. But now, seeing the actual heart of a man he had killed and gutted with his own hands beating serenely inside the box, it was almost too much to comprehend.

Almost.

Max feasted his eyes, not wanting to move, wanting to drag this moment out forever. This was what it must feel like to be God. He could hear Raven's ragged breathing as she peeked around him and into the box, getting her own view of what could fairly be described as a miracle.

The possibilities were endless. Max's brain swirled with possibilities. He had always craved power, and in fact was a natural leader. The impressive following he had built up over a very short time in Arizona testified to the truth of that statement. Max was handsome and charismatic and inspired loyalty in his followers. He was Jim Jones minus the suicidal tendencies.

But this discovery, this stone he had liberated from that idiot Indian back on the reservation, was a game-changer. A world-changer, in fact. Max now had in his grasp the key to the acquisition of more power than even he had ever had the temerity to envision. His own heart, the one beating inside his chest, soared as he allowed himself to visualize all the possibilities.

But first things first. He had a job to do that must be completed to everyone's satisfaction before beginning to fulfill his true destiny. The job involved a transaction which would earn Max money, lots of it, money which would give him the freedom to pursue his bold vision.

Behind them, a crinkling noise coming from the heavy plastic tarp on the floor brought Max back to the present, reminding him of the short-term significance of the miracle he had just wrought. He and Raven turned simultaneously and he gasped at the sight greeting him despite being prepared for it. Raven stumbled backward, beginning to scream and then clapping her tiny hands to her mouth. She took shelter behind Max, squeezing into the space between his body and the table holding the two wooden boxes.

Atop the heavy tarp, Manning's dead body began to stir. Already the deathly grey pallor of the corpse was receding, replaced by a more life-like hue. His cheeks couldn't be described as rosy, not exactly, not even by the most wide-eyed optimist, but the skin-tone appeared slightly more alive.

It was impossible, of course, all of it; Manning had no heart in his chest with which to pump blood through his body. And he was dead. There was no question about that. Max had done the job himself, making absolutely certain the poor sucker's heart had stopped beating. Then he had frozen the man for a week and cut his heart out.

Dead.

This was impossible.

But right here on the basement floor was proof of the opposite: Earl Manning, his legs and arms moving in more or less a random manner, before seeming to coordinate themselves and forcing his corpse into a sitting position. His back was to Max and Raven, facing the other end of the basement, and he swiveled his head nearly one hundred eighty degrees—another impossibility, but there it was—and gazed at the two of them with clear, questioning bewilderment in his eyes.

The milky caul was gone. His eyes were blue and piercing. Lifelike. The corpse opened its mouth as if to speak and then closed it again. Behind Max, Raven was breathing heavily. He thought she might pass out. He didn't care.

"Hello, Earl," he said.

The corpse blinked once and behind him Raven screamed again, this time long and loud. "Who are you?" the thing that used to be Earl Manning asked. Its voice was low and rough and Max didn't remember it sounding like that when the drunken loser appeared at their door on Raven's arm. Whether the change was a result of the Navajo stone's magic or the gaping hole Max had cut in the man's chest he had no idea.

Max smiled. "I'm your owner," he said. "Your God. My name is Maxwell Acton, but I don't believe in standing on formalities, so you may call me Max."

"Owner? God? What the hell are you talking about?" The corpse adopted an aggrieved look, then spied Raven and continued. "What did you do to me, bitch? The last thing I remember is you coming on to me at the Ridge Runner and us leaving together. Just what's going on here?"

Max snickered, mumbling to Raven. "Apparently this transformation doesn't add any brain power to the stiff, does it?"

She didn't answer and he addressed Manning. "You were duped, my friend, suckered, played, used, hornswoggled. You were had. We needed a subject for our little test, and you volunteered. Unfortunately for you, it was unknowingly, but, hey, if you were stupid enough to believe a once-in-a-lifetime piece of ass like Raven Tahoma would give a loser like you a second look, then in my book you deserve what you got. And my book is the only one that matters now, at least to you."

Earl Manning looked back and forth between the two of them, head swiveling slowly, uncomprehending. Finally Max said, "Run your hand across your chest."

The corpse did so, a look of confusion crossing his reanimated face as his hand dipped into the cavity in the middle of his chest caused by the missing heart muscle and broken rib bones. "What have you done to me?" he whispered. The sound was paper-thin and plaintive, and the look of confusion on his face was replaced in an instant by one of anger and utter, undiluted hatred.

"I told you," Max answered, "I own you now. You see, you are what is known in technical parlance as a 'revenant.' Fancy word, I'll admit, especially for someone of your limited intellectual capacity, but it's one with a pretty simple definition. You're dead, Earl, I'm sorry to say, but on the bright side, you've been reanimated. Brought back to life. By me. I am now your God, and your sole purpose from this moment on is to do what I tell you. You'll find you have no choice in the matter, literally; your actions will be exactly as prescribed be me, no matter how you feel about your instructions. Agree with them, disagree, it doesn't matter in the least. You *must* do as you're told."

Manning shook his head, either in disagreement or disbelief, Max wasn't sure which, but the look of loathing on his face never changed or diminished. Max decided it was time for a demonstration. Manning needed to understand the truth of his words.

"Stand up," he said simply.

"Screw you," Manning replied, but began to rise even as he spit the words out. The corpse pushed itself up to its knees, then ever so slowly shifted its weight so that its feet were beneath its body, eventually rising to a standing position. It stood unsteadily, body swaying slightly as if still as drunk as Earl Manning had been when he took his last reeking breath more than a week ago.

Max turned and closed the lid on the Navajo box, snapping the latch and sealing the beating heart inside it next to the perfectly round stone. Then he faced Manning again and said, "Come over here." Raven whimpered behind him.

The Manning-thing again said, "Screw you," louder this time, but again began moving even as it spoke. It lifted its left foot and almost immediately slammed it back down onto the floor, maybe twelve inches in front of where it had begun, as the corpse fought to maintain a sense of balance. It staggered sideways and then fell backward, slamming into the wooden staircase leading from the basement up to the first floor.

The silence was broken by a loud *Crack!* as something snapped inside Earl Manning, perhaps another rib, from the force of its body's impact against the stairway. The reanimated corpse didn't seem to notice, however, immediately rolling awkwardly to its feet and trying again.

This time Manning managed to move in the proper direction, gazing steadily at Max as he staggered forward across the basement floor, skirting the tarp upon which he had recently lain dead, lurching to a stop directly in front of him. "What have you done to me?" he whispered.

"We've gone over all that," Acton replied dismissively as Raven cowered behind him. She whimpered again and was ignored. "To clarify, and I'll try to use as many single-syllable words as I can, I killed you. I cut out your heart.

You were—you *are*—dead. Your heart now resides inside this breathtakingly beautiful box, next to a stone containing a mystical power: the power to reanimate the dead.

"The possessor of this box controls the stone. As you may notice, I possess the box, thus you belong to me. As long as your heart resides next to the stone inside this box, you will continue to, for lack of a more accurate word, live. If the heart is removed from the box and taken away from the stone you will, again for lack of a better word, die.

"You may have noticed, even with your limited brain capacity, that you have control over your body to a certain extent but are completely beholden to me. While in possession of this box, I am able to divine your intentions as well as force your compliance with my instructions. As I believe I have already mentioned, I am your God.

"That's about as simple as I can make it, Mr. Manning, and whether or not you choose to believe what you've been told is irrelevant to me and, in point of fact, also to you. It is all completely true, as you have already discovered and will continue to discover.

"Now, we have a limited amount of time to accomplish what needs to be done before your body . . . shall we say . . . *deteriorates* to the point where you will be of no further use to me, so let's stop wasting it and get started. Would you like to know what you're going to do for me?"

"No."

Max told him anyway.

11

"The obvious place to start would be the Ridge Runner," Mike said, leaning back in his chair and eying Sharon across the desk. The atmosphere inside the office was tense and awkward, each person trying to concentrate on the job at hand, each well aware of the eight hundred pound gorilla of their breakup inside the room. "That was the last place anyone saw Manning, as far as we know, so that's where we need to go."

Sharon sat silently and Mike studied her face before speaking gently. "I know you had a history with this guy. Would you rather I took Pete Kendall with me to do the interview?"

"Of course not," she answered as her face flushed bright crimson. Mike wondered whether it was from anger or embarrassment. "My 'history,' as you call it, with Earl Manning consisted of one highly regrettable night spent humping in the guy's pickup truck, for crying out loud, while trashed out of my mind years ago when I was young and stupid. Believe me, I can handle this job."

Mike sat, thinking. "What about us?" he said. "Would you rather not be around me, considering . . . you know. No one would blame you, certainly not me, if you chose to sit this one out. Like I said, I can bring—"

Sharon cut him off. "Listen, if we're going to be able to work together, we might as well start now, don't you think?"

Mike's head snapped back as if he had been slapped. "Of course," he nodded. "That's fine. Let's go, then."

***

The ride across town to the Ridge Runner was conducted mostly in silence. There didn't seem to be anything to say so no one said anything. Mike piloted the cruiser into the lot and felt the eyes of the patrons and staff on them as he and Sharon walked to the door. It was early, Happy Hour hadn't even officially begun yet, so only a small phalanx of hard-core drinkers was in attendance, but Mike didn't mind. They were the ones he wanted to talk to, anyway.

The soft buzz of activity ceased as the two officers entered the rectangular concrete building. The half-dozen or so regulars stopped talking, stopped drinking, stopped everything. They simply sat and stared.

The hostility was evident. Most of the people—all of them men—holding down stools at this time of day had had occasion at various times to make their acquaintance with the Paskagankee Police Department, some for more serious issues than others, but the one thing they all had in common was a mutual dislike and distrust of law enforcement.

Mike didn't care about that. The guys who thought themselves the toughest and the baddest in this little town were small potatoes compared with some of the truly evil people he had come in contact with while serving on the force in Revere, Massachusetts. Gang members, drug dealers, wife beaters, gun runners, all of whom had little or no regard for human life, had been nearly a day-to-day reality back in Revere. These people in Paskagankee might be tough, but they held no power of intimidation over Mike McMahon.

Bo Pellerin stood behind the bar, as motionless as his customers, waiting for Mike and Sharon to cross the floor. He wore a dirty apron that might at one time have been white but was now a dingy grey, wiping glasses with a rag that looked as though it had last been washed in the same load of laundry as the apron.

"Chief," Bo said.

Mike nodded a greeting and extended his hand. Pellerin took it reluctantly. "To what do we owe this pleasure? It ain't even dinnertime yet, so I figure none of my customers have been arrested for DUI."

"It's nothing you've done, or any of your customers, either, as far as I know," Mike replied. "We're here about Earl Manning."

"Ain't seen him in over a week. He hasn't been in here since a week ago Friday."

"Is that unusual?"

"Hell, yeah, it's unusual. I don't think Earl's missed more than one day at a time on that stool over there," he nodded to the empty barstool closest to the wall, "since, well, since as long as I can remember, and I took this place over from my daddy almost ten years ago."

"Last Friday night was when he was last here?"

"That's what I said."

"That was eight days ago. How can you be so sure it wasn't Saturday night, or Thursday, if he comes in here all the time?"

Pellerin chuckled. "Oh, it was Friday, all right. Ask anyone that was here; they all remember, even the ones that can't remember what they had for dinner five minutes after they put their fork down."

"Why's that?"

"Because last Friday night was Earl Manning's wet dream come true. *Sorry,* ma'am," Pellerin said, leering at Sharon in a way that made it clear he wasn't the least bit sorry.

Mike waited for the bar owner to continue and when it became clear he had no intention of doing so, said, "What are you talking about, Bo?"

"I'm talking about this little girl who came in just before midnight, after Earl was well on his way to liquid oblivion. She's the hottest thing to hit this town since, well, since *her,*" he said, nodding and leering again in Sharon's direction.

"HEY!" Mike said, getting in Pellerin's face and refocusing his attention on the question. "Keep your opinions about Officer Dupont to yourself unless you want to see your liquor license disappear like your common sense."

Pellerin's lip curled but he said nothing. Mike prompted him. "So, some young lady came into the bar and she was very good looking. What happened then?"

Pellerin smiled. "Okay, we'll do it your way. Yes, she was *very good looking*. She comes sauntering in like she owns the place, walking through very determinedly like she knows exactly what—or who—she's looking for. She walks around the entire bar and then stops next to Earl. She sits down and starts chatting him up like he's freakin' Matt Damon or something. Next thing you know, they get up and walk out together.

"That was the last I seen of him," Pellerin said. "I called up his Ma a couple days later to get his piece of shit truck out of my parking lot. She came and got it that same day, and I ain't seen neither one of 'em since."

"Can anyone verify your account?"

"I told ya," Pellerin said in exasperation. "*Everyone* can 'verify my account,' as you call it. This chick could get a rise out of a dead man and she zeroed in on Earl like maggots on spoiled meat. I guarantee everyone can 'verify my account;' it's all anyone could talk about around here for days."

"What did she look like?"

"Holy shit, she was hot."

"Could you be a little more specific?"

"Well, let's see. Maybe five foot four, darkish skin like she spent a lot of time in the sun, jet-black hair halfway down to her butt, and the nicest butt to be jammed into a pair of jeans in this town since . . ." he glanced at Sharon and seemed to feel the chief's stony glare and finished, ". . . well, since a long time, anyway."

Mike nodded as Sharon jotted the description down in a small notebook. "I'm sure you won't object to us asking your regulars a few questions? From the sound of things, they'd probably love the opportunity to relive the big moment."

Bo Pellerin smiled, revealing a mouth full of stained and yellowed teeth. He wiped his hands on the greasy apron and said, "I don't mind at all, Chief, knock yourself out. But you haven't asked the most important question yet."

"Really. And what might that be?"

"Don't you want to know her name?"

"You have her name?"

The grin widened. "Sure do."

"You didn't tell me you talked to her."

"I didn't."

"Listen, Bo, you're not doing yourself any favors, here. This young woman is potentially a witness in a missing-persons case. You'd better stop screwing around and tell me what you know, and right now, because I'm just about out of patience with your little boy games."

Pellerin raised his hands in surrender. He seemed satisfied now that he had gotten under Mike's skin in front of his customers. "Okay, okay," he said. "You know my sister Rose operates a little gift shop downtown, *Needful Things,* right?"

"Bo, I've lived in this town for almost a year now. Of course I know Rose's shop. She named it after the Stephen King book."

"That's right. Well, anyway, this little chick you're looking for was in there a few weeks ago with some rough-looking dude old enough to be her father. Hell, maybe he *was* her father, I dunno, but here's what I *do* know. Rose said the chick was farting around, looking at glass figurines or some such crap, long after the guy had found whatever the hell he had come in to buy. He finally lost patience and said . . ."

Pellerin paused theatrically and Mike waved his right hand in a tight circle—*get on with it.*

". . . He said 'It's time to go, Raven.' Her name is Raven."

"Did Rose get her last name? Or the other guy's name? The older one that could have been Raven's father?"

"Not that I know of, but you'll have to ask her to be sure."

"We will, don't worry. And thanks for the information, Bo, it will go a long way toward finding Earl."

"Yeah, well, hurry up about it," Pellerin said. "Sales are down in this place twenty percent since that gin-soaked bastard disappeared."

Mike shook his head. "Your concern is touching. We're going to talk to your regulars for a bit, then we'll be out of your hair."

"Like I said, have at it, but they won't have anything of value to add to what I already told you."

And he was right. They didn't.

12

Earl Manning picked his way through the woods, staggering more than walking, tripping over fallen logs, scrub brush littering the forest floor, even occasionally the tiniest of harmless twigs. It seemed that overnight, or rather over the week he lay at the bottom of a freezer, his muscles had somehow forgotten most of the subtle techniques involved in ordinary locomotion. It was like being drunk only without the accompanying fuzzy alcoholic haze.

He had been driven to a point along one of the most desolate stretches of Route 24 by that devil Max Acton and the treacherous beauty Raven. They pulled to the side of the road and as the car crunched to a stop on the gravel, Acton had reviewed his instructions one last time and then sent him on his way.

A medium-sized fallen birch tree, perhaps eight inches in diameter, loomed in front of him and he spent a moment studying it, determining after a fashion that it would be better to climb over it than to try to work through the thick brush on either side. He threw his right leg across the trunk and half-vaulted, half-crawled over the tree, falling to the ground on the far side and rolling to his hands and knees before struggling to his feet and marching on.

Before his transformation, eight days and a lifetime ago, Earl would have spent at least a few seconds brushing the dirt and leaves and detritus of the forest floor off his clothes had he fallen like he just did. He may have spent his entire life, nearly thirty years, in the tiny, remote village of Paskagankee, but no one would ever have accused him of being some kind of Daniel Boone. Earl had never been comfortable in the great outdoors, much preferring to spend his time atop his personal barstool at the Ridge Runner or sprawled on the ratty old couch inside the trailer he shared with his mother, drinking Budweiser and watching the Sox on TV.

Now, however, the twigs and rotting leaves and clumps of damp, musky north woods dirt clung to his jeans, dropping off slowly, unnoticed. Keeping his clothes neat and clean had not been included in his instructions and thus was a non-factor for the new but definitely not improved version of Earl Manning.

The orders he *had* received were simple. He was to keep to the cover of the trees fifty or so feet east of the rutted and pothole-strewn dirt track in order to avoid detection, following the obscure road—he had lived his entire life in this area but had never had the slightest inclination this road was here—for a mile or so north. Eventually he would arrive at a brand-new home, a cabin constructed by some billionare software developer from the west coast. Then he would do what he had to do and get the hell out.

The bitch of it was that Earl Manning had no desire to do it.

Any of it.

Earl couldn't have cared less about some billionaire software developer, unless the guy was having a party and offering free beer and maybe beautiful women, which was clearly not the case. If left to his own devices, Earl would not have been within five miles of this isolated road in this eerie, God-forsaken forest. He would be sleeping one off in his own lumpy bed, waiting for Ma to wake him up with the smell of sizzling bacon and frying eggs.

It wasn't much of a life, Earl knew that—he might not have been a Rhodes Scholar, but he wasn't completely stupid, either—but it was *his* life, and certainly far preferable to the nightmare he now found himself thrust into. He ran his hand over the frightening cavity in the middle of his chest, the cotton of his shirt pushed into the hole which had been stitched up so carelessly by his new master, and shuddered.

He had no heart. The asshole jocks he had grown up with, the kids on the Paskagankee High football team who had tortured him mercilessly as a kid, scoring with the prettiest girls while being no or smarter or better looking than he, had told him exactly that thousands of times when he was a kid—"You ain't got no heart, Manning"—but they had meant it as nothing more than an insult, a nasty and hurtful way of telling him what everyone already knew anyway: that they were better than he was.

But this was different. He literally had no heart. *His heart was gone.* It was actually gone, carved out of his chest, somehow beating by itself and fueling his body despite being stored inside a plastic bag in that goddamned Max Acton's special box in the basement of his rented house of horrors a few miles away.

What had Acton called him? "Revenant," that was it; that was the word he had used. Earl was a revenant. Earl wasn't sure of the exact dictionary definition of the word, it wasn't one he had ever heard before and a dictionary wasn't exactly within reach at the moment, but based on his personal experience of the last few hours Earl thought he was becoming quite the expert on revenants.

He was dead; there was no question about that. That fact was indisputable. His heart had been removed from his body and was being stored in a room miles away.

Dead.

Hard to argue that point.

And yet, here he was, walking (sort of), thinking, feeling more or less like the old Earl, except with one critical difference: Free will was no longer a part of his life. He was no longer calling the shots.

In some small ways he was still able to control his actions, sure, the fact that he had determined on his own how to circumnavigate the fallen birch tree moments ago was testament to his ability to puzzle out problems, but in a much larger sense, Earl was now no better than a marionette. He was nothing more than an empty husk of a former human being whose purpose was being dictated by Max Acton's string-pulling, as much in charge from miles away as if he were standing right here next to Earl in the forest.

When Earl had awakened in the basement of Acton's rented home, confused and frightened and knowing something was very wrong but having no idea what it might be, he had had no intention of standing upon command or of walking to Acton when summoned, and yet he had done exactly that, because he had had no choice in the matter.

He cursed at Acton and refused to stand, yet his body performed the activity all on its own. He cursed again and refused to walk, yet his body performed *that* activity all on its own, too. If free will, the ability to determine one's own future through one's own independent choices and actions, was what ultimately defined humanity, then Earl Manning was not only dead, he was no longer human.

And that was terrifying. He was on a mission for which he had not volunteered and did not wish to undertake, but still, here he was, plodding along approaching the point where he would either accomplish it unwillingly or die trying, if that was even possible. Could you be killed once you were already dead? Or would a more accurate question be, could you be killed once you were "undead?"

Earl mopped his brow by force of habit. It was an unnecessary and futile gesture, since whatever black fucking magic was powering this whole nightmare had not insinuated itself into his sweat glands. Despite the heat and the intense physical activity—Earl was working harder on his first day as an undead man than he had ever once worked in his last decade as a live one—his skin remained as cold and dry as a stone.

He trudged along and tried to think. Thinking and planning were two things he had never been particularly good at when he was alive, and they seemed like even more elusive concepts now that he was dead. He couldn't seem to force his mind to focus on any one thought for more than a second or two at a time. It was like there was a mosquito buzzing around his head at night, constantly moving, landing for a second and then disappearing again when he swatted at it.

And that was frustrating, because Earl had the annoying sensation that this inability to focus was important in some way. That it might make a difference, somehow, in his—literally—damned existence. That maybe he could use it to his advantage. He concentrated on that notion as hard as he could. Acton was controlling his existence and his activities like some evil, black-hearted god, but he wasn't controlling his every precise move right down to every muscle twitch. The Fucking Devil Acton could sense Earl's *thoughts* and *intentions* but could not control his every precise *action*.

Important.

That was an important distinction; maybe a critical one. But why? What the hell difference could that small detail possibly make? And why did it matter, in the long run? He would still be dead no matter what. But there was a significance to that distinction that was eluding him. He tried and tried to concentrate on the question but simply could not make the mosquito stay in one place for more than a second or two.

Earl staggered through the forest, struggling to walk and think at the same time. He caught his foot in a root sticking out of the forest floor and pitched forward, banging his forehead on a tree. He cursed out of habit, despite the fact that what a little over a week ago would have caused a nasty headache and probably a blooming purple bruise had not caused any real pain at all.

It didn't matter, he was still pissed. He wondered if walking would ever become second nature like it had once been, or whether he would be forced to move like Frankenstein's monster for the rest of his life, or death, or whatever the hell it was. He wondered if Max Acton, sitting in his broken-down house across town could sense his frustration. He hoped so; it would serve the miserable bastard right.

And then Earl forgot all about the mystery of being a revenant and why it seemed so important that Acton could control his purpose but not his every action, because as he raised his eyes to a shaft of bright sunlight stabbing through the thick forest canopy, Earl spotted a clearing. A man-made clearing.

At the far end of the man-made clearing, in the middle of the thousands of square miles of virgin forest in extreme northern Maine, a log cabin loomed in the distance, shimmering in the heat, massive and impressive and newly constructed.

He was here. And it was time to go to work.

13

"Well, that was pleasant." Sharon tucked a stray lock of black hair behind her ear as she accelerated out of the Ridge Runner parking lot.

Mike chuckled darkly. "Yeah, that Pellerin's a real engaging guy. He certainly doesn't have a whole lot of respect for women, does he?" He thought about the tavern owner's leering comments to Sharon and pursed his lips angrily.

"I had two strikes against me the moment we walked into the bar," she said. "My uniform — he's not a big fan of cops, in case you hadn't noticed — and the fact that Earl Manning is probably his biggest customer. I'll bet he was barely exaggerating when he said his sales are down twenty percent since Earl's gone missing."

"Well, then, he shouldn't have been dicking us

around. He should have been glad we're out trying to hunt Earl's sorry ass down."

"I'm sure he is, but Earl has spent countless hours sloppy drunk in that bar, undoubtedly pouring his broken heart out to Bo about how I blew him off all those years ago. I'm sure he doesn't include the part about using alcohol and drugs to get in my pants while he's telling his sob story. Undoubtedly that part is conveniently overlooked."

"Two strikes," Sharon repeated. "Actually, the process went much better than I expected it to. At least we walked out with something resembling a lead, which we certainly didn't have before."

The atmosphere inside the cruiser was better than it had been on the way to the Ridge Runner. It wasn't exactly the same as when they were together, but Mike was relieved not to have to sit through the stilted, awkward, tense silence of earlier. It was obvious Sharon was trying to keep the mood light. At least, as light as possible under the circumstances. "So, where are we headed now, boss?"

Mike smiled and cut a look sideways at her. "Where would we be headed if you were in charge of this investigation?"

"Rose Pellerin's shop," she answered immediately.

"Right you are."

***

The air felt dry and somehow brittle, like the inside of an elderly person's home, as they walked into *Needful Things*. Sharon had always felt the name of the shop—a tiny cubby which had been around as long as she could remember—to be an unnecessary reach, as if its owner might be trying to convince the world Paskagankee was some gothic little New England town of horrors, and that something strange and eerie and otherworldly might be found here.

The reality, Sharon felt, was that the attempt was mostly wasted. Paskagankee was so far off the beaten path in northern New England that visitors and vacationers rarely came around, and when they did it was usually because they had gotten lost and wanted nothing more than directions back to the interstate highway fifteen miles away. The natives of this little town certainly weren't falling for the Stephen King comparison. They already knew exactly what Paskagankee was—a sleepy little hamlet where nothing much ever happened. At least that's what it *had* been until last fall, when the murders had begun occurring.

Sharon thought about those bizarre few days and shivered unconsciously. Maybe there was more to the name of Rose Pellerin's shop than she had previously realized. Maybe when the old lady named this place a couple of decades ago she had smelled the evil coming; had somehow just been better attuned to it than anyone else.

A tiny bell hanging at the end of a brass bracket mounted on top of the door announced their arrival. The shop was tiny but jam-packed with knick-knacks, greeting cards, collectibles. They were the sorts of items you might expect to find inside the elderly person's home with the dry and brittle air.

Rose Pellerin stood behind the counter next to the door and stared at them as they entered, her expression guarded. It was as if she had been expecting them, and clearly she had. Undoubtedly, her brother had called as soon as they left the Ridge Runner to warn his sister that she could expect a visit from the police.

Sharon wondered if Rose was any friendlier than Bo and decided she couldn't very well be any more hostile. She tried to recall whether she had ever spoken to the store owner and didn't think she had, despite living in Paskagankee virtually her entire life. She had seen her around town, of course, plenty of times—you couldn't live in a place this small and not know mostly everyone, at least by sight—but their paths had never directly crossed.

"Hello, officers," the shopkeeper said, and smiled, and it was as if the sun had just peeked out from behind the clouds after a heavy rain. Rose Pellerin's face turned from wary to welcoming and suddenly she looked nothing like her brother.

Mike extended his hand. "Ms Pellerin, I'm Chief Mike McMahon and this is Officer—"

"—Oh, I know who this young lady is," she said. "Hello, dear, how are you?"

"I'm fine, Ms Pellerin," Sharon answered, puzzled. "Have we met?"

"Not officially, I suppose, but you used to go skipping past this very front door every day on your way to school when you were just a little thing. I could tell, even way back then, that you were going to turn into quite the heartbreaker, and good Lord, I was right on the money, wasn't I?"

Sharon's could feel her face flush. She decided Bo Pellerin's blatant hostility and aggression would be preferable to this torture, especially with Mike standing right next to her. He was obviously enjoying the exchange immensely and Sharon knew she would be hearing about it the moment they closed the doors of the cruiser. *Heartbreaker! 'Good Lord' was right.*

After a few seconds that felt more like hours Mike took pity on Sharon and forged ahead. "Ms Pellerin—"

"Rose, please, everyone calls me Rose," she interrupted.

"All right then, Rose. I assume Bo called you to tell you we were on our way?"

"Why yes, chief, he did."

"Then you know why we're here."

"I do, but I'm afraid I can't shed much light on the couple you're looking for beyond what my brother has already told you. I remember them quite clearly, even though they came into the store only once, and for a fairly short amount of time at that. The young woman was breathtakingly beautiful, almost as pretty as Officer Dupont, here. Unfortunately, the older man paid cash for their purchases, so I don't even have a credit card receipt I could look up to tell you his last name."

"Your brother said the man called the young woman 'Raven,' is that correct?"

"That's right, and the older man's name was Max."

"Really. Bo didn't mention that you heard the man's name."

"That's because I never told him," she explained. "I don't speak with Bo very often. He's always so negative about everything I try to stay away from him for the most part. You know what I mean?"

"Of course," Mike answered with a smile. "You were saying? About their names?"

"Oh yes, about the older man's name. I never told Bo that I heard his name. The only reason I even mentioned the young woman to him is because she was just so incredibly beautiful I wondered if he had seen her around town, too. But of course up until that point he hadn't. Anyway, as the couple was walking out the door after paying for their purchases, the young lady said, quite clearly, 'Thank you, Max, these things are lovely,' and then they disappeared."

Sharon jotted the name in her tiny notebook as Mike asked, "Have they been in your store since that day?"

"No, they walked out the door and I've never seen either one of them again."

"But you're certain the woman was named Raven and the man's name was Max."

"Completely certain, at least to the extent that's what they were calling each other. Whether or not those were their real names, I couldn't say."

Mike smiled again. "I don't suppose either one of them happened to mention where they were staying in town, did they?"

"No. They really didn't say much of anything at all while they were in here except for the very short snippet of conversation Bo mentioned, and then the couple of words I heard as they were walking out the door. I'm afraid I don't know anything else; I'm sorry."

"No problem," Mike answered. "You've been very helpful. If you see either of them again, would you please call me right away? It's a matter of considerable importance." He handed her a business card with the Paskagankee PD telephone number as well as his personal cell number printed on it.

"Of course," she said, walking them to the door. The bell tinkled as it opened, the sound warm and inviting, and Sharon wondered how two people who had grown up and lived their entire lives in the same town could have turned out as differently as Bo and Rose Pellerin, one dour and uncooperative, the other pleasant and helpful.

They walked into the warm June sunshine, crossing the paved parking lot to the cruiser. Sharon asked, "Want me to drive?"

Mike grinned. "It's up to you, Princess. You're the heartbreaker, after all."

Sharon groaned and rolled her eyes as she made a fist around the car key. Mike was still laughing as she pulled onto Main Street and gunned the engine, turning toward the center of town. For a few minutes it was almost like the old days.

14

The plot of the TV soap was hard to follow, but Josh Parmalee was trying like hell to keep up. One chick was sleeping with another, stringing along two guys, engineering a plot to kidnap the baby of her former lover, while faking her own death in order to defraud a life insurance company out of millions of dollars. Josh loved soaps. They were the only thing on television that even came close to approximating some of the bizarre shit he had seen during his days on the Seattle PD.

Treachery, backstabbing, random violence, drug deals gone sour, bad people cutting down even worse people in hails of gunfire, Josh had seen all of it and more before retiring and somehow, against all odds, landing squarely in the middle of this unbelievably cushy job.

It was the sort of once-in-a-lifetime incredible shit luck

that never happened for guys like him. Josh was under no illusions about what he was: a mostly unmotivated cop who had spent his entire career in the shadowy grey area between strict enforcement of the law and earning dirty money by discreetly looking the other way during the commission of certain illegal activities.

Josh had been careful to protect his back at all times, but had always been willing to do business with the right people at the right time—or the wrong people at the wrong time, depending on how you looked at it—if those people showed a willingness to contribute enough cash to his secret retirement fund. Then the shit luck that never happened for guys like him had actually happened.

Looking back on it, Josh could still hardly believe his unlikely good fortune. It almost seemed like a dream. Only it wasn't a dream, because if it had been, he would not be sitting here today, lounging in front of the big-screen TV in the living room of Brett Parker's brand-new vacation hideaway watching two gorgeous soon-to-be Hollywood starlets make out with each other while stuffing his face with Doritos.

Brett Parker, for crying out loud! One of the richest and most influential men in America, the guy *People Magazine* had named one of the Sexiest Men Alive two years running, not that Josh cared about how sexy any dude was. But the point was this guy was the Real Deal, and Josh Parmalee, of all people, had been hired to provide his security. Unbelievable.

The soap went to a commercial just as things were getting hot and heavy between the two girls, and he thought back to the day that had changed his life forever. He was a patrolman, stuck in the world of the law enforcement foot soldier, unlikely ever to receive the promotion to detective that he craved, thanks to questionable decision-making skills and his tendency toward over-reliance on the enthusiastic employment of fists and baton in keeping suspects in line.

On that fateful day, Josh had been patrolling a local park where rich and influential native son Brett Parker, local software magnate extraordinaire, was scheduled to dedicate a brand-new baseball field for underprivileged children he had financed out of his own pocket. A podium was set up on the pitcher's mound, with television cameras and print reporters gathered around home plate to memorialize every second of the Great Man's appearance among the unwashed masses.

Josh had been patrolling the outfield, ostensibly on the lookout for trouble but mostly eyeing the hordes of beautiful young women who always followed Parker around, drawn to the man's wealth and power like moths to a flame.

He trailed along behind one particularly scrumptious young thing; a girl dressed in a tiny t-shirt barely covering her ample assets and the tightest pair of jeans Josh had ever seen. He wondered whether she would even be able to slide them off if she ever managed to corral Parker.

As he did his best to look inconspicuous while keeping her in his sights as long as possible, a sudden furtive movement ahead and to the girl's right caught his eye. He almost ignored it; after all, you didn't see female specimens like this one every day; not unless your name was Brett Parker, of course. But something about the activity raised his hackles.

He glanced to his right, annoyed at the distraction,

and his eyes widened in shock as he saw some dude who looked as though he had just woken up under a bridge abutment—long, dirty beard and filthy jeans that probably had never seen the inside of a washing machine—pull a handgun out of his pocket and begin bringing it to bear on Parker.

And no one noticed, except for Josh.

It was freaking unbelievable. Here they were, smack in the middle of a huge crowd of who knew how many thousands of people, and a grubby bum most people would cross the street to avoid was brandishing a gun, *and nobody noticed!*

The bum was positioned almost directly behind Parker now, the Great Man's back completely exposed to the commoners as he addressed the reporters and TV cameras transmitting his words to the millions of other commoners not fortunate enough to attend the ceremony. The moment the guy fired, Parker would go down. There was no way he could miss. It was the perfect angle and the perfect opportunity for this sleazeball—probably crazy as a loon, suffering from paranoid delusions or something—to make his nutty statement to the world by assassinating Parker.

And Josh reacted.

He reacted immediately. Just because he was a semi-dirty cop, willing to take his money where he could get it, didn't mean he wasn't a halfway decent officer when he wanted to be. He knew instinctively if he drew his gun dozens of people would die, there was no question about it. He would spook the nut-job, the crazy bastard would spray the crowd with bullets, and people would die.

So he left his sidearm in its holster and instead,

launched himself at the man. No bullshit fair play warning like the cops always gave on TV; Josh wasn't about fair play, he was all about getting the upper hand by any means possible. He launched himself like the middle linebacker he had been back in high school, hitting the guy with his powerful shoulders and driving him sideways into a crowd of teenagers.

The gun flew up into the air as it was jarred out of the asshole's hand, and as if someone had flipped a switch, chaos erupted. People started screaming and running and Josh brought the guy to the ground, shoving his face into the dirt, grinding a little more grime into the bum's already filthy beard, not that anyone would notice.

And just like that, Josh Parmalee became a hero. He was the flavor of the day, receiving a commendation from a grateful mayor, whose finely tuned political instincts told him it was the right move despite the singularly uninspired nature of the record in Josh's personnel folder. There was a ceremony on the steps of City Hall, presentation of a medal, and a sincere handshake from Brett Parker himself at the end of a moving speech where he thanked Officer Parmalee for saving his life. All of it captured by the greedy eye of the Seattle TV news cameras, then transmitted around the country by virtually every network.

But the best part, the unbelievable part, came after the ceremony, while Brett Parker and Josh relaxed in the Mayor's office, sharing a beer and casual conversation. That was when Parker had sprung the job offer on Josh, admitting the events that afternoon at the park had shaken him up badly. "I need personal security," he said, and Josh nodded, still with no freaking clue where the conversation was headed.

By the time Parker got around to spelling out the job offer, Josh had stared at him for at least thirty seconds, mouth hanging open like a damn fool, unable even to formulate a response. He waited for the billionaire to begin laughing, to pull the rug out from under him and declare the whole thing a joke, but he never did. He simply waited for a response from the man who had saved his life, the man he now wanted as his head of personal security.

And Josh had accepted on the spot.

Now he sat munching on Doritos and shaking his head at his unlikely good fortune. One moment in the right place at the right time, a few seconds of sheer luck, had given him this cushy gig with all of the trappings of wealth and power. One moment of action—the whole crazy incident had taken maybe ten seconds from beginning to end—and now he had life by the balls.

The commercials ended—laundry detergent, diapers and tampons were all they ever seemed to advertise on soaps; that was the worst part of watching—and the show came back on. Josh was disappointed but unsurprised to see they were now focusing on a different storyline for the time being, one which didn't feature beautiful young actresses French-kissing each other.

He assuaged his disappointment with another Dorito, crunching away happily, when he heard a drawn-out *creeeeeak* just outside. The sound seemed to come from the porch, and although this brand-new house creaked and groaned all the time as it began the process of settling on its foundation, this particular noise seemed somehow different. Furtive, like the movement he had detected so long ago at the park, and which had ultimately been

responsible for changing his life.
    Josh stopped chewing and listened hard.

15

There were less than a half-dozen real estate agents in the Paskagankee area who might have rented a home to the mysterious Max and his beautiful companion. The pair wasn't living in the small downtown area—it would have been impossible to do so and remain as invisible as they had—and the only apartments for rent in Paskagankee were all located within a fifteen minute walk of the police station, so Mike assumed if they were living in the area at all it would have to be in a house somewhere on the outskirts of town.

This still left them with a vast expanse of territory to consider, given the sheer geographical vastness of Paskagankee. But the handful of local realtors became the logical starting point for the search. If none of them panned out, Mike knew more research would be required to uncover names and contact numbers for homes available for rent by individuals outside the immediate area.

He eased into the wheeled chair behind his desk and picked up the telephone, gazing through the glass office wall at Sharon, busy working the phone out in the mostly empty squad room. They had split the numbers evenly, three for him and three for her, and he watched as she sat with her feet on her desk, holding the telephone receiver to her ear and biting her lip as she tried to coax information out of a realtor clearly unwilling or unable to part with it.

For those few minutes back in the cruiser, after leaving *Needful Things,* the shroud of tension and regret which had been hanging over them since the breakup seemed to lift. Then reality reasserted itself. They drove into the police station parking lot to continue the search for Earl Manning and the easy familiarity they had shared disappeared like the popping of a child's balloon. They trudged into the station and split up, Mike disappearing into the chief's office and Sharon sitting down at her desk, the moment rich with symbolism and pain.

Mike sighed and looked at the telephone numbers he had printed out, selecting the top one and punching the digits into the keypad on his phone with more force than necessary.

"Green Mountain Realty, Barb speaking, how may I help you?"

Mike was surprised but grateful for the opportunity to talk to a real human being rather than a machine. "Hello, Barb, how are you today? This is Chief Mike McMahon of the Paskagankee Police Department."

"Chief McMahon, hello! Finally decided to get out of

that little apartment you're renting downtown and enjoy the advantages of home ownership?"

Mike laughed. "No ma'am, I don't think I'm ready for that kind of responsibility just yet. Actually, I'm calling on police business. We are investigating the disappearance of a Paskagankee resident, Earl Manning, and believe a newly arrived couple in town may have information which could be helpful in the search. The problem is we don't have a last name for either the man or the woman. We only know that they are likely renting a home on the outskirts of town. We believe their first names are Max and Raven. I don't suppose you've rented any homes within, say, the last three months to a couple with these names? The man is considerably older than the woman."

"No, Chief, but the rental market has been very slow recently. Between the slow economy, which will continue to struggle in a remote area such as this even after the rest of the country has gotten back on track, and that horrible business with Chief Court killing all those people last fall, residential home sales and rentals have virtually dried up. I'm certain I would remember if I had served a couple such as the one you mentioned. I'm sorry I can't help you."

"No problem. Thank you anyway, Barb."

"Good luck with your search, Chief, and give some thought to what I said about buying a house. There are tax advantages, not to mention the pride of ownership."

"I'll think it over, Barb, and when I'm ready to buy, you'll be hearing from me. Thanks again."

Mike hung up and glanced out through the open blinds into the bullpen to see the front legs of Sharon's chair slam down on the worn tile floor as she stood, writing furiously in her notebook. She looked up and caught Mike's eye, gesturing with her head for him to come out of his office. He could see, even from twenty feet away and through a window, that she was onto something. Her eyes shone and her body crackled with an electric energy that made Mike's heart ache.

He left his office in time to hear the end of Sharon's telephone conversation with the realtor. "Are you kidding me?" she said into the mouthpiece. "That place was run-down ten years ago. I'm surprised it's even inhabitable. Thank you so much for your information; you might just have helped locate a missing person."

She hung up the phone and turned to Mike. "Bingo. Max Acton is the guy's name, and he's renting the old Higginson house out on Depot Road, way out in the woods. The place was empty and falling apart when I was in high school—"

"—Way back then?" Mike interrupted, and Sharon smacked him on the arm.

"The point is," she continued, "the place was a piece of crap a decade ago and it has undergone virtually no maintenance or restoration since. No legitimate couple would ever rent that place unless they were trying to keep as low a profile as they possibly could."

Mike smiled and fist-bumped his officer. "Looks like we're in business. Let's go."

16

Josh Parmalee listened for the creaking sound a second time, his mouth hanging half-open, Dorito crumbs littering his jeans and his Nine Inch Nails T-shirt. He was careful to dress professionally when in public on the job with Parker—the Great Man would expect nothing less—but out in the woods in the middle of nowhere a suit seemed a little bit like overkill.

He was certain he had heard a noise, furtive and hushed, like someone (something) sneaking across the newly constructed wraparound porch Parker was so proud of. The hairs on the back of Josh's neck stood on end and he felt a worm of fear wriggle its way through his intestines.

He shook his head and grunted. He was being ridiculous, a freaking little pansy. Next thing you knew he would scream and piss his pants. He was just unused to being way out here in the forest, that was all. He was a city guy, had been born and raised in Seattle and spent his entire life there. All of this vast emptiness, with its three hundred year old towering pines and its millions of frigging mosquitoes and its mooses or meeses or whatever the hell they were called, it was all a little unnerving. That was all.

Besides, he had now been listening closely for at least a minute and had yet to hear a repeat of the sound which had caused this massive overreaction. He was glad his old compatriots on the Seattle PD couldn't see him now, cowering inside his rich boss's house, all because of a little *noise*.

He grunted again and stuffed another Dorito into his mouth and that was when the front door slammed open with a *Crash!* banging into the freshly painted living room wall with enough force to gouge out a chunk of drywall. A puff of delicate white dust floated into the air like a miniature explosion and Josh's eyes widened in shock.

Looming in the doorway, swaying side to side as if drunk or high, stood a haggard-looking skeleton of a man, hair unkempt, dirty clothes hanging off his rail-thin body, his face somehow . . . *off* . . . as if the features couldn't quite coordinate with each other. His eyes seemed off-kilter, glazed and unfocused and looking in two different directions, and one side of his mouth curled up as if attempting to smile or perhaps sneer, while the other side bent down in studious concentration.

The man shook his head side to side slowly and his eyes came together, focusing on Josh, who was so surprised he hadn't moved, hadn't even put down his bag of chips. The intruder shambled forward a couple of feet and stopped. "Brett Parker?" he asked, the voice issuing from deep inside his chest, low and rumbling, and that was what snapped Josh out of his shocked inaction.

Josh leapt to his feet, orange-yellow crumbs scattering all over the freshly varnished hardwood floor, and he had the absurd thought that he had better get the mess cleaned up before Parker saw it or his boss would flip out. He reached for his weapon, a Sig Sauer P229 shoved into the waistband of his pants at the small of his back. He yanked it out, holding it—for the moment—with both hands at his side, barrel pointed toward the now-messy floor. Josh had instinctively checked the intruder's hands the moment he crashed through the door and they were empty, and he knew he could bring his weapon to bear, if it came to that, before the man could get within arm's length of him.

Josh had had plenty of experience dealing with drugged-up losers back in Seattle, usually young men, assholes hopped up on meth or angel dust or any of the other crazy shit these idiots were stupid enough to put into their bodies, and that's what it appeared this dirtbag had done.

Sort of.

Something was off about the guy, that much was plain as day.

"Why don't you just stop right there," Josh said calmly, his insides churning with the adrenaline rush he used to experience almost daily but had nearly forgotten about since hiring on with Parker. He raised the Sig to punctuate his point and almost lowered it to the floor again, but thought better of it and held it eye-level, barrel now pointed at the intruder's chest.

To his surprise, the man *did* stop. In Josh's police experience, losers as far gone as this guy appeared to be didn't normally pay the slightest attention to a weapon, whether pointed at them or not. But this guy looked quizzically at Josh and repeated his question. "Are you Brett Parker?" The voice really was spooky as hell.

"Who wants to know?" Josh countered, and the man standing three feet inside the damaged doorway, swaying on his feet like a stoned teenager at a heavy-metal show, shook his head. "You ain't Parker. Where's Brett Parker?"

And that was when everything went to shit. Because at that moment Brett Parker, the *real* Brett Parker, the man this loony-tune was searching for, came wandering into the room from the hallway, forehead wrinkled, demanding to know just what in the holy hell was going on here. And the hallway was behind the intruder, meaning the crazy bastard stood between Josh and Parker. Meaning the intruder was closer to Parker than Josh was, meaning also that if Parker came any closer to the man standing in front of the door, there would be no way he could get a shot off without risking hitting his boss.

It was decision time. Josh had to make a split-second determination whether to fire his weapon or not. The answer was simple. This crazy-looking motherfucker had burst into a private residence uninvited and unannounced, lunacy written all over his features, ranting and raving about Brett Parker, a man worth billions and who had dozens—if not hundreds—of enemies throughout the business world.

It was a no-brainer. Sure, the intruder was unarmed, but Josh could take care of that minor detail later; maybe put a steak knife in his dead hand or something.

He fired. Flame belched from the barrel of the Sig and the weapon blasted, the noise loud and shocking inside the enclosed room, and a sharp, tangy smell filled the air, and the crazed-looking, drugged-up stranger took a direct hit in his chest. The impact blasted him backward and he smashed into the partially open door, falling against the wall he had damaged with his violent entrance.

Parker instinctively dove to the floor and Josh had to give him credit, he never screamed. Josh figured a prepped-up Ivy League pussy like Brett Parker would crap his pants with the discharge of a weapon, but he did nothing of the sort. He hit the deck and rolled into the hallway and instantly rose a notch in Josh Parmalee's eyes.

Josh lowered his weapon and looked down the hallway. His hands were shaking and he was breathing heavily and he could feel the adrenaline pumping through his system. It felt good. "Are you all right, boss?"

"What the hell is going on here?" Parker demanded, rolling onto his hands and knees and looking up at Josh, waiting for an answer. His sandy blond hair hung in his eyes and he looked more angry than afraid.

And before he had a chance to explain, before he could tell Parker about the door slamming open and the crazy fuck bursting in, swaying on his feet and jibbering about looking for Brett Parker in his drugged-up, spooky voice, before he could say any of that, the intruder, the guy crumpled in the corner who by all rights should be dead, the guy who had taken a 9mm hollow point right in his drugged-up chest and been blasted five feet backward, that guy, began to rise.

The stranger pushed himself up on his hands and knees slowly, until he was in virtually the same position as

Parker. Then he lurched to his feet, his hands exploring the hole that had appeared in his chest when the slug punched through his body, a look of annoyance mixing with wonder on his face.

Josh stared, mouth agape, too stunned to move. This guy could not possibly stand after being shot in the chest—Josh would bet a week's paycheck he had hit the man right in the heart—at practically point-blank range. It was inconceivable. The druggie's shirt, already dirty and threadbare, was now shredded and torn where the bullet pierced it on its way into the man's body.

Josh could see a ragged hole in the man's chest around the fluttering remnants of that shirt. The hole seemed much larger than it should have been, even considering the damage his round could do. But the most unbelievable part, the part that had Josh staring in wonder when he should have been preparing to defend himself and his employer, was the utter lack of blood.

The man's chest should have been gushing; blood should have been pumping out of him with the force of a small fire hose, spurting out with every beat of his heart, leaking and flowing and soaking his shirt as the life ebbed out of him. But it wasn't. It wasn't gushing or pumping or flowing or doing anything else; it simply wasn't there. *There was no blood.*

The crazy-ass stranger who was hopped up on drugs and didn't seem to know how to bleed began shuffling forward across the floor, moving toward Josh, shambling like some kind of fucking zombie out of a two a.m. horror movie on cable. Except it wasn't two a.m. and this wasn't some stupid zombie horror movie. Incredibly, the guy still hadn't taken note of Brett Parker, but Josh wasn't thinking much about Parker or anything else at the moment. All he could think was *this is not freaking possible.*

The stranger spoke again as he shambled toward Josh, demanding for the third time, "Where is Brett Parker?" His voice now sounded ten times worse even than before. Because now Josh could now hear his words coming out of the hole in his chest as well as out of his mouth.

This is not freaking possible.

Finally Josh thought to raise his gun and train it on this weird intruder who didn't seem to be able to die or even to bleed. He brought it to chest level and fired just as the guy clamped one impossibly strong hand around his neck and tossed him effortlessly across the room. Josh heard the sound of the gun discharging and felt it buck like something alive in his hand. He caught the flash of fire as it flew from the barrel, saw it in his peripheral vision as he felt himself flying through the air, not with the greatest of ease or even any small amount of grace.

Josh slammed into the granite fireplace and the last two things he thought before his world went black were, 1) He must have blasted that motherfucker to hell this time, and, 2) Parker was going to be really pissed when he had to clean all of Josh's blood off his brand new chimney.

He wavered for a moment, lost somewhere in that fuzzy grey expanse between alert and unconscious, thinking of nothing besides what a relief it would be when his body finally shut down. Somewhere outside of himself he heard a long moment of complete silence. Then the screaming started.

Parker hadn't screamed before, but now he did, he made up for his lack of expression earlier by shouting out a symphony of terror, screaming until he went hoarse, screaming for mercy and for his mother and for nothing in particular besides a sane moment in a suddenly insane world.

And then Josh Parmalee's world disappeared, going up in a puff of smoke as his brain shut itself down.

17

Earl grabbed the guy who had shot him and tossed him effortlessly across the room as the man fired his gun again. This time the bullet missed Earl and the shooter's body smashed into the fireplace with a thud and crumpled onto the polished granite hearth. His strength surprised him. He wasn't especially tall and had always been scrawny and that was even truer now that he was dead, but he lifted the much heavier gunman with no trouble at all and threw him like a pitcher firing strike one across home plate.

Getting shot had been a trip—the bullet broadsided him right smack in the chest with the force of a speeding freight train, slamming him backward into the wall, but there had been no pain, just a momentary sense of intense, imploding pressure. Then he stumbled clumsily to his feet and continued on as if he had simply tripped and fallen.

His chest was a mess. The bullet blasted through the empty cavity where his heart had been, punching a hole the approximate size of a dime in the middle of his sternum. Earl could feel a jagged, baseball-sized canyon where the slug had exited out his back, rocketing into the wall behind him.

But all-in-all, Earl felt pretty damned good about the situation. He had been shot but was still standing and wasn't even bleeding. He knew Parker was here and although this house was about the biggest damned thing he had ever stepped foot inside that wasn't called a mall, it was only a matter of time before he hunted down his target and accomplished his goal.

He looked away from the unmoving body of the dude who had shot him and spotted what he had come for. He smiled, the left side of his misshapen face beaming while the right barely moved. Earl had discovered it wasn't easy coordinating all of the various movements of your body when you were dead and his concentration wavered when he turned, because rising slowly and quietly to his feet, clearly doing his best to will himself invisible, was a man. A man who had to be the elusive Brett Parker.

Earl stumbled forward, closing the distance between the two of them quickly despite his difficulty walking. It was obvious Parker was in shock, his brain trying to process what he had just seen, and thus the man wasn't moving anywhere near as quickly or as efficiently as he should have been able to. Not that it would have made a damn bit of difference.

The bizarre little dance continued as the pair moved down the hallway, Earl advancing, Parker retreating. The software magnate still hadn't said a word, but his eyes grew steadily larger as he took in the ruined figure stalking him. Earl couldn't decide whether to be offended or pleased. He decided that didn't make a damn bit of difference, either.

Finally Parker ran out of real estate, bumping into the closet door which formed the end of the hallway and trying without any measurable level of success to push his way through it. Earl attempted another smile and that was when the billionaire started screaming. He yelled loudly and enthusiastically, sometimes calling for help, sometimes demanding Earl leave and promising him he could have whatever he wanted if he did, but mostly hollering panicked words and half-phrases that didn't seem to have any meaning at all.

Earl waited patiently. He had nowhere to go and no pressing business awaiting him beyond his current assignment, and he certainly wasn't going to get tired—he could stand all day now that he was dead. Eventually Parker reached the inevitable conclusion that yelling for help was pointless in a place where the nearest neighbor was located almost four miles away, across a nearly impenetrable forest, and he shut his mouth.

Parker looked up in fear, cringing in the corner of the hallway, still pushing futilely against the closet door. It was as if his brain had forgotten to tell his feet that backing through the end of the house was impossible. Earl could sympathize. He was getting used to dealing with a certain amount of mental confusion himself.

"Where is it?" Earl asked, and Parker gasped in terror but surprisingly did not begin screaming again.

"Where is what?" he whispered back, eyes still huge,

goggling at Earl like he had never seen a reanimated dead guy before.

"Don't play stupid," Earl said, falling back on the script he had been forced to memorize by his god, The Fucking Devil Max Acton. "What is it that everyone from the biggest software corporations in the world to the smallest startups would kill to get their hands on?"

"I don't know what you're talking about."

"BULLSHIT," Earl rumbled, leaning down and screaming in Parker's face, giving the man a whiff of the smell of death, a corruption that no amount of Navajo mysticism and no magic stone could completely erase. Parker whimpered, breathing heavily, and tried to fold his body up into itself but still said nothing.

"I'm talking about The Codebreaker," Earl explained, speaking softly now. "The hush-hush software you developed for the U.S. Department of Defense that's supposed to be some big secret but that everyone knows about, the software that will crack any encryption known to man within seconds, military or civilian. *That's* what I'm talking about. The Codebreaker"

Parker sighed; a long, shuddering sound that Earl took as resignation. "I won't continue to pretend I don't know what you mean. You're holding all the cards and I'm holding none. And I want to live. But I don't have The Codebreaker here, it's not with me, it's back in Seattle under lock and key," Parker stammered, exactly as Max Acton had said he would.

"Bullshit," Earl replied again, reaching out and grasping Parker by the throat. His fingers began to close like a pair of vice grips, slowly cutting off the man's air supply. "I know you always keep a copy of the software with you on a thumb drive to protect yourself in the event something were to happen to the master copy. I want it and you're going to give it to me and if you don't you're going to end up just like your gun-toting friend out there."

By now Earl's hand was practically closed. Parker could no longer talk but nodded violently, his hair falling down his sweaty forehead and into his eyes. Earl released his grip and waited while the man choked and gagged, a high-pitched whistling sound accompanying his desperate lung-fulls of air. Earl wondered momentarily if he had done permanent damage to the man's windpipe before realizing he didn't care. At least the guy was still alive; that was more than Earl could say.

Finally the man seemed to have regained his breath, more or less, and sat with his head bowed between his upraised knees. Earl rumbled, "Thumb drive," the creepy sound emanating from his ruined chest as well as his mouth, and Parker nodded.

"Okay," the billionaire whispered. He reached into the right front pocket of his cargo shorts and Earl wasn't even concerned that he would withdraw a weapon. What was the guy going to do, kill him? It was way too late for that.

Parker pulled out a small portable hard drive, tiny, no bigger in size than a pack of gum. Earl shook his head. Could it really be this easy? Did this software big shot really carry a copy of his precious breakthrough, the thing everyone in the world was after, in his pants pocket?

Apparently he did. Parker held it up for Earl's inspection with a trembling hand. "This is it," he whispered.

Earl shrugged. "How am I supposed to know?" He grabbed the tiny hard drive out of Parker's hand and shoved it deep inside his own pocket, wondering how much of the activity inside this cabin Max Acton was able to discern back at his house through their strange, mystical connection.

As he did so, the seed of an idea began germinating inside his scrambled brain and he instinctively pushed it away, not wanting his god, the man who held his very existence in his hands, to catch even a whiff of it.

"That's the software, I swear," Parker said, and Earl looked at him and smiled.

"I believe you," he said. "Now let's go."

"Go? Go where? Where are we going? I gave you what you came for, now just leave!"

"That's not part of the plan," Earl told him with genuine reluctance in his voice. "And I couldn't change the plan even if I wanted to."

"But what do you need me for? You have the software, you don't need me!"

"You *say* I'm holding the software and I actually believe you. But what if you're lying? What if this is nothing but a decoy, a phony hard drive with no purpose other than to hand to anyone managing to make it past your armed guard? What if this thumb drive contains nothing but a list of your favorite rock songs, or the names and phone numbers of all your mistresses, not that that wouldn't be totally cool, too. What then?

"Besides," he continued, "I can't very well leave you here to your own devices. As soon as I walked out that door you would be on the phone to what passes for the local law around here. I can't very well have that, can I?"

"You could cut the phone lines," Parker argued, desperately looking for a way to make the nightmare go away. "And cell coverage here is pretty much nonexistent, so I couldn't contact anyone, at least not for several hours, and by that time you could be three hundred miles away in any direction."

Earl reached for Parker's throat and the man shrank back against the closet door. The conversation was getting repetitive and was irrelevant to begin with. He *had* to do what Max Acton had instructed him to do; he literally had no choice, and Acton had told him to bring Parker *and* the software back to the house. So that was what he would do. Period. It was the end of the story, even if Parker didn't understand that fact.

Closing his hand around Parker's throat one more time—he didn't know where this superhuman strength had come from, he supposed it must be part of the whole revenant vibe but was thankful for it in any event; it certainly made dealing with reluctant assholes a hell of a lot easier—Earl lifted the man with one arm and plopped him back down on the hardwood floor of the hallway.

Immediately Parker began gagging and choking again but seemed to get the message. He raised his hands in surrender and lurched painfully to his feet. He began stumbling toward the front door.

Together the odd-looking pair crossed the devastation of the living room and meandered their way into the front yard, Parker moving shakily thanks to mortal terror and his injured throat, Earl moving shakily because he was dead. Earl noted with satisfaction that the guy who had used him for target practice was still lying in a heap in front of the fireplace where he had fallen, not moving, not moaning or groaning, not giving any indication of being alive at all.

Earl knew how the guy felt.

18

Max swung the ancient Dodge Caravan around in the middle of Route 24, then coasted to a stop on the gravel shoulder and left the vehicle idling as he waited for Earl and their new guest to come stumbling out of the forest. He very much missed the compact power and sheer penile masculinity of the Porsche, but had reluctantly decided to leave it at home in favor of the nearly invisible minivan with the blacked-out windows.

For one thing, there would be too many people riding back to the house to fit inside the little sports car. Plus, that flashy rocket would be far too memorable to continue driving in this hick burg now, where almost everyone owned either a four wheel drive pickup or a four wheel drive SUV. Better to be inconspicuous. The Porsche would have to be retired for a while.

It had not been an easy decision, though. Max had grown up with less than nothing, scrabbling on the streets of Boston with his crack-addicted mother, never knowing when his next meal was coming or where it was coming from, and had quickly grown accustomed to the finer things in life after developing the co-op scam out in the Arizona desert. It was still incomprehensible to Max how much *stuff* people would give you if they viewed you as their hero, their savior, their . . . well, their *god*.

He thought about the co-op and smiled, his mind twenty-five hundred miles away, reliving what had—until meeting Raven and learning of the existence of the mystical Navajo stone—been his greatest triumph. The "co-op" had started out as nothing more than a dusty little commune constructed around the remains of an old abandoned mining camp where members eked out a living making and selling trinkets to tourists while they "simplified their lives" by signing over their most valuable possessions to their leader, Max Acton.

It was all so easy. People wanted to believe in something larger and more important than themselves and their empty lives, and yet so many had no use for organized religion. Max had started with a handful of followers, most of them street people, bums so down on their luck they had almost nothing to give, but Max didn't care. Nothing worthwhile comes without effort, and he knew that once the word started getting around about the little slice of Nirvana he was running out in the desert, people would begin flocking to him.

And he was right on target. He was more on target than even he had anticipated. Before long the little ramshackle village had been demolished, torn down and replaced by a brand-new barracks constructed for the followers, and a majestic, soaring home for the leader, complete with vaulted ceilings and Italian terrazzo floors and marble countertops and sinks with gold fixtures and old-fashioned solid-brass fittings.

And then Raven Tahoma had come to him. A young girl from the reservation who had abandoned her home and her heritage search of something else. A young girl so strikingly beautiful and yet so completely lost that he had no trouble convincing her she belonged with him.

One night, cuddling in bed after screwing his brains out, Raven had told him an unbelievable story, a story of an ornate wooden box containing a mystical stone being held in a safe by Don Running Bear, grandson of the last great Navajo mystic. According to Raven, the stone contained powers that were terrifying in their magnitude, powers enabling the possessor of the stone to bring the dead back to life, to reanimate them, and even more terrifying, to compel the reanimated subject—the revenant—to perform any task the possessor of the box commanded.

Anything.

The story was unbelievable, preposterous, but Max had known immediately it was all true. He couldn't say how he had known, exactly, but the important thing was that he *had* known. The implications of that knowledge were immediate as well. Everything he had achieved with the co-op in the desert—the beautiful home, the dedicated followers, the wealth and influence over his subjects—was a tiny drop in the bucket compared to what he would achieve if he could only gain possession of the mystical stone.

Max had begun planning and scheming to make the stone his own. He started by grilling Raven over the course of several weeks, learning everything she knew about the stone, every last detail, which was a lot. Her father had been very close to Don Running Bear, was his best friend, in fact, so close the young girl considered him almost an uncle, and her dad had confided all he knew to his only daughter.

Max had recognized immediately that he was destined to possess the stone and make use of its awesome power. That fact was as clear as day. Why else had he been led from the East Coast urban city of Boston, Massachusetts to the hot, dry western sands of Arizona if not for this? The co-op had been wonderful, he had thought until meeting Raven that *it* was his purpose in life, but the moment he learned of the existence of the Navajo stone, everything fell into place.

So he formulated a plan, using Raven's extensive first-hand knowledge of the reservation and of the Running Bear family to acquire the stone and its beautiful wooden box. The plan had been both simple and effective—there was no need to get fancy when simple would do, that was a philosophy Max had developed years ago and which had always served him well—and he had walked off the reservation with the stone, and thus his future, securely in his grasp.

Now he waited patiently for Earl Manning and Earl's undoubtedly terrified billionaire guest to come clomping out of the woods. There had been no need to wait here for the several hours it would take Manning to hike through the thick forest, disable whatever minimal security Brett Parker had brought with him, locate the software and then hike back to the road with his prisoner. Max had simply driven home after dropping off his revenant, confident that when the time was right, the special connection he now shared with Manning would serve to alert him when it was time to drive back and pick them up.

And that was exactly what had happened. Max had been lounging in bed, half asleep, recovering from a romp with Raven when he felt a psychic "Bump," a tiny, almost imperceptible push in his mind, so slight it would be easy to miss if he weren't waiting for it. The bump told him Manning had accomplished his mission and was now on his way back through the woods with software mogul Parker in tow.

The obvious problem was that Max had no way of knowing whether the software Manning recovered was the real Codebreaker or a clever fake designed to trick anyone somehow managing to accomplish what Max had just done. He was reasonably computer literate but certainly no kind of software expert and thus would have no way of verifying the authenticity of the program. This was the weak link in the entire scheme. Max would be forced to deliver the software to the North Koreans blind and hope it performed as advertised.

One thing Max had learned years ago, though, on the streets of Boston as a child, was always to have a backup plan. He was well aware of the expression, "Don't take a knife to a gunfight," but Max subscribed to the theory that just taking a gun to a gunfight wasn't such a great idea, either. It was far preferable to bring *lots* of guns to the gunfight, so if you happened to drop one or it jammed or the other guy brought a bigger gun, you could still overwhelm him with superior firepower.

Thus, the most critical part of the plan, the part that would save Max from brutal Asian vengeance if it turned out they had been duped by Parker, was to keep Parker close. It would certainly have been much easier to instruct the revenant to kill Parker and bury him in a hole in the forest—the area surrounding Paskagankee, Maine was so thick and virtually impassable that he could have dug a grave fifteen feet into the great north woods and the body would never have been found—but Brett Parker would serve as Max's bazooka should a gunfight break out with the North Koreans.

Manning would be rendered irrelevant—the irrelevant revenant, Max thought with a smile—once he had completed his designated assignment, and furthermore, Max had no idea how long the revenant's deteriorating body would hold up. He wasn't sure exactly how the mystical stone performed its magic, reanimating a corpse, but the fact of the matter was that Manning was still dead, and, being dead, would inevitably begin to decompose over time.

That was why he had been frozen after being killed. Max had wanted to be certain everything was ready to go before thawing him, cutting out his heart and putting him to work. Time was the enemy of the revenant.

But Max had another use for the now-empty freezer sitting in the basement of the wreck of a home he had rented in Paskagankee. He had unplugged it and hosed it out after reanimating Manning, but it would soon be humming away, storing another body—Brett Parker, the soon-to-be murdered software genius. Max would kill him and freeze him, exactly as he had done with Manning. If the North Koreans came back at Max after delivery of the software, angry and vowing revenge because they had been sold a worthless fake, Parker's corpse would become Max's backup plan.

Max would simply cut Parker's heart out as he had done with Manning, thaw him out, and force him to duplicate the software. As a revenant he would be unable to refuse the command even if he wanted to. In fact, that had been Max's original plan, but upon further reflection he had decided it would be much faster and more workable simply to steal the valuable software. He wasn't sure how long it would take Parker to duplicate it if necessary and instead of risking a long, drawn-out process, Max figured once the man got a look at the shambling, terrifying sight that was the undead Earl Manning, he would in all probability comply and hand over the real Codebreaker without even considering any kind of double-cross.

And that was apparently what had happened, because as Max gazed into the thick northern Maine forest, Manning appeared, shambling directly into his line of sight, pushing a clearly terrified and now also exhausted Brett Parker, billionaire software developer and soon to be frozen dead guy, in front of him.

The pair stumbled to the minivan, Parker collapsing on the floor in back, too tired even to attempt sitting in a seat. Manning climbed in behind him, sliding the door closed, presumably to keep watch on their prisoner although it was clear the man didn't have the energy even to think about escape.

Max could only imagine how difficult the hike had been through that virgin forest, but Manning didn't even look winded. Apparently one of the few advantages of being reanimated—maybe the only one—was the inability to tire.

Looking at the hideous condition of Manning's body, though, Max didn't think many people would consider the trade-off to be worthwhile. Decomposition had begun, and although it was still in its early stages, Max could see his revenant's skin beginning to sag, especially on his face, under his eyes and on his cheeks. It was turning waxy, with a sheen that made Manning look a little bit like a replica of himself, as if Madame Tussaud had been crazy enough to construct a statue of a drunken Maine hick loser.

No matter. Soon enough Earl Manning's part in this project would be over—in fact, it was almost over already—and then he could go back to being dead. He could begin his journey to hell or whatever awaited him in the next phase of his non-existence.

No one said a word as Max turned the wheel and accelerated smoothly off the shoulder. He performed an expert three-point turn and headed off toward the crumbling, beaten-down rented home that seemed an apt metaphor for this whole miserable little town. But that didn't matter, either. Soon Paskaganee, Maine would be nothing more than a bad memory. Better days were coming. They were almost here.

19

Mike and Sharon made it as far as the reinforced glass front door before being called back by dispatcher Gordie Rheaume. "Chief?" he called across the nearly empty station house.

"What is it, Gordie?"

"I just took a 911 call from the new house out on Route 24. Someone there claimed there had been a break-in, seemed disoriented."

Mike frowned at Sharon. "That's Brett Parker's brand-new retreat. I was up there this morning meeting with his security guy." He hollered back across the station, "Who's on patrol right now?"

"Hadfield," came the dispatcher's answer.

He leaned toward Sharon. "I don't think I want Jimmy Hadfield representing the Paskagankee Police Department to someone like Brett Parker. I think we're going to have to split up. You go check out the B and E complaint at Parker's house and I'll head up to the rental by myself. Radio me as soon as you know what's going on over there."

"Will do," Sharon nodded, and pushed through the door into the warm Paskagankee afternoon.

Mike walked back to Gordie Rheaume's desk so he wouldn't have to shout. "Send an ambulance to the Depot Road address. Don't bother radioing Jimmy. I'm going to let him continue his routine patrol; I sent Officer Dupont to the home instead."

Rheaume smiled. "Good call, Chief. Oh, and the ambulance has already been dispatched. It should be on its way even as we speak."

Mike nodded and walked toward the same door Sharon had just exited. He could smell her perfume, all musk and cinnamon and implied sexual energy, still hanging in the air. It made his heart ache despite, or maybe because of, the fact their breakup was less than a day old. He realized he felt worse right now than he did after his marriage had dissolved. Kate had been drifting away from him even before the accidental shooting of Sarah Melendez, and the change that tragedy had wrought in him simply represented the tipping point in their relationship.

The heat radiated off the pavement in the parking lot as Mike approached his cruiser. Some of the realities of life as a small-town police chief were still sinking in, even though it had been nearly a full year since he had taken the job. Back in Revere, dozens of officers manned every shift, so he would never have had to consider how best to allocate resources just because two situations had developed at the same time. Here, though, when only two or maybe three officers were on patrol at once, using officers in the most efficient way became a very real issue.

Fortunately there was no need to worry about Parker's B and E. He would be in very capable hands with Sharon responding to the call. Mike was in love with the beautiful young woman but he was still quite capable of objective observation and it was clear to him that, given a little time and experience, she would develop into an outstanding law enforcement officer. The FBI had undoubtedly concluded the same thing, snapping her up and sending her to their academy in Virginia before she was forced to quit and return to care for her dying father last fall.

Mike mused about the vagaries of life as he swung onto Main Street and turned toward Route 24. If it hadn't been for Sharon's father dying—a man who had basically ignored his only daughter after the death of his wife when Sharon was in her early teens—she would certainly have been well into her career in the FBI, probably never returning to this tiny town. Mike would never have met her.

But Sharon's father *had* fallen ill, and Sharon *had* returned home to the last place in the world she wanted to be. She *had* cared for the old bastard until he died and she had met Mike and fallen in love with him and nearly been killed by the vengeful spirit last winter.

And Mike McMahon had been foolish enough to give his heart to another woman after swearing he would never make that mistake again. He had been foolish enough to think this relationship would last, in spite of their more than ten year age difference, in spite of the fact that her career was just beginning and she had nowhere to go but up, whereas his was heading—plummeting, really—in the other direction.

He chuckled bitterly. It was true what they said. There really *was* no fool like an old fool. Mike forced his thoughts into the present and tried to decide how he wanted to approach the man and the woman who, he hoped, would be able to shed some light onto the mystery of Earl Manning's disappearance.

20

Sharon was amazed at the sheer isolation of Brett Parker's retreat. The county road leading to the property was lightly traveled, even in the summertime. In the winter it became impassable, closed from the first significant fall of snow until the last of the melting occurred in the spring. After finally reaching the access road, a nearly two-mile drive through some of the thickest and most imposing forest she had ever seen was required before eventually she burst out of the trees into a newly cleared lot with a massive log cabin set in the middle. Parker's desire for privacy was legendary, but this seemed excessive, even for a noted hermit like him.

Sharon shut down the cruiser, parking well clear of the ambulance idling a few feet away from home's front door. Its twin rear doors stood open and its warning lights were flashing busily, which seemed like a dramatic bit of overkill. There was nobody to warn of anything for miles in any direction. She wondered how badly Parker was injured, as she hoped to question him before the EMT's hauled him away to the hospital, if that was necessary.

Shattered glass crunched under her shoes as Sharon crossed the threshold into the house. She paused a moment in the doorway, taking in the damage, which was extensive. It looked like a short but violent war had taken place in here. The heavy wooden front door was cracked nearly in half. A gaping hole had been punched into the wall, doorknob height. Tables were overturned, fine white drywall dust coated every surface, and blood had been splattered on the massive granite fireplace which took up most of the far wall.

In the middle of the room, EMT's were in the process of strapping a man onto a gurney. Sharon took one look at the victim and knew immediately it was not Brett Parker. She had never met the billionaire software mogul, but had seen him on the news plenty of times, and this was definitely not him. *Must be the security guy, the one Mike met with earlier this morning.*

Sharon approached the two EMT's, who were so caught up in their work they had yet to notice her arrival. She cleared her throat and one of the men jumped in surprise. They both glanced at her and then went back to work without uttering a word. The victim lay motionless on a backboard with his eyes closed. A bloody bandage had been wrapped around his head, ballooning out on the left side where they had wedged a thin ice bag underneath. The man was average height but blocky, built like a football lineman who had bulked up years ago, but had since gone to seed.

"Is he conscious?" she asked, not bothering to introduce herself.

"Yeah, I'm awake," the man answered from the stretcher. He opened his bloodshot eyes and said, "Who are you?"

"I'm Officer Sharon Dupont of the Paskagankee Police Department. And you are?"

"I'm Josh Parmalee, security for Mr. Parker. Where's Chief McMahon?"

"He's busy on another case. I'm here to assist you."

Parmalee shook his head in disbelief, wincing from pain as he did so. "Are you fucking kidding me? Brett Parker gets kidnapped and McMahon sends some flunky? Mr. Parker isn't important enough to warrant a visit from the actual chief of police in this crummy town? What's he doing, rescuing a cat stuck in a tree, helping an old lady across the street? What?"

Sharon let the insults go and waited for the man to stop venting. He had said only one thing of any importance, but that one thing was a doozy. Finally he stopped to take a breath and she interrupted before he could start up again. "What do you mean, Brett Parker's been kidnapped?"

"Kidnapped, you know; stolen, removed, taken away against his will. Kidnapped. Maybe you oughta look it up."

"The only report we received was of a B and E. Nobody said anything about a kidnapping. Who made the call to the police?"

"I did," Parmalee answered sourly.

"Well, then, why the hell didn't you tell our dispatcher that someone had been kidnapped? Do you have any idea how much time has been wasted?"

"Listen, sweetheart," Parmalee shot back, "I was tossed into a granite fireplace by that fucking lunatic and knocked out. When I came to I was woozy and could barely think straight. So you'll have to excuse me if my call for assistance wasn't specific enough for you."

Now Sharon was beginning to get the picture. This guy was supposed to provide security for one of the richest and most influential men in the world, and he had allowed his boss to be spirited away right out from under his nose. He was angry and humiliated and was taking it out on her. No problem; she could let him vent against the Paskagankee PD if he needed to. Pride was the least of their concerns if Brett Parker had actually been kidnapped.

She pulled her notebook and pen out of her breast pocket. Time was of the essence and she knew she needed to get as much useable information as possible out of this man. The EMT's finished strapping Parmalee onto the gurney and began wheeling him toward the front door.

Wait," Sharon said. "Where do you think you're going?"

"To the hospital," the one in charge answered, looking at her like she had just farted in church.

"Not yet you're not. I need to question this man and I need to do it now. Can you wait a couple of minutes?"

They looked at each other doubtfully and one said, "I suppose, but he took a nasty shot to the head when he hit those bricks, and—"

"Granite," Parmalee interrupted.

"What?" the EMT said.

"It's granite, not brick."

"Whatever. The point is, this guy has a good-sized gash in the back of his skull that's going to require sutures to close and he has probably suffered a pretty serious concussion. You can have three minutes, and then we're outta here."

"Fair enough," Sharon answered, and turned toward the prone man. "Now, how many intruders were there?"

"One."

She stopped, pen hovering above her note pad as she reviewed the damage to the room, certain she must not have heard the man correctly. "Did you say there was only one intruder?"

Parmalee snarled. "That's right, missy, there was only one. But you wouldn't believe this guy. I shot him right through the heart, right smack in the middle of the chest with a nine mm hollow point, and he got up like it was nothing, like he had slipped on a banana peel or something, and kept coming."

"Wait a minute. You *shot* him?"

"Damn right I shot him."

"Did you miss him?"

"I told you already, I hit him right square in the chest. It was a fucking bullseye. Jesus Christ, try and pay attention."

Sharon took in the room. "Then where's the blood?"

"How the hell do I know? I was a little preoccupied; didn't get the chance to go over the room with a magnifying glass."

"Well, if you shot the guy in the chest, there should be some blood, don't you agree?"

"Of course I agree. He shouldn't have gotten up,

either, but he did. I'm telling you what happened. Whether you choose to believe me or not is up to you."

Sharon looked doubtfully around the room again. The only blood was the small amount of spatter gracing the granite fireplace and hearth, blood which had obviously come from Josh Parmalee himself. She shook her head. "Okay, what happened after you shot him?"

"I told you already. He sort of clambered to his feet all pissed off like a lead slug to the chest was nothing more than a bad cup of coffee. Then he came over and tossed me across the room. That's it. That's all I know."

"Are you positive Parker's missing? Maybe he hid when the break-in occurred and he's still in the house somewhere. This is a pretty big place, after all."

"Of *course* I'm positive. He ain't here; that's the first thing I checked when I woke up. I do know how to do my job, you know." He closed his eyes.

Sharon bit off her reply; none was necessary, and getting into a verbal jousting match with this clown would accomplish nothing. Brett Parker had been kidnapped. This was huge.

"Okay," the EMT in charge muttered. "It's been long enough. Time to go." They began moving toward the door, rolling the injured man across the wreckage-littered floor.

"One last thing," Sharon interrupted. "I need a description of the intruder."

Josh Parmalee opened one eye and fixed her in its glare. "A description? He looked like death warmed over."

21

The minivan rolled to a stop in front of the ramshackle house and before it had finished rocking back and forth on its rusted springs Earl had rolled the side door open. He dragged Brett Parker out onto the patchy grass of the front yard, his movements ungainly but his grip as strong as ever.

Parker had attempted a number of times along the way to reason with Max Acton but Earl could have told him his efforts would be wasted and they were. Now he allowed himself to be manhandled, having apparently reached the conclusion that Acton was just as dangerous as the frightening freak with the jagged hole in the back of his shirt. He had no idea.

The bizarre trio trudged up the front steps and before they had reached the front door it swung open. Standing just inside the entryway was Raven, copper-skinned and beautiful, looking like the little woman in Stephen King's worst nightmare as she welcomed home her man, his undead slave, and their billionaire ticket to the good life.

They walked inside and moved directly through the house to the basement stairs, Max leading the way, Parker directly behind him being prodded by Earl, with Raven bringing up the rear. No one said a word as they clomped down the stairs and into the cool air of the basement.

Parker was breathing heavily, panting almost, as it seemed to occur to him that he had perhaps arrived at the end of the line. Earl watched as the software developer took in his surroundings; the unplugged floor freezer at the opposite end of the room, the small table next to it upon which rested the mystical box with the stone inside—not to mention Earl's heart—the collection of tools which had been used to cut that heart out of Earl's body, the gigantic tarp upon which the impromptu surgery had taken place.

The seed of an idea which had been planted inside Earl's brain back at the Parker cabin, and which he had pushed quickly away, again demanded Earl's attention and again he forced it from his mind, stealing a glance at Max as he did so. His "god" stared back at him, an unreadable look on his face. The look told Earl that while Max had no idea what was coming, he clearly realized something was not quite right.

There was no way Max could use his psychic connection to "read" Earl's plan because Earl had no idea what his plan might be. He had refused even to dwell on the seed of an idea for more than a second or two, knowing that if he did, Max would be able to sniff it out, and then *snuff* it out. Earl was counting on the ability of his unconscious mind to take over and implement the plan at the appropriate time, and until that time, his only chance for success was to pretend the seed of an idea didn't exist.

Max continued staring at Earl, a strange little smile on his lips, as he attempted to divine what was taking place inside Earl's head. For the first time since he was a little boy, Earl Manning could honestly say he was *glad* there was nothing much happening in there.

Max finally gave up, shaking his head and waggling his finger in Earl's direction, the meaning perfectly clear. *Whatever you're thinking about trying, don't do it. I'm your god. I control your fate, so don't even think about pissing me off.* Earl kept his face neutral and shifted his gaze to Brett Parker, who didn't seem to have gotten any calmer during the few seconds of silent drama between Max and Earl.

At last Max turned his attention to their unwilling guest, unleashing a high-wattage smile and extending his hand to Parker as if this were a business meeting and not a kidnapping. "Thanks for coming," he said, continuing the charade. He fished the thumb drive out of his pocket—he had relieved Earl of the item before even turning the Caravan away from the forest—and held it in the air, inspecting it a few feet from Parker while the man looked on dully.

"I'd like to thank you for the wisdom you've shown in agreeing to share this technology with me," Max said. "A lot of good can come from it, especially where I'm concerned." Parker said nothing and Max continued. "As you might have guessed by now, I have a buyer lined up for this item for whom money is, quite literally, no object."

"Then you're a traitor," Parker interrupted.

Max waved the interruption aside airily, his good

humor intact. "Call it what you will," he said, "but surely you don't believe you are the only software genius working on such an item? Perhaps you were out in front of the development curve, but undoubtedly there are brilliant minds all over the world working on creating software exactly like The Codebreaker. You perfected it first, that's true, but within a few years, maybe less, maybe *a lot* less, other Codebreakers will begin to crop up, and soon every developed country in the world will have their own version.

"That being the case," Max continued, "I might just as well profit off this little baby before it loses all value. If you had any kind of marketing sense, you would have come to the identical conclusion yourself. It's not my fault you're blessed with innate brilliance in one area but not a lick of common sense in another."

Brett Parker shook his head, his face impassive but the color rising into his cheeks an indicator of his anger. "You're a traitor," he muttered again.

"Anyway," Max continued as if he had not heard, "you're undoubtedly curious as to why you had to be a part of this gathering, since you were so kind as to share your invention with my friend Earl." He paused and Parker stared resolutely at the floor, saying nothing.

Then he shrugged and continued. "You, my new friend, are my insurance policy."

22

Earl Manning had never been the sharpest knife in the drawer or the brightest bulb in the lamp. He understood that. Growing up, his father made a point of telling him how stupid he was every chance he got, and even his mother had once scolded, "Earl, if brains was butter, you couldn't grease a pan." His own mother!

But he had always possessed a measure of animal cunning, more than once wriggling out of tight spots with the Paskagankee Police—often involving excessive alcohol consumption followed by a high-speed joyride in his ancient F-150—with a more or less believable lie or story that didn't stretch the credulity of the officer who had stopped him too badly. He had spent plenty of nights in a holding cell but had mostly avoided legal trouble on a larger scale.

It was that innate sense of cunning Earl was counting on now to save his ass one more time. He didn't know exactly what The Fucking Devil Max Acton had in store for him, but he could sense his body beginning to decompose at a faster rate. It didn't take a genius to conclude his usefulness to his "god" had pretty much ended with the kidnapping of Brett Parker and the recovery of the man's precious Codebreaker software.

Acton was preening and posturing, two activities Earl had already discovered the man lived for. They had herded Parker into the basement, the thumb drive with Parker's software secured in Acton's pocket, and the guy was lording it over the terrified software designer, taunting and intentionally frightening the man.

Earl stood at the base of the stairs. Raven was positioned directly in front of him, hanging back as usual, both fascinated by and afraid of Max Acton. Standing in front of her was Parker, perhaps the most reluctant house guest ever. And at the very forefront of the group Acton stood holding court, approximately one-third of the way across the basement, like an actor commanding the stage.

The moment Max addressed Parker and began telling him he had been brought here as an insurance policy, Earl knew what was coming and began readying himself for action without thinking about it in any specific terms. It was not an easy tightrope to walk. It was also, he knew, his only chance, and he was determined to make the most of it.

Finally the moment he had been waiting for arrived. Max smiled like a game show host telling the lucky contestant what he'd won. "As my insurance policy, it's not completely clear yet how much of your assistance I will need, if any, but rest assured, Mr. Parker, that while you're with me your living quarters will be adequate to your situation."

He hesitated. "Well, not *living* quarters, precisely, but . . . ah, it's difficult to explain. Perhaps a visual demonstration would be more appropriate. Mr. Manning, would you kindly show our guest where he will be bunking for the foreseeable future?

Acton indicated the industrial floor freezer at the other end of the basement with a flourish of which Bob Barker would have been proud, and Earl began staggering toward it. He knew instinctively this was the chance he had been waiting for, probably his one and only opportunity to salvage what was left of his miserable existence. He crossed the concrete floor in a few seconds, reaching the freezer and opening the cover like a mortician giving the hard sell on a top-of-the-line casket to a prospective client.

Max turned his attention back to the horrified software designer, whose facial expression indicated his growing understanding of the situation. The second he did, still acting without conscious thought, Earl grabbed the box containing the mystical Navajo stone and his still-beating heart off the table next to the freezer. He tucked it away in the crook of his forearm, cradling it against his chest like a sleeping baby, and strode rapidly back toward the tiny group clustered in the basement of the crumbling home.

No one had noticed a thing; not yet. Raven and Parker were watching Acton, both riveted, and Acton himself seemed so wrapped up in his little presentation that for the moment at least he appeared to have forgotten all about Earl.

So far, so good.

As he passed the open chest containing the tools the rotten bastard had used to slice open his frozen body and remove his heart, Earl reached in and plucked out the first item he could find which might suit his needs. It was a forged steel Phillips-head screwdriver with an impact-resistant plastic handle and twelve-inch long tempered-steel shaft.

The handle of the screwdriver rattled against the metal toolbox, Earl's grip betrayed by his steadily deteriorating physical condition, and suddenly all hell broke loose. The eyes of all three observers turned to Earl, Max Acton swinging around and adopting a defensive position. It was clear he knew something was going wrong, even if he was not entirely sure what that might be.

But by now it didn't matter. The physical strength Earl had gained as a result of the mysterious change he had undergone, combined with the advantage of surprise, was more than adequate for his purposes. There was now no need for Earl to try to shield his thoughts from his "god." *He* now possessed the box containing his heart, and thus—he hoped—*he* was now the one who controlled his destiny.

Earl lurched forward and slashed at his captor, wielding the screwdriver like a butcher knife, catching Max in the side of the neck. The screwdriver's long shaft entered just under his left ear and plunged straight through the man's throat, reappearing under his right ear in a gush of blood that looked as though it was being blown out a garden hose.

Acton issued a strangled cry, the sound moist and

bubbly, like he was trying to talk underwater, and then Earl yanked the handle of the screwdriver savagely, twisting as he pulled. The blood came out in a wave, splashing onto the floor. Ripped veins and blood vessels, along with unidentifiable gristle and gore, hung from the man's throat and Earl thought, *so this is what the expression "cutting a man's throat from ear to ear" means,* and Acton's desperate gaze locked onto Earl, his bulging eyes angry and accusing, and Earl watched as the life drained out of them with a swiftness that was astonishing, and then Max fell straight down, his dead body dropping with a thud into his own blood on the concrete floor.

23

Mike rolled to a stop on the gravel driveway outside the rental home on Depot Road. A beat-up old minivan pocked with rust sat at the end of the driveway next to a candy-apple red Porsche 911. The effect was incongruous, like looking at your eighty year old grandfather sharing a chaise lounge with Mila Kunis at the family picnic.

The big house loomed over the two parked cars, shadowy and silent, imposing. From the outside it appeared barely livable. Long strips of peeling paint hung from the window frames. Entire sections of wood siding had rotted away, leaving great sheets of exposed plywood. It was as if some invisible blight was attacking the home in sections, and the entire structure appeared slightly askew, like the foundation might be crumbling literally out from under the rest of the house.

The summer air hung heavy and still as he exited the cruiser. Mike's unease was palpable. It was plainly evident this was not the sort of place any couple would consider renting, not unless their names were Herman and Lily Munster. The only potential advantage offered by this home was its extreme isolation. If privacy was uppermost in the mind of a renter, then this dilapidated testament to shoddy maintenance would be ideal.

Dust kicked up around Mike's shoes as he crunched across the driveway. Even the gravel seemed tired and listless. Mike's sense of foreboding intensified as he became aware of total silence in the air. There was quite literally no noise. No crickets chirping; no birds tweeting. There wasn't even the rustle of a breeze in the majestic eighty foot tall pines surrounding the home. The complete stillness was unnerving. It felt to Mike as though nature could sense evil in the air just as he could.

He kept walking and reached down, feeling the radiators of the two vehicles as he passed by on his way to the front door. The Porsche's was cold, the minivan's warm, its engine block ticking as it cooled. He wondered what was happening at Brett Parker's retreat, the brand-new home that was the polar opposite in terms of quality from this one. Sharon should be calling in soon with a report of exactly what had been taken in the robbery.

One thing at a time. Mike pushed thoughts of Sharon from his mind as he punched the doorbell button mounted next to the front entrance and was unsurprised to discover nothing happened. The bell had either been disconnected or was broken, like seemingly everything else about this place. He lifted his fist and pounded hard on the door.

"Paskagankee Police. Is anyone home?"

Silence greeted the knock and Mike looked over again at the two cars in the driveway, one of which had been recently driven. Two cars, one still-warm engine. Two people supposedly renting this piece of crap house.

Nobody answering the knock.

Someone was here.

He reached up to pound on the door again, harder this time, and as he did he thought he heard a vague sound that set him on edge, raising the tiny hairs on his arm and causing him to freeze with his fist in the air. The windows were cracked slightly open and through the one to his right, covered by a ratty screen which had long ago stopped providing any protection from insects, came a weak, strangled cry for help.

Maybe.

He stood unmoving, waiting, not one hundred percent certain he had actually heard anything.

There it was. Again.

A sound that was more like a moan than the articulation of any actual words floated through the window once more, so weak and nearly inaudible Mike was surprised he had even heard it. But this time he was sure. He wasn't hearing things. The sound was human, and whoever was making it was in trouble.

Mike reached down to his hip and unsnapped the leather strap securing his Glock, lifting it clear of the holster, holding it in his right hand with the barrel pointed at the floor of the small wooden landing. The weapon felt solid and reassuring. He grasped the doorknob with his left hand, hoping it would be unlocked. It was.

Mike turned the knob and pushed, taking cover

behind the frame as the door opened noiselessly inward. He waited half a heartbeat, then peeked cautiously around the frame into an empty room. Another half-second wait and then he stepped clear of the door. Crossed the threshold.

The atmosphere inside the house felt hot and stale, stuffy and humid. The air smelled musty, Mike thought, exactly like what you would expect of a home that had been closed up tight for years. But this home had been recently rented, and the occupants hadn't even gone to the trouble of airing the place out.

And there was something else.

The scent of corruption, of death, of decomposing flesh, lingered in the air, barely perceptible but there nonetheless. Mike McMahon had been present at more than his share of murder scenes in his fifteen years as a patrolman back in Revere, and the smell of decomposing human tissue was something he would never forget. The scent in this crumbling house was less noticeable, more of a hint than anything else, but it was here.

His grip tightened on the Glock. He flexed his fingers subconsciously and moved slowly deeper into the house. The moaning noises he heard outside had faded away the moment he entered the house. Silence reigned, but to Mike it felt false, stealthy, like the determined efforts of a prowler to avoid detection.

Mike crossed the empty room—not a stick of furniture had been placed in it, no attempt at all to make the place even the slightest bit homey—and arrived at an open doorway leading to the home's kitchen. This room, at least, showed signs of habitation. Dishes had been rinsed off and piled in the sink, awaiting a cycle through the dishwasher, if it even still worked. A refrigerator hummed quietly in the corner, its compressor clicking on while Mike examined the rest of the room.

There was no indication the couple who had rented this house were here, yet the pair of vehicles parked outside indicated otherwise. And that somehow artificial silence continued to scream a warning in Mike's head. Something was very wrong here. The smart move would be to backtrack out of the house and call for backup—get Harley's ass up here, and maybe Sharon's, too, if she had finished up with the B and E at Parker's.

That would be the smart move. But those faint cries he had heard earlier were eating at Mike. They sounded exactly like the sounds a human being would make if he—or she—were suffering and in extreme pain. What if Earl Manning had been kidnapped for some unknown reason and was being held here, injured? Or what if the couple renting this home had nothing to do with Earl Manning, but had been hurt in some sort of home-improvement accident and needed immediate medical attention?

Mike grimaced and continued on.

A partially closed door in the corner of the room opposite the refrigerator creaked and Mike jumped, startled. He stood unmoving, gazing at the door intently, flexing his fingers again on the grip of his service weapon.

The air inside the house was still and unmoving, the air outside heavy and damp, with no hint of a breeze. There was no reason in the world for that door to have creaked. Mike padded silently across the kitchen, moving faster now. His pulse pounded and adrenaline quickened his breathing. He raised his Glock and held it in his right hand, head-high, the business end now pointing at the ceiling. Using the doorframe for cover, he took a deep breath and eased the door open further with his left foot. It gave way reluctantly, issuing a loud screech that sounded almost exactly like a scream of pain.

Dammit. There goes the advantage of surprise. Mike turned the corner, taking the stairs slowly, descending into hell.

24

Things happened quickly. None of Earl's actions had been planned out, at least not consciously, as any conscious thought would have alerted Acton to what was coming, so Earl was forced to react, to make things up as he went. But that was okay with Earl; things had worked out pretty well so far. He felt as alive right now as he had at any point since, well, since he had been killed.

A wet, squishy sound filled the basement as Acton's dead body struck the concrete floor. Earl tensed for a scream, so certain one would come that he paused for just a second and cringed slightly.

Nothing happened.

He glanced from Acton's prone body up into the eyes of the two people still alive in the basement. Raven, the green-eyed beauty who had lured him here with the promise of a night he would never forget—*boy, she hadn't been kidding about that one, had she?*—stared disbelievingly at the sight of the older man on the floor. She had clapped a hand over her mouth in horror but a tiny mouse-like squeak escaped around her splayed fingers anyway. "Ahhhhhh...' It was almost as if she wanted to scream but could not quite summon the breath necessary to make it happen.

The other guy, Parker, looked more composed, but only slightly. His bright blue eyes were open wider than Earl would have imagined possible, and he had slapped a hand over his mouth in a pose almost identical to Raven's.

And he was moving, edging toward the stairs. He stopped the moment Earl glanced his way, freezing in mid-stride, but it was clear he had been trying to take advantage of the diversion provided by Max Acton's untimely death to make a break for freedom. That sort of quick thinking was actually quite impressive, Earl thought. No wonder the guy's net worth was greater than that of some small countries.

Earl smiled and the software guy's expression changed from one of horror to one of . . . well . . . even greater horror. Earl decided he must look a lot more imposing in death than he ever had in life. This whole undead thing did have its advantages. "Going somewhere?" he rumbled.

That was when he heard the pounding on the front door. A second of absolute silence followed, and then the words, "Paskagankee Police" floated through the stillness of the house. "Is anyone home?"

The irony of the timing was inescapable, coming just as Earl had accomplished his goal. He was free of The

Fucking Devil Max Acton, who had apparently selected him at random out of all the drunken bums in the world to lure away from the bottle and curse with a fate worse than anything he had ever imagined. Acton was dead, and Earl's plan, which had never really been a plan to begin with—gain control of the box containing his heart and send Acton back to hell, where he clearly belonged—had been accomplished, and with shocking finality.

But this pseudo-plan had never really extended beyond the vague notion of grabbing the heart and stabbing Acton, and Earl now realized he didn't have the slightest idea how to proceed. The police were at the door, he had two wide-eyed, terrified hostages, and despite the satisfaction of getting the drop on the man he hated more than anyone else in the world—next to that stunningly beautiful bitch, Raven, of course—Earl knew he was no better off than he had been ten minutes ago. He was still dead, still holding his heart cradled in the crook of his arm like a goddamn football, and the process of decomposition was still proceeding along as nature had always intended, thank you very much. He could feel his skin loosening and slackening on his body as it prepared to slide right off his bones, and there was not a fucking thing in the world he could do about it.

One thing he *did* know, though, was that after a lifetime of scrapes with law enforcement over issues mostly small but occasionally large, he was not about to simply cower down here in the basement of this house of horrors and wait for the pig upstairs to find him, take his heart away from him, and send him off to some research facility where geeks in white lab coats would poke and prod at him like he was some freaking specimen under a microscope.

Earl moved with a speed and economy of motion that must have surprised the two people in the basement still breathing. It certainly surprised him. He shambled three steps forward and grabbed the software nerd with his right hand, bunching the guy's shirt up in his fist and lifting him onto his toes without even really trying. His strength had by now stopped surprising him.

The dude looked too shocked to scream, or even to say anything, but the chick, Raven, she had obviously heard the cop at the front door just as Earl had and she looked ready to launch into one massive yell for help. Earl's left hand shot out just as she took a deep breath. He hooked her throat in the webbing between his thumb and forefinger, slamming her up against the wall as she began a scream which quickly died away to a wheezing, "Help me..."

The wooden box containing Earl's heart tumbled to the floor with a clatter. Earl expected it to smash into a million pieces, dumping his heart onto the concrete, but it bounced once, twirled on one corner like a coin spinning on a table, and fell still.

Raven clawed at his hand ineffectually as her face began to redden and then turn purple. He realized he was suffocating her and he didn't care. She deserved to die a horrific death for what she had done to him, and he would have enjoyed drawing it out, too. See how she liked the idea of dying.

But there wasn't time to give Raven what she deserved. Not yet. A cop was at the front door, and in Earl's experience, cops didn't just turn around and go away once you had drawn their attention. The pig was probably even now nosing around the house, and if that was the case, it was only a matter of time—and probably not very much of it—before his nosy porker ass ended up in this basement.

Earl looked from one captive to the other, trying to decide what to do next. The software dude had begun babbling quietly, begging for his release, saying something about Earl keeping the fucking Codebreaker software, as if maybe a dead guy might give a shit about a goddamn computer program. Raven, of course, was saying nothing, occupying herself with her futile attempt to fight her way free, or at the very least to get a little air.

And just like that his next move became crystal clear. Earl took one step backward and smashed the software guy's head into the beautiful bitch's head, bringing them together like an enthusiastic cymbal player. Earl had never played a musical instrument, but he thought if being a musician was anything like this, he had truly missed out on something special.

There was a hollow-sounding thud and the two bodies dropped to the floor in a rough approximation of the swan dive Max Acton had performed a couple of minutes before. Parker, the software guy, hit the concrete and lay perfectly still, arms and legs splayed, while Raven's extremities twitched and jittered and she gasped for breath and then let out a surprisingly loud moan. Earl thought he might have to hit her again, but then her arms and legs stopped thrashing and she fell silent.

Earl bent down and picked up the wooden box, thankful it had stayed in one piece. He didn't know what would happen if the rock and the heart sharing space inside the box were to get separated, but he had a pretty good idea he wouldn't like the result. He hugged his prize to his chest like a new mother cuddling her baby and tried to figure out his next move.

25

Whatever had happened in this basement was bad, Mike could tell that much before even reaching the bottom of the stairs. Bodies were sprawled atop the bloodstained concrete floor, two men and one woman, none of them moving. One of the men he recognized immediately as Brett Parker, still dressed in the khakis and dress shirt he had been wearing this morning during Mike's visit. How Parker had gotten here and what the hell had gone down at his house was open to question, but obviously the report of a break-in at Parker's home had been woefully inadequate.

The other two people Mike did not recognize, but he knew immediately they must be the couple he was looking for. Older man, strikingly beautiful young woman. The woman lay next to Parker a few feet away from the body of the man, who had taken the worst of whatever had gone down here. His head, bent back at an unnatural angle, lay in a pool of blood that had clearly come from his neck, most of which was currently missing.

Mike raised his weapon and stopped on the stairs, taking in the scene, looking for whoever — or whatever — might have caused all this damage. The basement was mostly empty aside from the three prone adults littering the floor, with just a top-loading floor freezer taking up space in the far corner, along with some tools and a couple of small tables littered with junk.

The perpetrator of whatever had happened seemed to have disappeared. Mike had a lot of things to do in the next few minutes; he needed to prioritize. Number One was to check on the condition of the three victims, although it seemed patently obvious at least one of them was dead. He also had to get backup out here and secure the scene, as well as call for medical assistance for anyone left alive. And he had to contact Sharon to find out just what the hell had happened at Brett Parker's home.

But first things first. Mike holstered his weapon and stepped off the stairs to assess the condition of the three victims. The assailant was gone, but Mike could not shake his feeling that something was wrong, that he was missing something of importance. The smell of death and corruption was much stronger down here, enough to make it hard to concentrate. He knelt at Parker's body and felt for a pulse. Strong and steady. He looked for any obvious wounds and could find none. Parker would live.

Next he moved a couple of feet to his left and performed the same quick examination on the young woman. Same result: strong, steady pulse and no obvious sign of serious injury. He looked her over and realized that whatever Bo Pellerin's faults were, and there seemed to be plenty, he was right about one thing—the girl was a knockout. Literally, Mike thought.

He stood and crossed half the length of the basement to the third body. Given the amount of blood on the floor and the severity of the man's wounds, there was no doubt in Mike's mind he was dead, but he refused to take anything for granted. He had to be sure. Careful to avoid stepping in the blood, he knelt next to the man as he had done with the other two victims. He placed his finger lightly on the side of the man's neck—what was left of it—searching for a pulse. He found none. His sense of unease, his feeling that something was not right, intensified.

Out of the corner of his eye, he noticed a river of blood had dribbled off across the floor, the trail roughly paralleling that of the freezer's electrical cord, which ran from the back of the freezer in a meandering trail to where the plug lay on the floor just shy of a wall socket. . .

The freezer was unplugged.

Holy shit, the freezer is unplugged. Nobody moves into a new residence and goes to all the trouble of carrying a freezer into the basement and setting it up, only to leave it unplugged, with the cover closed.

And Mike knew.

He cursed and fumbled for his Glock as he felt rather than saw a lumbering presence moving up behind him. He pulled his weapon clear of the holster and threw himself to his left, twisting his body as he slid through the victim's cooling blood, which was already beginning to coagulate, becoming sticky and viscous.

He ended up on his back and raised his weapon,

pointing it at the spot he had just vacated.

And then he froze at what he saw.

It was Earl Manning, the missing man. Only it wasn't Manning. Not exactly. It was a shambling mess wearing filthy, tattered, bloody clothing. It was a frightening-looking shell that more closely resembled a walking skeleton than a human being. The skeleton carried a small wooden box in one arm and in the middle of its chest was a ragged hole, a hole Mike thought might almost be big enough to see straight through and out the other side if the angle was right.

This couldn't possibly be the Earl Manning Mike had had occasion to bust for drunk driving once or twice since his arrival in Paskagankee. That guy was no great physical specimen, but at the very least he resembled a living, breathing human being, more or less. This thing looked less than human, somehow *in*human.

But it had to be Manning, and Mike realized it didn't really matter whether it was or not, because whatever it was, it was coming after him with murder in its cold dead eyes and a long, bloody steel screwdriver in its hand.

Mike sighted down the barrel and barked, "Stop right there."

The thing smiled a ghastly smile and kept coming.

Mike said, "I mean it. FREEZE!"

The hideous face grinned wider and kept coming.

The Manning-thing was less than three feet away when Mike fired, blasting him to kingdom come. The disturbingly thin body flew backward, smashing to the floor and lying still.

Mike stood, shaking from the adrenaline coursing through his body and cursing himself for not seeing the obvious. A top-loading freezer in the basement, unplugged but with the lid closed. The thing, whatever it was, must have been hiding in the freezer, holding the lid slightly open so it wouldn't latch, waiting for Mike to turn his back.

And he hadn't noticed. What the hell kind of cop was he?

He cursed again and walked slowly over to Earl Manning, or whatever the hell it *really* was, goddamned box still cradled in the crook of his arm, even after being shot. He reached down and felt for a pulse and found none. Manning was dead; no question about it, but the lack of blood from the bullet wound was mystifying. So was the general condition of the body, which was horrendous. And he was stone cold. It was as if he had been dead for quite some time, rather than just a few seconds.

Mike gazed at Manning's chest. The whole thing was sunken, like it had fallen in on itself, like his ribs had been broken and no longer provided a support structure for the skin, which appeared paper-thin and somehow rubbery. There *was* a hole in his chest, too, just as Mike had suspected, a hole besides the one he had put there with his 9 mm slug. It was big and dirty and slimy, with unidentifiable gore surrounding it, but no blood, not even a trace.

Something was seriously wrong here, but the time for worrying about what had happened to Manning would be later. Right now, he had a dead body on his hands—two, he supposed, now that he had killed Manning—and a pair of injured civilians to worry about. He wiped the fingertips which had touched Manning's skin on his pant leg and grimaced, wondering briefly about communicable diseases. Then he looked inside the open freezer. It had recently been cleaned, that was obvious, but it still smelled foul; no amount of scrubbing or hosing out would be able to remove the putrescent stench of decaying flesh. Of death.

A stealthy scraping sound came from behind him and Mike whirled, concerned that a second person had somehow been hiding in the basement, wondering how that could have been possible. He turned to see the scarecrow figure of Earl Manning launch himself across the floor, shoulder lowered like a battering ram.

He had just enough time to begin dropping into a defensive crouch when Manning plowed into him, the wasted body of the undernourished, alcoholic dead guy packing a punch Mike could not believe. His Glock flew out of his hand and they tumbled to the concrete, Mike underneath Manning. The back of his head bounced off the floor with an audible *Crack* and his vision blurred and a black curtain dropped over his eyes like someone had flipped a switch.

Mike shook his head, desperately trying to regain his senses. An intense, white-hot bolt of jagged lightning fired through his brain and Mike thought, so *this is what it feels like to suffer a concussion*. Then the black curtain lifted and his brain started accepting images from his eyes again and he knew he was in big trouble. He sucked in a breath, gagging from the ungodly stench, wondering how he could have not noticed the smell the moment he had descended the stairs.

He unloaded a right cross to Manning's jaw, smacking his elbow on the floor on the backswing, connecting solidly. Manning's head snapped back absurdly, nearly bouncing off his shoulder before returning to a more or less upright position. Mike took another breath and gagged again.

Then the man who should have been dead but was not wrapped one bony hand around each side of Mike's head and lifted it, smashing it down on the floor a second time. The box Manning had managed to hold on to during the entire fight was finally jarred loose and fell with a clatter, but Mike didn't hear it. A loud buzzing noise filled his ears and the curtain dropped over his eyes again, and this time it stayed there.

Mike's last thought was, *this is all impossible,* and then the buzzing noise disappeared, and so did everything else.

26

Sharon wrestled the cruiser around the idling ambulance and started down the access road. The moment the EMT's had begun loading the injured Josh Parmalee into the back of their vehicle, she had sprinted to her patrol car, anxious to get out in front of the bulky truck. The access road was narrow, and if she didn't depart first, there was a good chance she would be stuck behind it until reaching Route 24, and time was of the essence. One of the richest men in the country had gone missing in this tiny town, and every second would count in the search.

Once out of the driveway, she accelerated as much as she dared on the dirt trail which was barely wider than Parker's driveway. She drove with her left hand, plucking the handset for the car's radio off its stand with her right.

"Unit Two to Base," she said.

"Go ahead," came the reply, weak and staticky.

"Yeah, Gordie, how come you didn't tell me you had dispatched an ambulance to Parker's place?"

"I tried, Sharon, but I guess you had already gotten out of your vehicle by the time I could get to it. Sorry about that."

"No problem," she said, shaking her head, wondering whether dispatcher Gordie Rheaume could sense the frustration in her voice. She didn't feel like she was doing much to hide it. "Has Unit One checked in yet?"

"Nope. Haven't heard from Mike since he arrived at the Depot Road address."

Sharon paused, wheeling the cruiser around a fallen branch taking up two-thirds of the trail. The left side of the vehicle dropped off the shoulder and she applied power, fearing sliding into the ditch. The wheels spun and then caught, and the cruiser climbed back up onto the narrow dirt road. Sharon breathed a sigh of relief that was short-lived. Mike should have checked in by now. Even if he had located and interviewed the couple they were looking for, he had been out of touch for far too long.

Something was wrong, she was sure of it. She wondered how to proceed. It was imperative they get every available member of the force onto the search for Brett Parker, and as soon as possible. Undoubtedly they were going to have to call in outside help; to Sharon that seemed like a given. But all of that was for the chief to decide. Where was he?

"Uh, Unit Two, you there, Sharon?"

She glanced at the mike as if hoping it would give her some kind of clue how to proceed. It didn't, so she picked it up and said, "I'm here, Gordie. Have you tried calling his cell?"

"Of course," he answered, his exasperation apparent.

"Okay, I'm going to give it a try, too. Let me know the second he checks in, will you?"

"Roger that," the dispatcher answered, and the radio went dead. Sharon hung the mike back on its stand. The things they needed to talk about were best left off the radio, anyway. The disappearance of Brett Parker in an assault at his home was not the sort of thing Mike would want the public learning about until he was ready for them to know, and anyone could listen in to the radio traffic on the police frequency.

But still. He wasn't on the radio and he wasn't answering his cell phone. Mike took his responsibilities as chief very seriously—maybe too seriously, sometimes—and Sharon knew he would answer if he could. Her concern morphed into outright worry as she fished her cell phone out of a small leather holster on her belt, not slowing the cruiser as she punched his number on her speed-dial.

She had nearly reached Route 24 by now, where she would need to make a right turn if she planned on returning to town. The phone buzzed electronically in her ear and there was no answer. Cell coverage in this remote village had been nearly nonexistent until the killing spree last fall. News media had swarmed the town in the aftermath of the tragedies, and almost overnight, a cell tower had been constructed. Service was still spotty, though, for reasons no one could quite explain.

The cruiser reached the end of the trail, pulling up to the intersection of Route 24. Sharon stopped, wondering how far behind her the ambulance was. The cell phone transferred her to voice mail. A robotic-sounding voice informed Sharon she should "leave a message at the tone."

She disconnected the call and tossed her phone onto the seat next to her. Leaving a message was pointless. Mike would get in touch as soon as he could; Sharon was certain of that. Despite the pain she knew their breakup had caused him, Mike would not hesitate to talk to her on any job-related matter.

The cruiser idled patiently at the intersection. Right turn to head back to town and the police station. Left to go out to the home on Depot Road, where Mike's last radio transmission had originated. It was no contest. Sharon wheeled the vehicle to the left and goosed it. She could be there in ten minutes.

27

Earl sat astride the unconscious cop's body and pondered his next move. Bitter experience had taught him there was never just one pig, they tended to move in pairs or groups, like junior high girls at a dance. So, either a second police officer was already in the house somewhere—a possibility which seemed unlikely, given that a shot had been fired and gunshots never seemed to fail to get the attention of the law—or reinforcements would be along any minute now.

That being the case, he knew he had a limited amount of time in which to make his escape. Even if he got away cleanly, though, Earl suspected his time was running out. His strength was still superhuman, and he didn't feel any different than he had since being awakened from death by The Fucking Devil Max Acton, but the process of decomposition was continuing, and sooner or later he knew his body would simply fall apart and drop to the ground, magic stone or no magic stone.

The billionaire software geek and the beautiful but treacherous Raven were both beginning to stir on the floor over by the stairs. They moaned softly and their arms and legs had begun twitching in what was still a more or less random fashion. Their eyes remained closed, but Earl figured before long that would change.

It was kind of ironic, Earl thought. Brett Parker was a billionaire, but none of that money was doing him a lick of good at the moment. He was just another unfortunate dude. He had gotten his head smashed and he dropped to the floor just like anyone else would have, regardless of his money.

All that money.

Billionaire.

Earl gazed at Parker, eyes narrowed. He was a billionaire. Billionaires were special. They had access to all kinds of resources; things unimaginable to small-town Maine alcoholic loser corpses. Another plan began to take shape in Earl's brain. It was a long shot, of course it was, probably doomed to failure like everything else in his miserable existence, but it was better than wandering aimlessly, waiting to die. Again.

He struggled to his feet, clutching the box containing the stone and his heart—his lifeline—with an enthusiasm born of desperation. He wished the hole in his ruined chest was a little bigger, so he could simply stuff the box inside and carry it that way. He smiled ruefully at the thought and then got down to work, placing the box reluctantly on the floor at his feet. The thought of letting it out of his grasp for even a second was panic-inducing, but he needed both arms for what was to come next.

He bent over the cop and slid a hand under each of the pig's armpits. "Nothing personal," he whispered. This particular cop wasn't so bad, as cops went. McMahon had arrested him a couple of times for DUI and was living with the chick, Sharon, who had, against all odds, fucked him silly one glorious night back when she was still a drug-and-alcohol-crazy high school slut.

It had been perhaps the best night of his life, and while he had known even then it was too much to expect lightning to strike twice, he had spent hundreds of hours daydreaming about someday getting his shit together and hooking up with the now-cleaned-up cop, maybe sharing an apartment or something. Becoming a couple.

But he had known all along that was a patently ridiculous notion, and in any event didn't hold anything against this cop for shacking up with Sharon Dupont. She was every dude's dream, a chick with a body that wouldn't quit, but with a sweet personality that suggested she wasn't even aware of her effect on men. It was a magical combination, one no guy could be expected to pass up. He certainly hadn't.

So there was no malice in what Earl was about to do, although he wouldn't lose any sleep over it, either. Not that he actually needed sleep any more. He snickered. There would be plenty of time to sleep when he was dead. Again.

Earl half-carried, half-dragged the cop across the floor. The cop groaned once and his eyelids fluttered and Earl thought he might be about to wake up, then he quieted again. His eyes remained closed.

They reached the freezer and Earl struggled to toss the unconscious man inside. The cop's upper body flopped down and he hung up on the side of the metal box, suspended at the waist, half in and half out of the big freezer. Earl reached down and lifted his knees, then pushed them over the side, depositing his lower body into the freezer where he lay crumpled and unmoving. Then he slammed the lid and turned toward Parker and Raven.

He was running out of time, he could sense it. He had to move. Now. He picked up the wooden box, relief flooding through him to once again have it in his grasp, and trudged across the basement floor, stepping around the bloody mess that used to be Max The Fucking Devil Acton. Earl wished his mouth still produced saliva so he could spit on the dead body.

He reached Raven and the software guy and paused, thinking hard, trying his damnedest to concentrate. He badly wanted to teach the little bitch Raven a lesson. She was directly responsible for the mess he was in right now. If not for her treachery, Earl would be lounging on his couch with a beer in his hand, watching The Price is Right and waiting for the Ridge Runner to open for Happy Hour.

But he knew he could only take one of the pair with him. There was no way he would be able to control two hostages, especially with his body deteriorating so quickly. And as much as he wanted to take revenge against Raven, the billionaire software guy was a gift which had fallen right into his lap. A gift he could not afford to pass up.

Maybe there was no way out of this cursed half-life he had awoken to. *Probably* there was no way out of it. But if anyone could get to the bottom of the mystery of how he was moving and talking and thinking—if you could call it that—while his heart pumped away inside a plastic bag, it had to be a guy with the resources of Brett Parker. And if Parker could get to the bottom of *that* mystery, maybe he could even figure out a way to reverse it.

Earl knew the chances of that happening were one in a million. Hell, probably one in a billion. But a microscopic chance was better than no chance at all, and he wasn't going to pass it up. He kicked the unconscious chick in the ribs just for fun, then bent down and picked up Parker the same way he had picked up the cop now trapped inside the freezer. Instead of dragging him across the floor, though, Earl tossed the software geek's body over his shoulder and staggered to the stairs, climbing them as quickly as he could.

He crossed the grungy kitchen and moved through the empty living room, weaving like the drunk he had been for most of his life. Parker's weight didn't bother him, he still had plenty of strength thanks to the magical stone in the box, but coordinating his movements was becoming more and more difficult as the decomposition process continued. His body was giving out.

Earl cursed and plucked two sets of keys from a hook which had been pounded into the wall next to the front door. Then he stumbled out of the house and across the weed-strewn lawn to the driveway. He eyed the ancient minivan. He didn't know how long it would take for his body to give out and die again, but he wasn't about to spend what little time he had left in that beat-up piece of shit. *Porsche, here we come.*

He eyed the two car keys in his hand, one attached to a plain metal ring, the other to a fancy fob with buttons and the distinctive Porsche horse-head logo. He dropped the minivan's key at his feet and moved to the sports car, muscling Parker into the passenger seat and crossing to the driver's side. He turned the key and the 911 growled to life.

Earl jammed the car into reverse, almost stalling it in the process, and scattered gravel across the front lawn as he backed down the weed-strewn driveway, moving fast, the big engine barely straining. He hadn't given any thought to how difficult the manual transmission might be to operate in his present condition, with his coordination shot all to hell. He considered changing vehicles for just a moment, then decided, *Fuck it. For once in my life—or death—I'm going to drive the best.*

The Porsche careened wildly into the road, tires screeching as Earl hit the brakes and shifted into first. Then he hit the gas. And stalled the engine.

He twisted the key and tried again. Again the car stalled.

He screamed in frustration and Parker stirred next to him. This time, he focused his limited powers of concentration on shifting the gears and easing out the clutch, and the car began rolling slowly along the deserted roadway. Once he was moving, shifting gears became a little easier, and Earl gunned it, rocketing away from the scene of his gruesome death and subsequent horrifying rebirth.

Where he was headed was a mystery, but he had his hostage, and that was a good start. Now it was time to get the fuck out of Dodge while the getting was good.

28

Sharon rolled slowly up the driveway that at one time had been gravel but was now comprised mostly of sickly-looking greenish-brown weeds that had forced their way between small rocks scattered along a wide pathway. She parked behind Mike's cruiser and studied the dilapidated house from the front seat. It looked empty. Felt empty, too, but that didn't mean much, especially given the fact Mike had parked next to a rusting minivan. A gap of several feet stood between the two vehicles, meaning there may have been another car parked there when Mike had arrived.

Sharon punched redial on her cell, knowing what the result would be but unable to stop herself from trying anyway. Mike would have called her if he was able. She waited impatiently through the electronic buzzing, hanging up when the same robotic voice she had ignored earlier began telling her to leave a message. She thought about radioing Gordie to see if Mike had checked in and didn't bother. Gordie would have alerted her if he had.

She opened her door and stepped out of the cruiser, uneasy, her right hand resting lightly on her weapon. She stepped forward and ran a hand over Mike's radiator. Warm, but not too warm, a temperature she felt might be consistent with his arrival almost an hour ago. She guessed the car had not been driven since then.

The front of the minivan felt cooler than the cruiser, but not cold. This car had been driven fairly recently, also, probably parked here not too long before Mike's arrival. Sharon took one more long look around, not sure what she was looking for, then moved quickly up the steps to the front door.

It was standing half open.

The door appeared to have been pulled or pushed closed, but without sufficient force to cause it to latch securely. She peeked through the opening into an empty room. It was a living room or some sort of sitting room. She figured she had probable cause to enter, but the question was how did she want to do it? Announce her arrival, as she probably should? Or proceed quietly?

The decision was an easy one. The chief of police had come here on a law enforcement matter and had been out of touch for far too long. There was no reason to alert whoever might be inside the home that a second officer was here, especially since it was *only* one officer, with no backup.

The issue of backup was a problem, too. She could hear Mike's voice in her head insisting she return to her cruiser and call for another unit. Harley was patrolling somewhere in town. She knew she should call Harley and wait for his arrival before entering the house.

But geographically, Paskagankee was massive. The odds were slim that Harley was close enough to get here within the next few minutes; the home's location was remote even by Paskagankee standards. He might take twenty minutes or more to arrive, and Sharon's uneasiness was increasing with each passing second. Twenty or thirty minutes was too long to wait with Mike out of touch.

She would enter the house and worry about the repercussions later.

She eased through the door sideways, her slim body almost but not quite able to squeeze through the opening without disturbing the door. It creaked open a few more inches, making more noise than she would have liked but less than she had expected. She drew her weapon and held it by her side.

This room was empty, not just of people but of furniture. She padded across the floor as quietly as she could and entered an out-of-date kitchen. It had probably been new somewhere around 1970 and never updated or remodeled since. Unlike the previous room, this one at least showed signs of habitation, although a quick glance gave no indication of how many people lived here or how long it had been since their arrival.

Sharon took a step and froze. Someone was sobbing, crying quietly. The sound seemed to be coming from an open doorway on the far side of the kitchen. The sobs were muffled, as though the person making them was trying to keep quiet but could not quite manage it. She strained to hear; it sounded like a female, or perhaps a child. It was definitely not Mike.

This changed everything. Whoever was through that door—probably a basement door, from its positioning—might be injured and in need of medical assistance.

Or it could be a trap. Whoever was sobbing might be trying to lure her down the steps.

Sharon cursed under her breath and crossed the kitchen to the door. It opened to her left and a set of stairs descended into the basement, as she had suspected. She started to holster her gun and then thought better of it. Taking a deep breath, she said, "This is the Paskagankee Police. Identify yourself."

The sobbing stopped instantly. There was no answer.

Sharon tried again, a little louder, although she was certain the basement's occupant had heard her the first time. "This is Officer Dupont of the Paskagankee Police Department. I need to know who's down there. Are you hurt?"

Another moment of silence. Sharon was debating how to proceed when a small voice said, "My name is Raven. I think . . . I think I have a concussion."

Sharon frowned in concentration. Raven was supposed to have been the name of the young woman they were looking for, but this voice sounded more like that of a young girl than a grown woman. "Can you walk?" she asked.

"I think so."

"Is anyone else down there?"

"Yes. . . No . . . Um . . ."

"Who else is down there with you, Raven?"

"Um, Max."

"May I talk to Max, please?"

"Uh . . . I don't think so."

"Why not, is he hurt?"

"He's . . . um . . . I think he's dead." The voice broke and the woman/child began sobbing again, this time more forcefully.

A chill ran down Sharon's spine and she raised her gun, not quite aiming down the stairs but not pointing the barrel at the floor any more, either. "Who else is down there besides you and Max, Raven?"

A short pause. "No one."

"Okay," Sharon said, much more forcefully. "I want you to move very slowly toward the stairs. Put your hands out directly in front of you, as far as they'll go, just like you're a zombie in a B movie. I want to see your hands first as you approach the stairs. Can you do that for me, Raven?"

"I . . . yes, I think I can do that."

"Okay, come on, then, slowly." Sharon doubted she could believe Raven about no one else being in that basement. Mike's cruiser was out front. Mike was not. So unless he had left the house on foot or as a prisoner, he was here. Somewhere. *Goddammit, don't you dare be lying down there dead, Mike McMahon!*

She forced herself to focus, despite her fear and her nearly overwhelming urge to scream at the young woman, *hurry up!* Every second counted, especially if Mike was injured and lying helpless in the basement or somewhere else on the property. But this was the wrong time to rush things. If she didn't handle this situation properly, she could end up injured or dead herself. How would she help Mike, then?

A pair of small hands appeared, fingers spread apart,

floating as if by magic beyond the wall to the right of the stairway. Raven's forearms followed, and then her entire body became visible. Even from the top of the stairs, Sharon could see a purplish-green welt forming on the side of her head.

"Okay, Raven, that's far enough. Are you armed?"

The young woman shook her head gingerly—she had to be suffering from one hell of a headache—and Sharon told her, "All right, I want you to lie face-down on the floor, Raven, and I'll come down and have you back on your feet in just a moment."

Without another word, the woman bent at the knees and lowered herself to the cement as instructed, spread-eagled. Sharon edged down the stairs slowly, still concerned about a trap, knowing her legs and lower body would be exposed before she had an opportunity to see into the rest of the basement.

She continued to move. When the entire basement had come into view she stopped, horrified. In roughly the center of the basement an older man lay in a pool of blood, his throat ripped open, veins and tendons and unidentifiable gore trailing out the wreckage of his throat and scattered around his unmoving body on the cement.

This had to be Max, the man Mike had come here to interview regarding the couple's connection to the missing Earl Manning. Rose Pellerin had said the man was considerably older than the woman, that his name was Max, and that he had called his companion "Raven" that day a few weeks ago inside *Needful Things*.

Max was clearly dead, and as relieved as Sharon was to see that Mike was not dead on the floor as well, her concern over his disappearance intensified. Was it possible this slaughter had occurred before Mike had arrived? If so, where had he gone?

"Dammit," Sharon muttered under her breath, and Raven whimpered.

In her concern for Mike, she had almost forgotten about the young woman lying virtually at her feet. Sharon holstered her weapon and leapt down the last three stairs, wrinkling her nose in disgust at the stench suspended in the basement like a noxious cloud. The air smelled like a bag of hamburger that had been left in the sun for a few hours. She glanced at the freezer in the corner and noticed it was unplugged. What the hell . . .?

She shook her head to try to clear away the smell with no measurable success, then knelt and patted Raven down quickly. The woman was unarmed. Sharon helped her to her feet and led her to the stairs, sitting her down on one and kneeling in front of her. "What happened here?" she asked roughly, still trying not to gag from the overwhelming odor.

Raven covered her face with her hands and whispered, "He killed Max," and began sobbing again, and Sharon's temper exploded. Time was ticking and Mike was missing and there was a dead guy on the floor in a pool of blood and it *smelled so bad down here* and she just didn't have time to coddle this whiny bitch.

"I can see that," she snapped. *"Who* killed Max is what I need to know right now, and *where* did they go?"

"The drunk killed Max, the skinny guy, the one Max killed. He killed Max." She spread her fingers and peeked through them at Sharon. Her cheeks were flushed and tear-streaked. "And I don't know where he went."

"You're talking in circles. Who's 'the drunk'? Are you

talking about Earl Manning?"

Raven nodded, reclosing her fingers over her eyes to avoid the intensity of Sharon's stare. "Okay," Sharon said. "Now we're getting somewhere. But you said Max killed Earl and then Earl killed Max. You can't have it both ways. Which is it?"

For a long moment Raven didn't answer. Sharon prepared to ask the question again, more forcefully, and then from somewhere under Raven's hands came the mumbled reply. "I think I'm going to puke."

Sharon had seen stories on the news and read reports in the paper of law enforcement officers beating up suspects in custody and had never understood how a sworn officer of the law could do something so stupid, so patently destructive, both to his career and his case, but now she understood. There was so much at stake—a murdered man lying on a cold cement floor, the kidnapping of a billionaire right out of his home, Mike's disappearance—and Sharon knew all three events had to be connected. She just didn't know how.

And now the only person who could shed some light on the situation was refusing to cooperate. She wanted to slap this little bitch silly, punch her square in her pretty face, shake her until she spilled whatever she knew.

Instead she stood and yanked Raven to her feet, ignoring the young woman's whimper of pain. Sure, she had a nasty knock on the head, she probably was suffering from a concussion as she had said, and the sudden rise had probably made her head feel like it was about to explode. Sharon didn't care.

"Fine. Have it your way. Let's get you some medical attention," she said evenly, marching Raven up the stairs faster than the woman would probably have liked. As she climbed, she took one last look around the basement, wondering distractedly why these people would have closed the lid on an unplugged freezer, especially if there was meat inside. And judging from the stench in the air, there must have been. That nasty smell certainly wasn't coming from the dead guy on the floor; his body hadn't begun to decompose yet.

Something wasn't right. She was missing something; she knew it. She just couldn't quite put her finger on what it was. The situation with the freezer seemed off somehow, but then, finding a dead body would shake your perspective. She exhaled sharply in frustration and the whiny bitch whimpered again and the freezer vanished from her thought process as she continued up the stairs. She needed to plan her next moves — call for an ambulance for Raven, get a crime scene team out here as quickly as possible, continue the search for Mike. Not necessarily in that order.

They clambered into the kitchen, leaving the death and destruction and stench of the basement behind. Sharon kicked the door closed with her foot so the smell wouldn't take over the whole house.

29

Mike struggled to force himself awake. It was hot in his apartment. Unbelievably hot. Stiflingly hot, especially for the middle of the night in northern Maine. He couldn't even remember moving back into the tiny piece of shit apartment yet after getting the boot from Sharon, but he must have done so because here he was. The place had never been *this* hot, though. Humid, too. Just taking a deep breath was a struggle.

And his head was pounding, like someone was drilling straight into his brain from the back of his skull, like he had—

—Wait a second. His head felt like he had fallen onto a concrete floor and smacked it, like he had toppled backward after being tackled by someone, which was exactly what had happened. He wasn't at home in bed at all, he had blacked out after hitting his head fighting Earl Manning.

Shit.

He reached for the service weapon at his hip and banged his knuckles against a piece of metal or some sort of wall. His holster was empty. His gun was gone.

And suddenly Mike knew exactly what had happened. He replayed it in his pounding head clear as day, as if he could see it happening right in front of him. Manning tackling him, packing a lot more of a punch than the wasted one hundred thirty-five pound body of a lifelong alcoholic should be able to manage. The pair of them tumbling to the floor, Mike's head bouncing off the concrete like a rubber ball. Trying to maintain consciousness but blacking out.

Manning must have tossed his unconscious body into the freezer in the basement of the crumbling house and then slammed the lid. The bastard had either killed the dead guy lying on the basement floor or had witnessed it and undoubtedly was long gone by now. But that wasn't the worst part. The worst part was that in all likelihood Earl Manning now had Mike's Glock.

"Jesus," he mumbled bitterly, and the sound went nowhere, not bouncing off the corrugated aluminum of the freezer's interior, not squeezing out of the airtight tomb. It simply seemed to shrivel and die, disappearing like his last hope.

Sweat dripped off his face, plopping onto the freezer floor, the sound reminding him of the ticking of a clock. Mike wondered how long an adult human being could survive inside one of these things and guessed it couldn't be more than thirty minutes, forty at the most, before all the air was used up and the victim began breathing his own carbon monoxide, eventually poisoning himself.

But even if his guess about the timing was right, it gave him nothing to work with. He had no idea how much air was left because he had no way of knowing how much time he had already spent inside the freezer. It probably wasn't long—more often than not when the brain gets scrambled and shuts down, it's for no more than a few seconds, a couple of minutes at the most, then it reboots like a computer hard drive—but it could have been thirty seconds or fifteen minutes or anything in between.

At least while he had been unconscious he had been breathing slowly, not using much air, unlike now when panic was starting to take over and he could feel himself breathing heavily, nearly panting, feeling like he had just run ten miles. He forced himself to slow down, to conserve air, to *think*.

Gordie knew he was out here, and the Paskagankee Police dispatcher had been doing his job a long time. He would expect Mike to check in after searching the house, whether he had found the couple he was looking for or not. If enough time went by and no communication had been received, Gordie would send another cruiser to investigate. Either Harley or Sharon would be dispatched.

And they would find an otherwise empty house with a dead body on the floor of the basement. Who knew whether either one of them would think to check the closed freezer? And, really, even if they did, what were the odds they would get here quickly enough to discover anything beside his cooling corpse huddled in the bottom of the thing?

Mike realized he was starting to breathe heavily again

and forced himself to calm down. Panicking would do no good. But it was definitely getting hotter in here, a sure sign that the oxygen was rapidly disappearing.

He forced himself to be still and think, although it was becoming harder and harder to concentrate. Brett Parker and the young woman had been lying on the floor when he first entered the basement. They had both been unconscious but not suffering from any apparent serious injuries. Manning was undoubtedly long gone, but what were the chances he would have killed both of them before leaving or taken both as hostages?

Maybe one or both of them were still out there and had awoken and recovered sufficiently to help him. Maybe if he screamed loudly enough, some of the sound would force its way out of this metal coffin and alert them to his presence.

Maybe.

But there was a risk; a big one, the way Mike saw it. If neither of them had regained consciousness yet, or if Manning had killed both before leaving, or if they had both already gotten up and made their way out of the basement, he could scream his fool head off and the only result would be to burn through the remainder of his oxygen that much more quickly, effectively condemning himself to death.

He tried to stay calm and weigh the options. Sweat continued to drip; he was soaking, he felt like he had jumped into a pool with all his clothes on. The decision was simple, really. In all probability he was going to die inside this freezer. There was no getting around it. And if that was the case, he wasn't about to go down without a fight. If yelling for help brought the end about more quickly, so be it. At least he would go to his death knowing he had tried.

Mike took a deep breath, wondering whether it would be his last, and bellowed as loudly as he could.

30

Driving a car was hard when you were dead, and coordinating all the muscular activity needed to shift a manual transmission properly was damned near impossible. All of the problems he was having took what had been a lifelong dream—putting a Porsche through its paces—and made it seem like more of a pain in the ass for Earl Manning than the joy ride he had been expecting. Plus, a fire engine red Porsche 911 would stick out like a sore thumb with the authorities, who would undoubtedly already be in the process of launching a massive search for Software Boy and the suddenly missing chief of police.

He should have taken the minivan. He knew that. It would have been easier to drive and might have made blending into the scenery at least a possibility.

Goddammit.

Thinking logically had never been Earl's strong point—he wasn't sure he had ever even *had* a strong point—and being dead had scrambled his faculties even more, but one thing he knew was that it would be suicide to return to that piece of shit house in the woods and try to change vehicles now, so all he could do was continue on in the Porsche and hope for the best.

It would be suicide; that was a good one. Could someone who was already dead even commit suicide? How could you kill yourself if you weren't alive to begin with? Earl wasn't sure, but he thought that might be what the eggheads called a conundrum. Whatever it was called, it was the sort of philosophical discussion that would have kept the alkies and barflies at the Ridge Runner busy for a good long while, that was for sure.

The Porsche weaved back and forth along the remote Paskagankee roads, mostly staying on the right side, occasionally drifting across the centerline whenever Earl became distracted, which seemed to be happening more and more. He knew enough to keep to the lightly-traveled roads as he headed out of town, and so far, since leaving The Fucking Devil Max Acton's house, had seen only a handful of vehicles.

He glanced over at his billionaire passenger, slumped in the sports car's other bucket seat. Parker had been moaning and occasionally twitching, and Earl guessed he would be regaining consciousness soon.

He wasn't sure whether that was a good thing or a bad thing. It would make him much harder to control, which was bad, but on the other hand, Earl figured a guy who had invented and sold enough computer software to end up one of the richest men in the world couldn't help but be smarter than he was, and he definitely needed some serious brainpower.

Because, well, here was the thing: Earl had no goddamn clue what to do next. He had outsmarted The Fucking Devil Max Acton precisely by *not* planning anything out, by just acting on instinct and attacking when The Fucking Devil's attention was elsewhere.

He had known enough to take cover in the only available hiding place when the cop showed up, catching the guy by surprise and somehow taking him down.

And he had even been bright enough to take a hostage.

But what now? Sure, Parker was rich. Maybe he even had research and development connections in the field of human reanimation, if there was such a thing. But he was from the west coast, his research facilities would be three thousand miles away, and the minute they even tried to use the guy's ATM card to get a little operating capital the authorities would be on him like, well, like Earl Manning on a free beer.

The situation was just about fucking hopeless. Earl felt himself getting worked up, agitated, like he did when his Ma tried to make him do stupid shit like take out the garbage or clean their ratty trailer. If he could breathe, he'd probably be hyperventilating right now, but, of course, that wasn't a problem, was it?

Earl spied a fire lane cut into the trees, coming up fast on the right. He hit the brakes, too hard, and the Porsche skidded along the deserted road, the car's ass end trying to overtake the front. Parker's limp body tumbled into the passenger side foot well and wedged itself into the tiny space. Earl concentrated on keeping the goddamn car from flying off into the trees and forgot to hit the clutch with his left foot and the fucking engine died and he slammed his hands on the steering wheel in frustration as the car came screeching to a halt, somehow stopping right in the middle of the road.

He wanted to cry or scream or hit something. Instead he turned the key to restart the car and it tried to jitter forward since it was still in gear. Earl forced himself to slow down, concentrating hard, and depressed the clutch before turning the key again and the engine fired up like the car had just come off the showroom floor, purring contentedly. Earl eased the Porsche into first gear and chugged forward, making the right turn into the fire lane and driving a couple of hundred feet until he was pretty sure the vehicle was out of sight of the road, not that anyone was likely to come by.

Then he shut the engine off and leaned down to the right. It was time the two of them had a little conversation, man to man. *Or at least corpse to man.* Earl snickered. He dragged Parker's body back up onto the seat and raised his hand to slap the billionaire like people always did on TV when someone was unconscious—it seemed to work every time—and noticed his hostage's blue eyes were open and he appeared more or less alert. He seemed to be working hard at looking anywhere but at Earl, but he was definitely awake, although he had not so much as uttered a word yet.

Earl smiled and Parker scrabbled his feet against the Porsche's firewall, doing his best to shove himself through the passenger side door and into the woods. He had apparently learned nothing from unsuccessfully attempting the same maneuver at his house. A terrified whimper escaped his lips and Earl's smile widened into a grin. "Welcome back to the land of the living," he said. "That makes . . . well . . ." he pretended to count on his fingers . . . "one of us."

"What do you want from me," Parker whispered. "I gave that other guy the Codebreaker already; I have nothing more to offer."

"That other guy," Earl mused. "Oh, you mean The Fucking Devil Max Acton, the man whose throat I ripped out? The man who murdered me and then desecrated my corpse by cutting my heart out and bringing me back to life to act as his personal slave? Is that the other guy you're referring to?"

Parker nodded slowly, clearly unsure where this conversation was going and whether agreement would be good or bad for his long-term health.

"Well, here's the thing," Earl said. "I don't give a damn about the fucking Codebreaker, I have other things to worry about. Things like getting my heart put back in my chest and getting my life back. And not this crazy half-life of being dead, forced to do someone else's bidding, either. I mean becoming a real, live person again, going to the Ridge Runner and drinking with my friends. It might not seem like much of a life to a rich snob like you, but it's mine, and I WANT IT BACK!"

Earl had felt himself getting angrier and angrier as he talked, pissed off at the unfairness of what he had been put through, and by the time he finished talking, he was surprised to discover he was shouting, screaming into Brett Parker's face. He would have been showering the man in spit, but, of course, he couldn't generate saliva; he was dead.

Parker's eyes were wild, his face white as a ghost. He shook his head. "What does any of this have to do with me?" He was still whispering, as if maybe he thought the sound of his voice at full volume might push Earl over the edge. And *that* pissed him off, too.

"What does it have to do with you? Are you really that stupid? You have all the money and all the resources. You're going to use that money and those resources to figure out how to get me my life back."

Parker shook his head. His bewilderment looked real. "I don't know anything about what happened to you, and I don't know anything about bringing the dead back to life. I . . . I don't even think any of that is possible. I'm a computer software developer, a tech geek, that's all. I don't see how I could help you."

Earl snapped. Parker was his only hope and the software billionaire had fallen right into his lap. That couldn't have been a random occurrence; the guy had to be able to fix him. The universe couldn't possibly be so cruel as to give him this rare opportunity and not allow him to use it somehow.

"BULLSHIT," he screamed, and he turned the key and the engine started on the first try. He jammed the Porsche's stick shift into reverse, remembering to depress the clutch despite the stress and his anger, and then stomped on the gas. The engine roared and dirt and dust and rocks flew from under the tires as they spun on the sandy surface of the fire lane and a second later they caught and the Porsche rocketed backward, Earl barely paying attention, somehow managing to avoid shooting off the narrow trail into a tree.

Parker screamed and Earl felt a rush of savage glee and in a matter of seconds, against all odds, the Porsche had reversed straight out of the fire lane. It bounced onto the crumbling pavement of Mountain Home Road, shooting sparks as it bottomed out on the slight rise of the shoulder and then flew into the air. Earl smacked the top of his head on the Porsche's carpeted ceiling and he felt the car begin to cant slightly to the left, and then they slammed back down onto the road, sparks flying, thick black smoke billowing from under the wheel wells as Earl kept the accelerator jammed to the floor.

The engine screamed and the tires screamed and Parker screamed and the Porsche shot across the empty road, disappearing into the forest opposite the fire lane. It blasted through the branches of an ancient fir tree like a bullet and slammed backward into the tree's massive trunk and the car exploded in a shower of smashing glass and twisting sheet metal.

And then it was quiet.

31

Sharon reached the top of the stairs and pushed Raven roughly through the doorway into the kitchen, anxious to get as far away from the overwhelming stench in the basement as possible. She was in a hurry to get medical attention for Raven and then transport her to a holding cell so she could continue her search for Mike McMahon.

She was frustrated and angry. There wasn't a doubt in her mind this young woman knew more than she was saying, both about the dead body in the basement and maybe also about Mike's disappearance, but she had clammed up and shown no signs of cooperating and Sharon didn't want to waste precious time on a lost cause. Maybe once she had tossed Raven into the back of the cruiser and they were on their way to the hospital she could get the girl to open up a little.

But she was still pissed. She kicked the basement door

closed after shoving Raven into the kitchen. The door slammed and the whole house seemed to shake, and she stalked forward and—

—What the hell?

A muffled sound came from somewhere she couldn't quite put her finger on. It might have been in front of her or behind her or even above her on the second floor. Or maybe from the basement. The sound was brief and aborted and perhaps even a figment of her imagination.

She stopped dead still, grabbing Raven by the crook of the elbow to keep her from continuing into the empty living room. What had she heard? Had she even heard anything? It had sounded almost like a puppy whimpering or maybe someone snoring enthusiastically under a blanket.

Or maybe a cry for help.

'What is it? What's going on?" Raven asked, turning her head to look quizzically at Sharon.

"Shut up," she hissed. "Did you hear that?"

Raven shrugged. "What?"

"Never mind," Sharon answered, concentrating, trying to focus all of her attention on her sense of hearing. Finally she shook her head. It must have been her imagination.

She took one step and heard it again, weaker this time, if that was possible. It was just barely intelligible. But it wasn't a puppy whimpering and it wasn't anyone snoring under a blanket. It was a cry for help, and it had come from the basement, Sharon was suddenly sure of it.

She looked at Raven and realized Raven had heard it this time, too. The young woman was watching her with sharp, clear, calculating eyes and Sharon knew if this girl had suffered an injury down in that basement, it definitely wasn't anything too serious. She also knew the minute she let Raven out of her sight, the girl would run like a greyhound.

"Come with me," she said, pulling Raven toward the kitchen sink. The girl stumbled and almost fell.

"What are you doing? What's going on?" she said.

"Get on your knees."

"What?"

"JUST DO IT." Sharon was out of patience. She couldn't tell whether the voice from the basement was Mike's or not, but someone was definitely still down there, and that someone needed help, and Raven's "poor me" game was getting old very quickly.

She forced the reluctant woman to a kneeling position and grabbed her handcuffs off her belt, leaning down and hooking one of the bracelets around the drain pipe under one of the kitchen sink's dual tubs. Then she pulled Raven's thin wrist toward her and slapped the other side around it. She had no idea how sturdy the pipe was, but this girl was even tinier than her—maybe 95 pounds soaking wet—and she was willing to bet Raven wouldn't be able to escape before her return even if the pipe had weakened with age.

"Don't you move," she said, standing quickly and trotting to the basement door. She yanked it open and the smell of rot and corruption struck her again and her eyes began to water as she descended the stairs. She was sure the cry she heard had originated in the basement, but the damned basement was wide open and practically empty. Where had someone been imprisoned that wasn't immediately apparent when she was down there?

She took the stairs two at a time, hanging on to the wooden stair rail and hoping she wouldn't stumble and twist an ankle. The minute her eyes cleared the wall she knew exactly where the call for help had come from. The floor freezer at the far end of the basement was almost exactly the perfect dimensions for stashing a body.

She realized she had been distracted by the murdered man lying in the middle of the cement floor, as well as by the injured Raven, but still Sharon mentally kicked herself for not investigating the freezer; for not at least opening the lid and checking it out.

Another cry came from inside the freezer, this one weak and barely loud enough to hear. She took the final four stairs in one flying leap—to hell with worrying about a twisted ankle—and landed with a smack on the floor, stumbling but keeping her feet, making a wide berth around the dead body and all the blood and then sprinting to the freezer.

She yanked on the silver latch and her nervous, sweaty fingers slipped off it. Another swipe at it and the latch gave way and she pushed up on the hinged lid and there was Mike McMahon, crumpled on the freezer floor. His face was bright crimson and sweat poured off every exposed bit of skin in rivers and he seemed unable to catch his breath.

"Sweet Jesus," Sharon muttered and clambered over the side of the freezer, hooking a hand arm under each of his armpits, struggling to lift his much heavier body. He smiled weakly and breathed deeply, his chest heaving, taking in the foul stench like it was crystal clear mountain air. He slipped out of her grasp and fell to the floor again, then pushed himself up to a kneeling position, hanging his head over the side of the freezer.

"What took you so long?" he whispered, and Sharon knelt down in the freezer, straddling his legs. She kissed him hard, knowing it was unprofessional but not caring.

She felt tears welling up in her eyes and forced them back. "You're not getting rid of me that easily," she answered. "This is a hell of a time to take a nap, though. In case you hadn't noticed, there's a lot going on right now."

"Thanks for the pep talk," he said, and grabbed the side of the freezer with both hands, forcing himself to his feet. He stepped over the side and stumbled to his knees on the cement and Sharon grabbed him, watching his eyes closely. "Are you going to be okay?"

Mike nodded. "I think so. A few more minutes inside that thing, though, and I think I would have been taking the long nap. Lights were blossoming in my eyes and I couldn't catch my breath to save my life. Literally. But I'm feeling better and better, just pissed off that Manning was able to get the drop on me."

"Manning?" Sharon said. "Earl Manning? Earl threw you into this freezer?"

"Yeah. What about it?"

"I have a witness that says she either saw Earl Manning get killed or she saw him kill someone. She wouldn't be any more specific and now she's clammed up."

Mike looked down at her, his eyes seeming to become clearer and more alert by the second. "Well, if Manning's dead, then he's a zombie, because he was moving around pretty damned good a little while ago. In fact, he hit me like a freaking freight train. He seemed to have had a lot more strength than a scrawny little drunk should."

Sharon shuddered. "Zombie? That's not funny."

"I wasn't trying to be."

32

The strange little group stumbled out of the house, Mike in the lead, clearly already more alert now than he had been just a few minutes ago, apparently none the worse for wear after nearly suffocating in the freezer. Raven followed him closely, with Sharon bringing up the rear, maintaining a tight grip on her prisoner's upper arm.

Sharon wasn't sure whether the young woman qualified more as a suspect or a witness, but one thing she *was* sure of was that Raven knew a lot more about what had gone down in that basement than she had thus far revealed. It seemed unlikely a woman as tiny as Raven could have gotten enough of a jump on the much bigger male victim to do the kind of damage that had been inflicted upon him, but Sharon had seen some strange things since returning to Paskagankee and had learned not to discount any possibility. Ever. Even if it was an *im*possibility.

They crossed the scraggly front lawn and Sharon said, "Wanna ride in my cruiser and then come back for yours after you get checked out at the hospital?"

Mike shook his head, wincing slightly as he did so. "No."

Sharon narrowed her eyes. "You took a pretty good knock on the head, are you sure you should be driving?"

"That's not what I mean," Mike answered. "I'm not going anywhere. I'll stay here and secure the area. I can get a head start on the investigation and be as prepared as possible when the evidence techs get here."

"You mean you're not even going to the hospital?"

"No reason to," he said. "I'm okay now and it's not like we're exactly overloaded with manpower. Harley can stay on routine patrol while you drive our friend here to the hospital to get checked out. I'm going to call Pete Kendall at home and get him out here to handle things on-scene, and I'll come join you at the hospital after I've passed this off to him. That will give Ms . . ."

"Tahoma," the young woman answered.

"That will give Ms Tahoma the opportunity to secure legal counsel if she wants it and we can begin interrogating her when I get to Orono."

"You're the boss," Sharon said reluctantly. She knew he should see a doctor before continuing, but he did have a point about the lack of manpower. Officers were hard to come by in a town as small and remote as Paskagankee, Maine, especially qualified ones. Investigating a murder, while simultaneously conducting a search for the missing

Brett Parker, was going to tax the tiny force to the limit.

Sharon knew Mike would have to call in outside help. He would be reluctant to do so, given how he had been shut out of the search for the killer roaming Paskagankee last fall by the Maine State Police investigative team, but she had known him long enough to know he would never allow personal feelings to get in the way of his job, especially when it involved something as important as a murder investigation.

She gazed into his eyes, holding his stare, wondering whether the intense fear she had felt when he went missing was showing on her face as plainly as she thought it must be. Breaking up with Mike had been the only sensible solution to an unsolvable problem, she knew that. She was surprised the Town Council hadn't taken action against Mike already for living with his subordinate.

But, goddammit, the pain was almost too much to bear. She had never felt whole until meeting Mike McMahon, and the thought of having to forego all the good he brought out in her for the rest of her life was unbearable. His going missing had only crystallized and clarified the feelings she had already known were there.

She tore her eyes away from his, aware that they had begun to tear up again, and hoped he didn't notice. She cleared her throat. "Okay, then." She pushed Raven Tahoma roughly into the back of her cruiser and slid into the front seat, firing up the engine.

"Hey," Mike said gently.

She looked up at him.

"Be careful driving."

She nodded, wiping the sleeve of her uniform blouse over her eyes, then gunned the engine, hitting the gas harder than she intended. She refused to return Mike's stare as she backed quickly down the driveway, giving the empty road her full attention. She slammed the car into Drive and accelerated away. Then she rounded a corner and the ramshackle house was gone.

33

Brett Parker heard the sound of airplanes buzzing overhead, nonstop, one after the other, like he was right next to the runway at Seattle-Tacoma International Airport. How the hell had he gotten here? He tried to remember. He had been working at the new summer retreat in Maine when—

—He opened his eyes, doing his best to ignore a pounding in his skull unlike any headache he had ever experienced, and realized it wasn't airplanes buzzing around his head at all; it was mosquitoes. The insects were everywhere, swarming around him, feasting on his flesh; great black clouds of mosquitoes, more of the vicious blood-suckers than Brett had ever seen in one place; more than he would ever have imagined *could* be present in one place.

He lay on his side, crumpled in a pile inside the wreckage of the Porsche, his body stuffed uncomfortably into the foot well on the passenger's side—again—like some giant had used him to try to plug a hole in the floor of the car. His head hurt and his arm throbbed painfully and his back felt like a soccer team had used it for kicking practice. But he was alive, and, it seemed, unharmed, relatively speaking.

Brett raised his head painfully and glanced up into the driver's side of the vehicle, looking for the freak who had kidnapped him right out of his own home and put this whole nightmare in motion. He was nowhere to be seen, and the car door on that side of the vehicle had been torn completely off its hinges. Safety glass from the windshield—and, apparently, all of the broken passenger windows—covered every available inch of surface, glittering colorfully in the muted light. A pine tree branch, at least two inches thick, had smashed through the rear window and then snapped off, the blunt end looking exactly like a battering ram, suspended inches from Brett's head.

But the creepy lunatic who had been driving the Porsche was gone. He had disappeared, maybe ripped from the car's interior by the force of the crash, maybe propelled through the windshield by the pine tree branch. Brett didn't know and didn't care. He was gone. In all likelihood he was dead. The guy hadn't been the picture of health to begin with—the smell of death hung on him like a shroud—and the odds of him surviving such a violent car wreck were absurdly low. Brett wondered how *he* had managed it.

He braced his right arm on the floor and pain flashed

up it from wrist to elbow. He sucked in a breath, trying not to cry out, not wanting to alert his captor he had awakened. He knew he was being foolish, Freaky Dude had to be dead, or at least badly injured and incapacitated, but the world had suddenly gone mad, tilting crazily on its axis, and he wasn't taking any chances.

He eased his right arm out from under his body. Something was obviously broken in that one. He tried the left arm, pushing gingerly until assuring himself it was okay. It held his weight. He pushed harder, wishing he could shoo away all of the mosquitoes. They seemed to be everywhere and had redoubled their attack when he began to move.

His arm throbbed and his back throbbed and his head hurt, he felt like he might be sick to his stomach at any moment, but gradually Brett rose up from the floor of the Porsche like a magic trick, pushing and straining, managing to slide his legs underneath his body until he was in a kneeling position, his stomach braced against the supple leather of the passenger seat, his face pressed against the backrest.

He reached for the door handle with his left hand and pulled. Nothing happened. He pulled again, and again nothing happened, and the old cliché about insanity being defined as attempting the same thing over and over and expecting a different result popped into his head and he almost chuckled.

The door was obviously jammed. He could pull on it all day and it was never going to open. He would have to go out the driver's side. No worry about *that* door being jammed; it was missing in action. Of course, there was the small matter of crawling under the broken pine tree branch, and trying not to cut himself to ribbons on all of the broken glass, but he was alive, and the freak who had caused all his problems was gone, and *he could do this.*

Brett pushed with his feet and slithered sideways, bracing himself with his good arm as the gearshift stabbed him in the belly. The branch pushed relentlessly down on his body and for a moment he thought there might not be enough room to squeeze through. Then the small of his back dipped under the branch and the pressure was gone and his upper body slid off the driver's seat and he fell into *that* foot well.

He landed on his right arm and this time he couldn't help himself; he screamed in pain. He shifted his weight, easing the pressure on his arm, resting for just a moment. He realized he was sweating and panting heavily and wondered when he would swallow a mosquito. It seemed inevitable. He was amazed he hadn't done it already.

Brett grabbed the rocker panel under the missing driver's side door with his left hand, hoping not to slice a finger off on the razor-sharp exposed sheet metal. He pulled mightily and his shoulder cleared the door. He pulled again and his upper body once again fell onto his injured right arm, this time on the soft carpeting of millions of pine needles. He screamed again but this time the pain was tempered with a sense of accomplishment. He was almost out of the wreckage!

He rolled to the left until his broken right arm was no longer pinned under his body, then pushed against the driver's seat with his feet, sliding along the bed of pine needles away from the car and toward the mammoth tree trunk. At last he was clear of the Porsche. He looked back at the wreck, amazed he was still alive. The back end of the vehicle had been compressed into roughly half the area it had previously occupied, crammed right up against the seats, which had been shoved forward until they were almost flush with the dashboard.

Brett now realized it was only by the most random form of luck that he had survived. By being unconscious, his unresisting body had simply been pushed into the foot well, the only place it could have gone without him being crushed to death. Had he been conscious, he would undoubtedly have tensed up—it would have been an instinctive reaction—and he would have been impaled by the pine tree branch. It would have run him through from back to front.

Brett waved his hand around his head weakly, trying without any measurable success to scatter the millions of mosquitoes, which seemed to have called in reinforcements once he had freed himself from the car. Now they surrounded his entire body, from head to toe, landing and feasting with impunity. It would be the ultimate irony to survive this horrific car wreck, only to die by having his blood drained by these parasitic insectile vampires.

All he wanted to do was rest, to close his eyes and sleep for a few minutes, but Brett knew that if he succumbed to that intense desire, he might never wake up. Even if he did, the daylight was passing quickly, and it would probably be night when he awoke. And an injured man in this remote area, defenseless and bleeding, would stand virtually no chance of surviving until morning. He would become nothing more than a midnight snack for some passing family of black bears.

Brett groaned and rolled to his knees, holding his

upper body off the forest floor with his left arm. He felt weak and lightheaded. He sat back on his haunches, doing his best to ignore the mosquitoes, and unfastened two of the middle buttons on his dress shirt. He lifted his right wrist with his left hand, sweating heavily from the pain and exertion, and slid the injured arm inside the unbuttoned portion of his shirt. Then he clumsily fastened one of the buttons, forming a makeshift sling for his broken arm. He didn't know how long it would hold, but it had to be better than nothing.

Now came the hard part. He would have to stand and fight his way out from under this gigantic tree, through the thick underbrush, and out to the road. Brett had only visited Paskagankee once before, when he purchased the land upon which his summer retreat would be built, and didn't know how Freaky Dude had gotten here, or even where "here" was. He might be a hundred miles from Paskagankee for all he knew. He had no idea how heavily traveled this road might be or how far he might have to walk to get assistance.

But Brett didn't care about any of that. He had survived the bizarre encounter with the lunatics who had kidnapped him, and he was going to be okay. He would fight his way to the road, he would stay conscious and clear-headed for as long as it took to get help, and he would get the hell out of this backwater horror-show of a town. He would sell his brand new house for whatever he could get for it—monetary losses be damned—and he would fly back to Seattle and never return.

Brett stumbled to his feet and the cloud of mosquitoes rose with him. His broken arm throbbed and his head pounded and his back hurt and the goddamned bloodsucking mosquitoes were relentless.

Getting out from under the pine tree was easier than he had expected it to be. The Porsche had punched a fairly significant-sized hole in the wall of branches and pine needles during its high-speed backwards run, and Brett took full advantage, dropping to his knees and duck-walking through the opening. On the far side he stood and continued to follow the path of destruction the Porsche had opened, stumbling forward, pausing every minute or two to catch his breath and try not to puke onto the forest floor.

It was amazing how far off the road the little car had managed to burrow through the underbrush before ramming the tree trunk. But Brett kept moving grimly forward, a death march of one, and eventually a black ribbon of pavement appeared before his grateful eyes. Suddenly he understood exactly what an oasis would look like to someone wandering lost in the desert. He broke through one last thicket of tangled thorns and he was through.

His watered and the sense of relief he felt was overwhelming. He had done it! He knew it might be hours before he was rescued, but even in an area as remote as northern Maine, Brett knew *someone* would come driving along this road eventually. If there was pavement in America, people would drive on it.

He was going to be saved. He smiled and picked a random direction and began walking, focusing his gaze downward so that he could avoid stepping in a pothole and falling one more time onto his broken arm. He almost felt like whistling a happy tune.

And that was when he ran straight into the stinking,

skeletal body of Freaky Dude.

34

Sharon hauled ass along the deserted roads, driving the cruiser too fast, angling into turns and tapping the brakes only when absolutely necessary. She wasn't specifically trying to put a scare into her passenger—her goal was to get Raven to the hospital in Orono and then back to a holding cell in Paskagankee as quickly as possible, then move on to some real police work—but the girl's drawn face and wide eyes were a nice little bonus.

She was annoyed and impatient. This young woman had somehow survived the slaughter which had almost gotten Mike killed, in all likelihood had information which could be critical to the investigation, and she had clammed up. A little scare might go a long way toward adjusting her attitude, but even if it didn't, Sharon had to admit it felt kind of good.

"How's your head feeling?" she asked gruffly in an effort to start some kind of dialogue. Raven Tahoma had barely said a word since being loaded into the cruiser, so a meaningful conversation seemed unlikely, but it was worth a try. Maybe the young woman would let something slip.

"He loves you, you know," Raven answered from behind the wire mesh separating the back seat of the cruiser from the front.

Sharon stared at her passenger in surprise, her gaze locked onto Raven's in the mirror as the cruiser wandered across the centerline of Mountain Home Road, heading for the forest on the opposite side. Raven's eyes widened in alarm and she raised her hand, pointing through the windshield at the rapidly-approaching thicket of fir trees. Sharon pulled the wheel to the right, thanking her lucky stars for the lack of traffic in and around Paskagankee.

The cruiser re-settled into the travel lane and Sharon eased off the gas. Being in a hurry was one thing, killing yourself by being in a hurry was something completely different. "He loves me? What are you talking about?" she asked, unsettled, too shocked at Raven's words to try to turn the conversation around on her.

"That officer back there, the one you rescued from the freezer. He's in love with you," she said simply.

"I heard you the first time. What I meant was why would you say that?"

"It's obvious." She shrugged. "I can tell just by the way he looks at you."

Sharon felt a flutter in her belly, which was stupid. She already knew how Mike felt about her; she felt exactly the same about him. The fact that he had nearly died this afternoon only served to clarify those feelings. But so what? It didn't change anything. They were still finished as a couple; she had broken off their relationship because there was no way they could be together. That hadn't changed.

Still, it threw her off her game to think she was so transparent that this stranger—a criminal suspect who had watched her interact with Mike for a total of maybe five minutes—could see right into the deepest reaches of her heart. It was disturbing. She needed to steer the conversation in a different direction.

She took a deep breath. "Yeah, well, did it occur to you that maybe he was looking at me that way because he had just come within a minute or two of suffocating to death? What happened down in that basement, anyway?"

Raven looked away, staring out the cruiser's passenger-side window as the woods flashed by. "It's the dead guy," she said flatly.

"The dead guy? The one with his throat slashed? He pushed Mike—Chief McMahon—into the freezer before he was killed?"

"No, no, not Max," Raven answered quickly. Sharon glanced into the back seat through the mirror and saw her passenger's eyes filling with tears. "The guy that *killed* Max had to have been the one that trapped Officer McMahon in the freezer. He knocked me and the rich guy out when the cop identified himself at the front door, and there was no one else down there, so it must have been him."

"Are you talking about Earl Manning?"

Raven nodded. A tear meandered down her pretty face. She didn't seem to notice.

Sharon shook her head. "But you said 'the dead guy'

did it. Manning couldn't be dead if he fought with Chief McMahon and trapped him in a freezer."

"Oh, he's dead all right."

"What are you talking about? You're not making any sense," Sharon said. She was annoyed at the bizarre turn the conversation had taken, but also felt a twinge of fear. She thought about Mike's mention of zombies and shuddered.

"It's the stone," Raven answered, unperturbed by Sharon's annoyance. Either she hadn't noticed or didn't care. "Once that Manning guy got control of the stone he regained control of his actions, and that's bad for everyone. I don't know how much damage he can do now, but I know it's a lot."

"Stone? What stone?" Sharon concentrated on the road as she drove. It would be a simple thing to get so caught up in trying to understand Raven's words that she drove into the woods, just as she had nearly done once already.

"It's a sacred Navajo stone," Raven answered. "Whoever gains possession of the stone harnesses an awesome power, the power to reanimate the dead and then control the reanimated corpse's actions."

"That's ridiculous," Sharon answered, trying to ignore the chill running down her spine, wondering if she really believed her own words.

"Think what you want; it doesn't matter to me either way." Raven gazed at Sharon through the rear view mirror. "I'm just glad that Manning guy is away from me. He killed Max and he has the stone, which means he's going to kill a lot more people before he's finished."

"Let's say for just a second I believe you. You killed

Earl Manning and—"

"—I didn't kill him," she interrupted. "The whole stupid plan was Max's idea. All I did was make the mistake of telling Max about the stone. After that, he was in charge. Max was like that," she said, sniffling. "He was an Alpha. You could never tell him what to do."

"Okay," Sharon said, anxious to guide the conversation back to Raven's confession. She hoped she wasn't jeopardizing the entire case with her impromptu interrogation, but what the hell. The young woman had never specifically requested a lawyer. Besides, she wasn't under arrest—yet—and this wasn't an interrogation room, and they were just having a casual conversation. She didn't know where this was headed, but her instincts told her they were going somewhere extremely important.

"Okay," she repeated, trying to gather her thoughts. "So, Max killed Earl Manning and then, what, reanimated him using this sacred Navajo stone?"

Raven was silent for a long moment in the back seat. She covered her face with her hands and Sharon began to fear she was going to refuse to answer. But then she did. "The process is a little more complicated than that," she said, "but that's basically it, yes."

Sharon's initial reaction was one of disbelief. Reanimating the dead? Impossible. Then she thought about the horrors of last fall, about ancient Abenaqui curses and about spirits occupying human bodies and about brutal killing sprees, and she bit off the response she had been about to spit out at Raven.

Again she thought about Mike's words as they walked out of the house he had nearly been killed inside. *If Earl Manning's dead*, he had said, *then he's a zombie, because he was moving around pretty damned good . . .*

She flicked her eyes to the mirror and saw her passenger still watching her intently. Then she concentrated on the road and hit the gas, picking up speed as she had done earlier. She needed to get Raven Tahoma to the hospital as quickly as possible. And she needed to talk to Mike.

35

Brett walked straight into Freaky Dude, who had seemingly materialized out of nowhere. He bounced off his captor's emaciated form and fell to his knees, skinning one on the pavement and wrenching his injured arm. The stench surrounding the man assaulted him and he gagged, eyes watering, bile rising into his gullet again. Whether it was a reaction to the smell or the pain in his broken arm he wasn't sure, and really, what did it matter? Freaky Dude wasn't dead after all; he had somehow survived the crash and made it to the road ahead of Brett. Then he had waited for him to stumble out of the woods.

He staggered to his feet and looked at his captor. The man's skin seemed ready to slough off his bones, and his bones looked like they might poke through that saggy skin at any moment. And the man was grinning at him. "What took you so long?" he rumbled. "I was beginning to think you weren't really trying. I could have pulled you out of the car, but I've recently become a big believer in self-reliance, you know what I'm saying?"

Brett's heart sank. His situation was hopeless. The lunatic had not only survived what seemed like an unsurvivable car wreck, he appeared spry and none the worse for wear, although in his present wretched physical state that wasn't saying much. Brett sank back to his knees and spit blood onto the road. He hadn't even noticed he was bleeding from the mouth until just now. Again, what did it matter?

"Where are we going now?" he asked dully.

"What are you talking about?" his captor answered. "Nothing's changed. We're going to find a way out of this piece of shit little town, and you're going to use your money and connections to reverse the damage that was done to me."

Anger flashed through Brett. He had tried to explain to this moron once already that he had no idea *what* had been done to him, and the notion that Brett Parker, of all people, could find a way to reverse it was nothing more than the craziest kind of pointless wishful thinking. He spit on the ground again. More blood. "How the hell are we going to get out of town? You just destroyed our vehicle, you idiot!"

"Watch your fucking mouth," the freak said. His foot flashed out and he kicked the kneeling Brett squarely in the chest. Brett dropped like a sack of potatoes, unable to brace himself with his right hand, falling onto his left and feeling his wrist crack. He had either just broken it or at the very least sprained it. He lay on the pavement, defeated, wondering what would happen next.

Freaky Dude loomed over him, the stink rolling off him in waves. "Well?" he said.

"Well, what?" Brett mumbled. The initial blast of pain in his wrist seemed to be receding. Maybe it wasn't broken, after all, or maybe it was, and the damage to his right arm by comparison was even worse than he had thought. It occurred to him that he didn't really care; what were the odds he would survive this insanity, anyway?

Well, let's go," the lunatic said. "We'll start walking until a car comes by, then when one does, we'll commandeer it and continue on. Like I already told you, nothing's changed."

Brett wanted to cry; he thought he might do exactly that. This horrifying, putrid backwoods idiot was completely delusional. Something awful had clearly happened to him, and whatever it was had apparently pushed him over the edge, because he certainly wasn't listening to reason.

Brett thought about Jenna and their little girl back in Seattle, waiting for him to return home, with no idea anything was wrong. She had probably tried to call him at least once since the beginning of this nightmare, but she wouldn't be concerned or upset that she hadn't been able to contact him. It wasn't at all unusual for him to ignore his cell when he was working on something important; he had gone as long as eight hours in the past before returning his wife's calls.

All of that is going to change, he thought. *I promise. Get me out of this and from now on, family comes first.* He wondered who this plea was directed toward. Brett had long ago stopped believing in God; he wasn't sure he had ever believed. But he had always maintained a firm grip on his own destiny before. Now that events were occurring which were completely out of his control, Brett realized the notion of some sort of Divine Being who could take charge of the situation and make everything normal again seemed not just desirable but necessary.

"I told you, let's go," Freaky Dude demanded and took one step in Brett's direction. He was now standing directly above Brett. Brett scrambled to his feet, which was easier said than done without using either hand to help himself up, but he managed it because he didn't want to get kicked in the chest again; the freak might look like he weighed a hundred ten pounds soaking wet, but he packed a punch that Brett had no desire to re-experience.

He stood unsteadily, swaying as a blossom of black and purple ballooned in his vision. He felt light-headed and knew he was going into shock; hell, he was probably already there. He hung his head and wished he could just sink back down to the pavement and rest. Then his vision cleared slightly and he felt a bit more normal and he began walking, moving past Freaky Dude without another word.

He trudged forward as fast as he could, not caring which direction he was going, intent only on escaping the smell. Apparently the freak didn't care which direction they went, either, because he simply chuckled once, low and gravelly and frightening, then fell in behind Brett, staggering along like an extra in *Night of the Living Dead*.

After the first few steps Brett began to find a rhythm and increased his pace. Shock waves of pain raced between his wrist and his elbow and his aching head throbbed steadily in time with his steps and his back wasn't all that happy at the moment, either, but he didn't care about any of that. Maybe if he moved quickly enough, the skeletal freak behind him would simply outpace the drugs or whatever the hell he was on—Brett had heard angel dust could give a person incredible strength, perhaps that was what Freaky Dude had taken—and just drop dead and fall to the ground. The prospect didn't seem likely, but it was all Brett Parker had going for him, and he clung to that fantasy for all he was worth.

36

Sharon punched the speed dial for Mike's cell phone and pondered a depressing realization: now that they had broken up, she didn't have a single non-work number programmed into the damned thing. She had no close friends, no brothers or sisters, no parents—mother long dead, father gone over a year now, not that he was worth much, anyway—and now, no Mike. She had never felt so completely alone in her life.

She forced her thoughts back to the matter at hand. She could worry about her pathetic personal situation later; right now, she had critical information to pass along. The information seemed ridiculous, and she had no idea what it might mean, but she wasn't about to dismiss it out of hand.

Static buzzed and the line whirred and then clicked as

Mike picked up. "McMahon."

"Mike, I'm at the hospital in Orono." There was no need for introduction—he would have seen on his caller ID who was on the line, anyway—and no time for preliminaries. "I had a bizarre but fascinating conversation with Ms Raven Tahoma on the drive over."

"Really. Didn't she ask for a lawyer? What were you doing interrogating her, Shari?"

"Interrogation? There was no interrogation, just a little girl talk, that's all. Besides, she never actually got around to requesting representation."

"Girl talk."

"Right. And what she told me sounds impossible to believe, but I thought I should get it to you right away and let you decide how much weight to give it."

"Okay, hit me."

"This chick's a Native American—a Navajo, specifically—and she left the reservation to join the murder victim, Max Acton, in a little commune scam he was running down in Arizona. Acton had a habit of getting close—intimately close—to the youngest and prettiest of his followers, and she fell for him like a stone, with the emphasis on 'stone'."

"Keep going."

"Well, apparently while she was unburdening herself to her new love in a particularly heartfelt pillow-talk session, she let slip information about a sacred Navajo stone her father's best friend had been charged with protecting."

"A sacred stone. Obviously, this stone has a bearing on our murder case, or we wouldn't be having this conversation."

"Oh, yeah. And not just the murder case; the Earl Manning missing-persons case, too, as well as the break-in at Brett Parker's home and his disappearance as well. It's the key to everything."

"I figured all three events were tied together, they had to be. I just couldn't quite put my finger on how. You're about to tell me, aren't you?"

"Yep. And the tie-in's a doozy, at least if you believe Ms Tahoma."

Sharon heard a long sigh on the other end of the connection and pictured Mike lifting his cap and running his hand through his thick hair. "Let me have it."

"Well, this sacred stone—again, if you believe Raven Tahoma—contains a powerful mystical property allowing its possessor not only to reanimate the recently dead, but to control the actions of the reanimated corpse, to force the corpse to do the possessor's bidding, basically." Sharon rushed through the last part, feeling ridiculous, knowing how silly her words sounded.

"And she's saying she and Max Acton murdered Earl Manning, then used the stone to bring him back to life?"

"Well, she's claiming it was all Acton's doing, but yes, that's about the size of it."

"To what end?"

"She's a little fuzzy on that part, but apparently it has something to do with a super-secret software project Parker's company been developing. This girl thought she was in love and was only too happy to team up with Acton, but now that he's cooling on a basement floor she's singing like a bird. She knows she's in line to take the fall for everything and she seems to be finding that prospect less than desirable."

Sharon waited for Mike to digest the information, knowing exactly what his next question would be. She didn't have to wait long. "But if Acton's dead and Raven Tahoma is in custody, who's controlling Manning now?"

"Raven said somehow Manning got the drop on Acton and killed him before he knew what was going on. She says the stone is far more powerful than Acton understood and it cost him his life. Anyway, Manning grabbed the thing and, as far as she knows, *he* is in possession of it now."

"So, what does that mean?"

"She doesn't know, but she seems pretty sure of one thing. It's not good."

Sharon waited for Mike to dismiss the information, to tell her she had just wasted ten minutes of his time in the middle of a murder investigation on a silly ghost story, a centuries-old legend that had nothing to do with anything.

He didn't do that. He didn't do anything. He simply stayed quiet on the line. She knew he was considering her bombshell logically, trying to deconstruct the information, looking for the most sensible next move.

"Is that it?" he finally asked.

"There is one more thing. Her father's friend, the one Acton stole the stone from? He was badly injured in the robbery, but she thinks he survived. She has his telephone number. She says he knows as much about the mystical stone as anyone alive. She's afraid to talk to him after what she did, but she thinks he will answer any question you have to the best of his ability and she's certain he'll do anything possible to get that stone back safely."

She heard him sigh again. He seemed to be doing a lot of sighing. "Give me the number," he said.

37

Mike paced impatiently in front of the crumbling home which had recently become a murder scene, his cell phone glued to his ear. The digitized series of beeps and hums indicated a phone was ringing at the other end, but no one was picking up. He cursed and decided to terminate the call—it was probably a waste of time, anyway—when a tinny voice floated out of his ear piece.

"Hello?" someone said, and Mike returned the phone to his head.

"Yes, hello," he answered. "My name is Chief Mike McMahon of the Paskagankee, Maine Police Department. May I please speak with Don Running Bear?"

"No, you may not."

Mike pulled the phone away from his head and stared

at it for a moment in confusion. "Excuse me?" he said. "This is police business. I'm calling regarding a murder and kidnapping which has occurred in my town, and I understand Mr. Running Bear may have information which could aid in the investigation. It's imperative I speak with him."

"Well, you're going to need one hell of a strong phone connection, Chief McMahon, because Don died more than three months ago, after being attacked in his own home and murdered in cold blood."

Mike froze. "I'm so sorry," he said. "I was told Mr. Running Bear had survived that attack. Who am I speaking with?"

"I'm Don's wife, Kai. You're calling about the stone, aren't you?"

"Why do you say that?"

"Because it was the only thing taken in the home invasion, and it's no ordinary rock. I've been waiting for a call like this ever since Don died. Honestly, I'm surprised it's taken this long."

"What can you tell me about the stone, Mrs. Running Bear?"

"I can tell you Don never wanted it, nor the responsibility that came with it, but he was not the kind of man who would have shirked that responsibility by forcing it onto someone else. He was deathly afraid of that stone, Chief McMahon, and rightfully so, as it turned out. It cost him his life."

"I don't understand. Why would someone kill to gain possession of a stone?"

"Don't pretend you know nothing of the stone's power, Chief. If you hadn't either heard or seen evidence of its terrifying mystical capabilities we would not be having this conversation. Please respect me enough to be honest with me, and if you will do me that courtesy I will help in any way I can."

"Fair enough," Mike answered, nodding thoughtfully despite the fact the woman was twenty-five hundred miles away. "You're right; I've experienced enough to at least believe there is something strange and unusual about the stone. But first, I have to ask—why was the stone your husband's responsibility and no one else's?"

"Don's grandfather was the last great tribal mystic, a man commonly referred to in your culture as a 'medicine man.' When he died, the stone—as well as all of the relevant teachings regarding it—passed to Don's care."

"What about Don's father? Shouldn't he have taken possession of the stone?"

"Don's father was already dead by then, killed in an automobile accident on the reservation."

"I see," Mike said, not sure how to continue. "Mrs. Running Bear, how much of the legend regarding the stone were you privy to?"

"My husband and I were very close," she said cryptically.

"So you could probably address a few of my concerns?"

"With Don's passing, I am probably the foremost living expert on the stone, I'm sorry to have to admit," the woman answered bitterly. "I wish I could say otherwise. Now, let's get on with this. I'll help you as much as I can, and then I intend to forget we ever had this conversation. I wish Don had never touched that stone."

"I understand."

"Here is a run-down of the most important things you need to know about that cursed stone. In order for it to function effectively, the heart of the deceased must be stored inside the ceremonial wooden box. It must be placed directly next to the stone. Whoever possesses the box then controls the actions of the deceased, also known as the revenant. The revenant's body takes on great strength, much greater than what the person would have maintained while alive."

"I can testify to that," Mike said. "I had a run-in with a revenant just a couple of hours ago."

"And you're still alive? You should consider yourself extremely fortunate, Chief McMahon."

"I do," he agreed. "But here's what I really need to know: despite the fact he's up and walking around, the revenant is still technically dead, correct?'

"Yes."

"And as such, isn't the revenant's body subject to the normal decomposition process? How long will it be before his body decomposes to the point it will simply stop functioning?"

"If your plan is to wait until the revenant's body decomposes and he falls over, you might want to reconsider, Chief. The normal decomposition process does not apply. Oh, sure, the skin will begin to slough off and the revenant will smell like last week's garbage, but part of the stone's effect on the body is to slow that natural process. It doesn't stop entirely, and yes, eventually the body *will* simply give out, but in the meantime, the revenant can and will do a lot of damage if not stopped.

"You see, Chief, the problem is that the brain of a revenant is affected differently than the rest of the body, at least that was what Don told me. After the heart is taken from the corpse and united with the stone, reanimating the body, you have an abomination: an unnatural, undead being. But for all intents and purposes, it is still the victim—the revenant's personality initially will be more or less true to what it was before he died.

"However, as time passes, the decomposition of the brain's tissue causes changes in the revenant, and none of them for the better. He becomes more aggressive, less subject to the normal tendencies we all have to curb our animalistic side. Mood swings will become more and more pronounced, and behavior less predictable, until eventually, before the body breaks down, the revenant will devolve into a killing machine, wreaking havoc, destroying anything in its path."

Kai Running Bear stopped talking and Mike remained silent. Finally she said, "Are you still there, Chief?"

"I'm here, ma'am, I'm just trying to comprehend the impact of all of this. It's a pretty bleak picture, if what you just told me is all true."

"Oh, it's true, all right, but that's just the bad news. And while I'll admit the bad news is quite horrific, there is good news as well."

"What might that be?"

"The good news is that no matter how badly the revenant's brain devolves, he *still remains* completely under the control of his master, the person who victimized him and who controls the sacred stone. The revenant is compelled to comply with his master's wishes, fully and to the best of his ability, to the exclusion of all else. So, while he may be uncontrollable and unstoppable on his own, the way to shut him down is to find and control the master, the person who retains the sacred stone. That is the key to stopping your nightmare, and mine, Chief McMahon."

"Oh my God," Mike muttered under his breath.

"What is it?"

"Earl Manning—that's the name of the revenant—is in control of the stone. He somehow managed to kill his master and gain possession of the box containing the stone and his heart. We believe he still has it in his possession. How do we stop him in that scenario?"

"The revenant is controlling his own actions?"

"I believe so, yes."

"Then, may your God help you, Chief McMahon. To my knowledge, that scenario has never occurred. I don't believe it will be possible to stop the revenant now, short of dropping a bomb on his head, and I'm not even certain that would do it. The blood will flow, Chief, and lots of it. You are going to have a virtually unstoppable killing machine on your hands very soon, if you don't already."

Again the silence dragged out, sadness and regret evident on Kai Running Bear's end of the line, desperation and fear on Mike's. "I just have one last question for you, Mrs. Running Bear, and then I'll let you go," he said softly.

"What is it?"

"If your husband knew how dangerous this stone was, why didn't he get rid of it? Why didn't he bury it somewhere in the desert where it could never be found? Why take on this enormous responsibility?"

"We don't always choose our responsibilities, Chief." She paused. "Sometimes they choose us."

38

The plan had been for Sharon to wait at the hospital. Mike would put Pete Kendall in charge of the investigation at the scene of the murder as soon as he could and then drive to Orono to interrogate their prisoner.

It was a simple plan.

But the way Sharon saw it, there were two problems with that plan: 1) There was no way of knowing how long it would take for Kendall to get to the crime scene, and thus no way to know how long it would take Mike to leave for Orono, and, 2) She could not stand the idea of cooling her heels away from the action while there was real police work to be done.

A young, movie-star handsome doctor had examined Raven Tahoma and informed Sharon that while the young woman's injuries did not appear life-threatening, she had suffered a fairly serious concussion and per hospital policy would be admitted overnight for observation. *Sure,* Sharon thought, looking the man up and down cynically. *I know how this works. She batted her eyelashes at you and complained about how the bad old police were out to get her, and now you're playing knight in shining armor.*

The last thing Sharon wanted was to sit here accomplishing nothing. But she knew someone who wouldn't mind hanging out in Orono doing guard duty for their beautiful and sexy prisoner: Paskagankee Police Patrol Officer Harley Tanguay. While Tanguay was a marginally capable officer, Sharon knew he would have no problem sitting inside the comfortable confines of Mercy Hospital, camped outside their prisoner's door reading a newspaper, sipping coffee and flirting with nurses.

She knew she should have checked in with Mike and gotten his okay before calling Harley. But the chief had plenty of things on his plate right now, all of which were higher on the list of priorities than swapping out officers assigned a boring duty like babysitting their witness/suspect while she dozed in a hospital bed.

Besides, asking permission meant giving the boss the opportunity to say no, and Sharon had long subscribed to the theory that it was better to apologize later than to ask permission now. So she had called Harley, and he agreed to take her place outside Raven Tahoma's room, just as she had known he would. Forty minutes later, about the time the patient was settling comfortably into her bed, TV remote in one hand and plastic cup of ginger ale in the other, Harley came strolling into the hospital and Sharon was free.

Now she piloted her cruiser north, anxious to get back to Paskagankee but thankful for a little time to think. The story told by Raven was a wild one, one she would have dismissed out of hand just a year ago as the nonsensical raving of a drugged up or delusional idiot. Now, thanks to the benefit of personal experience, she knew events of a paranormal or supernatural nature actually could happen; that the world was far from being as cut-and-dried as most people were comfortable believing.

She left the Orono city limits behind and the road gradually began to narrow, funneling from a wide, well-maintained avenue inside the thriving college town, down to a crumbling testament to overtaxed state and municipal budgets before she had made it halfway to Paskagankee. Thankfully, though, vehicular traffic also began to dry up, leaving Sharon free to drive without having to worry too much about the conditions around her, giving her the opportunity to scrutinize their prisoner's bizarre account.

A sacred Native American stone, bestowing on its owner the ability to reanimate the corpses of the recently deceased. A shocking betrayal, allowing a power-hungry con man to steal the stone and then attack and kidnap one of the richest men in the world. The law of unintended consequences, rearing its ugly head and allowing the reanimated corpse to strike back against his tormentor, killing the man and then escaping with a hostage.

It was a bizarre story, as far-fetched as it was horrifying.

And Sharon believed all of it. Why wouldn't she? She had known Earl Manning for a brief period in her life when, as a teenage girl, she was adrift and rudderless, using alcohol and drugs to escape a reality where she felt unwanted and unloved, her adoring mother dead and her uninterested father too lost in his own grief and his own struggles with addiction to care for a confused daughter.

She had lost her way, growing into the prototypical wild child, trading sex for drugs and booze, concerned only with scoring her next high. She knew now it was a miracle she hadn't died or been infected with HIV or some other communicable disease. She had been saved from herself by Paskagankee Police Chief Wally Court, a man who had seen something worthwhile inside her, giving her guidance and setting her on a path which would eventually lead to her present career in law enforcement.

She looked back on those years with a mixture of shame and disbelief, struggling to reconcile the person she had been back then with the person she was now. But it was during that period in her life that she had come in contact with Earl Manning, trading a night of sex for alcohol in what had been one of many one-night stands. Her recollections of that night were fuzzy, thanks to more beer than a petite high school junior should ever drink, but she felt certain she would have gotten some sense of the man's innate evil if Manning had been comfortable with committing murder.

She remembered him as unmotivated and unclean, a typical small-town loser willing to ply an underaged girl with liquor to get into her pants. Her impression of Manning was as negative as her memories of that night, as her memories of most of her teen years, but still she had a hard time believing he was the type of person who would wind up involved in kidnapping and murder, at least not of his own volition.

Of course, people could change. Sharon knew that; she

was a living, breathing testament to that fact. But morphing from a lazy, unmotivated drunken slob to a cold-blooded, calculating killer in the space of just a few years struck Sharon as too unlikely. She could believe he might get so trashed at the Ridge Runner he would drive off the road and kill himself or someone else—that was definitely believable, likely, even—but the scenario she had seen at the rental home, Max Acton lying in a pool of his own blood, throat torn out like he had been attacked by a rabid dog, just didn't fit.

She remembered a discussion with Mike last fall, when she was instrumental in convincing his relentlessly logical mind to accept the possibility of a paranormal aspect to the murders plaguing Paskagankee. The clincher had been a line from a Sherlock Holmes story that seemed to fit here as well: Eliminate the impossible and whatever is left, however improbable, must be the truth.

Manning had been missing for well over a week, his whereabouts a mystery not just to his mother, but to his drinking buddies at the Ridge Runner, where no one could remember him going more than two consecutive days without holding down a barstool. A mysterious couple show up in town around the same time Manning disappears, renting a crumbling home whose only redeeming value is its remote location. Manning resurfaces at the scene of a grisly murder, and the only available witness tells a tale of the paranormal.

And the smell, that was the kicker. The stench of death permeated the basement of the home where Raven Tahoma had been found and where she had rescued Mike from the freezer. ton's body could not have been responsible for such a smell, his corpse was fresh and had barely begun to decompose, and no other bodies had been discovered.

But a man who had been killed and then frozen a week before, only to be reanimated a couple of days ago, could certainly be responsible. And Sharon found herself believing that was exactly what had happened.

Her cell phone rang and she jumped. She glared accusingly at the phone lying on the seat next to her, then snatched it up and punched the "Send" button, seeing Mike's name on the caller ID.

"Yeah?" It came out harsh and scratchy.

"Sharon, it's Mike. Our witness-slash-prisoner resting comfortably?"

She thought about telling him she had switched places with Harley and was on her way back to town, but decided it would be too easy for him to send her back to the hospital if she mentioned it now. She would wait until she arrived at the crime scene to let him know. He might be angry—probably would be, in fact—but at least she would avoid babysitting duty.

"Yes, she's fine," she answered. "Is Pete there yet?"

"No, he should be getting here any minute."

"You sound preoccupied." Sharon had learned to read Mike's moods pretty effectively over the last few months and it was clear to her that something was eating at him.

"You wouldn't believe the conversation I just had."

"Try me. You called Don Running Bear, didn't you?"

"Yes and no. Don Running Bear is dead; he didn't survive the raid Raven's psycho boyfriend made on their home to steal the sacred stone. Acton either never told Raven her father's friend was dead or he didn't know. Either way, the guy's gone and unless there's a second sacred stone we don't know about, he's not coming back."

Sharon's heart sank. "So you didn't get any answers to your questions about the stone."

"Well, that's not exactly true. It turns out Don had confided many, if not most, of the secrets of the stone to his wife over the years. She seemed to have extensive knowledge of it. Unfortunately, none of the information she passed along was encouraging."

"What did she say?"

"A lot. The gist of it is that if we plan to stop Manning by waiting for his body to decompose, we're going to have a lot more corpses on our hands. Apparently one of the capacities of the stone is that it slows the decomposition process of the revenant."

"That's not good."

"It gets worse."

"What could be worse than that?"

"There's no way to stop him. Mrs. Running Bear told me the only way to control a revenant is to control its master. There's never been a case to her knowledge of a revenant gaining possession of the stone and thus controlling its own actions. To top it off, Manning's brain function is deteriorating rapidly, making him more aggressive and unmanageable, and he is basically unstoppable because you can't kill him since he's already dead."

An icy feeling of dread washed over Sharon. This was far worse than the situation last fall. At least when the renegade spirit was terrorizing Paskagankee, Professor Dye had had a plan to stop the madness. This time there was no plan. Only madness. "What's the good news?" she said weakly.

"Be sure to tell me if you think of any."

"What do you suppose the odds are Earl hasn't killed Brett Parker yet?"

"After talking to Mrs. Running Bear, I'd have to say slim. Maybe if Manning thinks Parker can help him he'll keep him alive, but it sounded to me like any ability for rational thought Manning still has will be gone soon. He's going to turn into a mindless killing machine if he hasn't already. Those were Mrs. Running Bear's words, by the way, not mine."

"And we don't know where he is."

"Nope. He could be anywhere within a fifty mile radius of this town by now, and it's widening rapidly. I'm going to have to alert law enforcement agencies all over the state, and I don't have a clue what I'm going to say to them. Who's going to believe a reanimated corpse is running around Maine killing people? Someone'll send a psych team up here and take me away to a rubber room, which may not be such a bad idea along about now."

Sharon's heart went out to him. Despite the fact she had ended their relationship, she loved Mike McMahon and always would, and the situation he found himself in right now could not help but end badly. He had beaten himself up endlessly over the death of a little girl during a hostage standoff a couple of years ago in Revere, Massachusetts, and then his career had nearly ended last fall during the Wally Court mess. He clearly recognized this situation was spiraling out of control, and if dozens of lives—or more—were lost in this situation, she felt he might never recover. "What are you going to do?"

She pictured him sighing and shaking his head. "Stick to the plan, I guess. I'll have Gordie send a BOLO out to all law enforcement agencies in Maine—maybe all of New England just to be safe—and then finish securing the murder scene and hand the scene over to Pete for a while when he gets here. Then I'll drive up to the hospital to interrogate Raven Tahoma. Maybe something will shake loose that will help us get this thing under control, or at least narrow down where Manning may have gone."

The plan sounded pretty thin to Sharon, and she knew if she recognized that fact, Mike must as well, but she didn't mention it. What would be the point? "Good luck," she said glumly.

"Thanks. There is one small thing to be thankful for," Mike added.

"I can't imagine what it might be."

"At least you're not in danger. It seems pretty unlikely a lunatic Earl Manning would show up at Mercy Hospital in Orono. I know you're not happy being stuck there, but it's a load off my mind knowing you're safe."

Sharon gazed out the windshield as the trees whipped by on the narrow road. She hadn't been paying much attention to the deserted thoroughfare as she talked and realized she was once again driving dangerously fast. She eased her foot off the gas and the cruiser began to slow.

"Uh, yeah," she said, feeling guilt and shame for misleading him. She was lying not just to the man she claimed to love, but to her direct superior as well. "Right. Safe."

Mike didn't seem to notice. "I'd better go," he said. "It's time to begin making a fool of myself and my department around the state."

"Okay. I know I said it before, but good luck." She wanted desperately to end the conversation with, "I love you," but she had thrown away the right to do so, hadn't she? "Talk to you later," she said instead, and disconnected the call.

Sharon tossed the phone back down on the seat. She was miserable. The Earl Manning she had known in the past may not have been capable of cold-blooded murder, but that individual was disappearing if he wasn't gone already. He was devolving into a killer. An unstoppable killer.

She rounded a corner, anxious to arrive at the crime scene in Paskagankee, anxious to offer an in-person apology to Mike for ignoring his orders, and slowed instinctively, stepping on the brake harder than she intended, stunned at the sight directly in front of the car in this deeply forested, remote location still miles from Paskagankee, miles from *anywhere*.

Walking along the side of the road—stumbling, really, staggering even—with his back to the cruiser, was a man dressed in rags, skinny to the point of emaciation, clothes tattered and filthy, fluttering in the light breeze. The man seemed to be struggling to match the pace set by another man, who, while dressed in much nicer clothing, was also filthy and covered in blood.

Sharon slowed further, now moving forward at barely more than a crawl. The rumble of the cruiser's engine finally alerted the trailing man to her presence and he turned and grinned, and Sharon gasped in shock.

It was Earl Manning.

39

Earl had guessed he wouldn't have to wait long for a car to pass by, and he was right. He had lived his entire life—and death, now that he thought about it—in Paskagankee, haunting these out-of-the-way back roads and fire lanes as a drunken teen and impaired adult, and one thing he knew for sure was that even way out here in the middle of nowhere, in the mole on God's butt-cheek, as he liked to think of his home town, people with nothing better to do would be out driving in the afternoon. Nighttime was a different story, but as long as the sun was out, townspeople would want to go to the store or to the movies or to any damned place.

He turned at the sound of the engine noise and instinctively took a couple of steps back when he saw the blue and white Paskagankee Police cruiser moving slowly along the crumbling pavement behind him. A lifetime of run-ins with the law, drunk-driving busts and petty scrapes with authority, had burrowed into his consciousness, and his first reaction upon seeing the Pigmobile was to look for an escape route.

Then he remembered. He was untouchable. He couldn't be killed—Max the Fucking Devil Acton had taken care of that problem quite effectively—and he couldn't be hurt. Hell, even if they shot his skinny ass, all that would happen would be he'd get knocked for a loop and another ventilation hole would open up in his body. Not ideal as far as aesthetics were concerned, but Earl had never been too concerned about appearance even in the best of times, and his current situation certainly didn't qualify as the best of anything.

So he smiled, baring his teeth at the pig driving up behind him, glancing at his traveling companion to make sure the software geek didn't get any bright ideas about using the distraction to take off running. No worries there. Brett Parker stood rooted to the spot, staring at the police cruiser like a starving man eying a turkey dinner. For a genius, the guy sure didn't have much common sense. Parker should have known a fucking cop wasn't going to be able to help him.

Oh, well. It was too bad for the geek, but good for Earl because the genius's stupidity would make him easier to control. He swiveled his head to look back at the cruiser and lost his balance, stumbling to his knees before scrambling quickly back to his feet. His body was definitely becoming less coordinated, and it was getting *much* harder to think straight.

His brain felt fuzzy and confused, like it did when he

was in the middle of a long bender, only instead of feeling mellow and happy like he did when he drank, he felt an undefined sense of anger and aggression building. *That's not surprising,* he thought. *I've been killed, had my heart torn out of my fucking body. Who wouldn't be a little twitchy?*

Earl stared hard at the cruiser, which had now come to a complete stop about fifteen feet away. His blossoming anger vanished—for now—and his smile returned when he managed to peer through the glare of the sun on the windshield and identify its lone occupant. Seated behind the wheel, staring out at him with wide blue eyes and her perfect angelic face, was his old drinking pal and one-time fuck buddy Sharon Dupont.

Earl heard himself cackle like a goddamned loon as he considered the possibility of expanding his little group to include the Paskagankee PD officer. He had only slept with her the once, back when she was a seventeen year old high school junior trashed on cheap beer, so desperate to get high or drunk that she would screw anyone or do anything.

He knew she had straightened her life out—Paskagankee was a small town; everyone was in everyone else's business—and was now living with the police chief. Of course, "living with" might be a bit of an exaggeration now that Earl had pitched the loser head-first into freezer and then slammed the lid.

So the chief was dead, or would be soon, which meant Little Miss Officer Goody Two-Shoes sitting there in the cruiser would be back on the market. Earl wondered if his pecker would still work since he was technically dead and decided there was only one way to find out.

He fixed Parker with a stare—easy enough to do, since

the damn fool was still gazing longingly at the police car—then began strutting toward the cruiser, wondering if Dupont carried as many pleasant memories of their night together as he did. He smiled. He would grab her around the neck, force her into the back seat along with Parker, then drive the cruiser somewhere nice and private where he could renew acquaintances with—

—The cruiser's door ripped open, rocking the vehicle on its springs. The little police chick leaped out of the car and took cover behind the door, which she had opened with such force it bounced back and hit her in the side. A hand appeared in the V-shaped space between the door and the car's body, and the voice he remembered so fondly from so many years ago commanded, "Stop right there, Earl!"

And Earl stopped right there.

Not because he was worried about getting shot—apparently Miss Law and Order was unaware of his new reality and thought threatening him with a gun was a strategy that might be effective—but rather, because he knew there was no way he could control the software geek at the same time he was locked in a battle with a cop who was busy filling him full of holes.

There was no possible way Parker would be stupid enough to stay standing on the side of the road when the gunfire started, and as much as Earl wanted to find out if dead people could have sex, he couldn't afford to take the risk of forfeiting Parker's money and technical savvy just for a little corpse nookie.

So stopped in his tracks and then began backing toward Parker, knowing there was no way in hell the young woman who had once screwed him in the front seat of his truck would now shoot him in cold blood. He took three shambling steps before she shouted, "I told you to stop. Now you freeze right where you are!"

He grinned at her for the third time, then turned and strode quickly toward Parker, who finally seemed to realize the cavalry wasn't going to be doing a whole lot of saving of the day today.

The software geek turned to run, but before he could take two steps Earl was on him. Earl wrapped his right arm around Parker's throat, careful to cradle the all-important box containing his beating heart in the crook of his left. He pulled his gun hand back toward his chest, squeezing Parker's throat closed, while at the same time twisting his body to the right, turning his prisoner into a human shield.

He straightened and faced the chick cop, who was still screaming something at him. He had tuned her out just like he tuned out his Ma when she told him to wash the dishes or pick up his dirty socks or stop farting in the middle of the living room. "Looks like we got us a standoff," he rumbled, cutting her off in mid-harangue, loosening his grip on Parker's throat just enough to allow the man a bit of air.

"Just calm down, Earl, nobody needs to get hurt today," Dupont called out, and Earl laughed.

"A little late for that, don't you think? I'm a walking corpse, I gave that fucking devil Max Acton what he had coming to him, and I suffocated your boyfriend in a freezer, you think for one goddamned second I'm worried about *anyone getting hurt?*" Earl's voice rose steadily in pitch as his fury returned, rushing back like a hurricane.

"Chief McMahon is fine," claimed Dupont. "He's

unharmed. And maybe Acton *did* get what he deserved, maybe it *was* a case of self-defense. But there will be no possible defense for harming an innocent hostage, no justification at all. Why don't you just drop your gun and let Mr. Parker go and we can sit down and talk about it?"

"Just like that? Really? I drop my gun and we all come together in a search for truth and justice? Maybe sing *Kumbayah* while we're at it? Because ain't you forgetting something, Sugar-britches?"

'What's that?"

"I'm fucking dead! Where's the truth and justice for me?"

"Earl, listen to me. Come with me and we'll figure something out, I promise, but nothing's going to come from us standing here in the middle of nowhere pointing guns at each other."

"Pointing guns at each other? But that's not really the situation, is it, sweetheart? Because you're pointing a gun at me, but I'm pointing a gun at *him*." Earl released his chokehold on Parker and raised Mike McMahon's Glock until the barrel was pressed against his hostage's temple. The man whimpered and Earl laughed savagely.

"So if you think about it," he continued, "I hold all the cards and you hold none."

He shoved Parker in the back and the two men stumbled forward. "So here's what we're going to do."

He shoved Parker again and again the pair lurched forward a few feet. "You're going to drop *your* gun . . ."

Shove, stumble. ". . . and we're going to take a little ride together . . ."

Shove, stumble. ". . . and then you and me are going to relive the good old days. Whaddaya say about that, baby girl?"

40

The thing that had once been Earl Manning stood swaying like he was drunk, gun barrel placed against the head of a clearly terrified Brett Parker, and Sharon knew she had just seconds to respond. Manning had pushed his hostage forward until he was now positioned no more than a few feet away, but he was using Parker quite effectively as a shield, giving her very little to aim at.

Still, she had been a crack shot at the FBI Academy, and she thought there was at least a decent chance she could hit Earl if he would just stop moving for half a second. He looked like he had just stepped off the Tilt-A-Whirl ride at the Fryeburg Fair, his head bobbing and weaving, now completely shielded by Parker, now hovering over his left shoulder, now gone again.

If she timed it just right, she could take him down. But then she thought about Mike's words. *He's basically unstoppable because you can't kill him . . . a mindless killing machine . . .*

What if she hit him and he didn't go down? Or what if she missed him entirely? It was a definite possibility, she was good with a gun but it was still a handgun, and he was still several feet away, and she *was* shaking like a leaf from the adrenaline coursing through her body. If she missed him or if he survived the shot, he would undoubtedly put a bullet into Brett Parker's head, and *he* wasn't a reanimated corpse, *he* would drop like a stone, and not a sacred stone, either, and an innocent man would be dead.

And it wouldn't just be any innocent man, it would be one of the richest men in America, a world-renowned software entrepreneur, and the fallout would be instantaneous and devastating. Moreover, he would have been killed with Mike McMahon's gun, and Sharon knew that after Mike's accidental shooting of seven year old Sarah Melendez two years ago, he would never recover. He still blamed himself for the little girl's death. If another innocent person were to die by Mike's gun, Sharon knew he would be lost forever.

So the decision was really no decision. Sharon tossed her weapon onto the shoulder of the road and stepped clear of the cruiser's open door. Brett Parker moaned in terror and disbelief. He had obviously been expecting her to take some kind of action, but what could she do?

She stepped forward reluctantly. "What now, Earl?" The stench was rancid and overwhelming, like spoiled meat. Sharon pictured maggots crawling all over

Manning's skin and gagged.

He leered. It was horrifying. "Now we see what this baby can do," he said, nodding at the Paskagankee Police cruiser, idling patiently on the side of the road.

Sharon moved toward the driver's seat and Earl shouted, "Hey!" and she froze. Earl chuckled, the sound like breaking glass. "Come on babe, how stupid do you think I am? You're not going to drive. Get into the back seat."

Sharon opened the rear passenger door and slid into the seat, her fear mounting rapidly. She had been thinking hard, hoping for an opportunity to use the cruiser as a weapon, to drive it into a tree or something, then grab Parker and run in the aftermath of the accident. Mike had said Earl's brain was deteriorating rapidly, what were the odds he would remain clear-headed enough to stop them?

But from the back seat she would be helpless. A thick wire mesh screen separated the front seat of the cruiser from the back, a precaution to ensure the safety of the officer after putting a suspect into the vehicle. There would be no way to get at Manning.

Sharon looked up and saw the horrifying skeletal body looming just outside. He maintained a firm grasp on Parker, who was now wide-eyed and pale-faced and appeared seconds away from a stroke or a heart attack. The stench intensified and she wondered how Parker had been able to stand being held against that corpse-like frame.

"Slide over," Manning ordered, shoving Parker into the back of the cruiser without waiting for her to comply. Then he slammed the door and they were trapped. There were no interior handles on the rear cruiser doors; they could only be opened from the outside, another vehicle modification made in the interest of officer safety that now spelled doom for Sharon and Parker.

"You've got to do something," Parker whispered fiercely, as if maybe Sharon could magically overcome the fact they were trapped inside a police car with no weapon and no way out. "What are you going to do?"

Outside the window, Manning bent down and snatched Sharon's gun off the side of the road, sliding it into the waistband of his filthy jeans at the small of his back.

"We stay calm," she answered quietly, "and wait for a break we can take advantage of."

"Why didn't you shoot him when you had the chance?" Anger seemed to be taking the place of fear now that he had been released from Manning's grip.

"Shoot him? When? While he was using you as a human shield? This isn't a movie set, Mr. Parker, the odds of hitting him were slim at best. I probably would have shot you instead, and then where would we be?" She didn't bother to continue, to explain that even if she *had* popped Earl Manning, even if she nailed him right between the eyes, there was still no chance of actually stopping him. He would simply get up, dust himself off, and then probably kill both of them on the spot. The situation seemed hopeless enough without adding that little informational gem into the mix.

"The guy's a raving lunatic," Parker continued as if she hadn't even spoken. His voice was laced with fear and maybe just a touch of wonder. "He says he's dead and that he needs me to figure out a way to reverse the damage that's been done to him. He's out of his mind, he's completely crazy, he—"

The driver's side door opened and Manning fell into the seat, banging his head hard against the door frame, the force of the blow rocking the car. He didn't even react. "Now, now," he said, speaking in a sing-song voice. "I know you two are conspiring against me and I won't have it, do you understand?"

He placed the box he had been holding—Sharon assumed it must be the box containing his heart and the sacred Navajo stone—onto the dashboard between it and the windshield, shoving hard until he had wedged it tightly into the space. Then he shifted the cruiser into drive and stomped on the accelerator and the car leapt forward, rear tires squealing on the pavement, the cruiser zigzagging down the road as Manning tried, largely unsuccessfully, to control it.

Sharon's cell phone rang. It was still sitting on the front passenger's seat where she had tossed it after talking to Mike a few minutes ago.

Earl moved his foot clumsily from the accelerator to the brake and the tires screeched again, this time screaming in protest from the rapid deceleration. Sharon and Parker were thrown forward and they smashed their faces on the wire screen at the same time, neither one able to stop their momentum with their outstretched hands.

Manning slammed the transmission into Park. He bent down, reaching with his long arms into the passenger-side foot well, snatching the cell phone off the floor where it had fallen as it continued to ring. He glanced at the caller ID and turned and glared into the back seat. "Well, well," he said. "Looks like someone has a call from her boyfriend." He seemed to be having trouble focusing his eyes and his tone had changed, losing its sing-song quality and becoming hard-edged and cruel.

Sharon had no idea what to say. She knew Mike would be on the other end of the line and that things were about to go from bad to much, much worse.

She was right.

Manning punched at the "Send" button, his finger missing three times before finally connecting, probably by accident. Before he had a chance to say anything, Mike's voice came from the earpiece, sounding high-pitched and far away, but still understandable in the silence of the police car. "Well, I did it," he said. "I just got off the line with the Maine State Police. They now think I'm either drunk or a raving lunatic, but they agreed to put out a BOLO for our friend Earl Manning."

"Isn't that nice," Manning said into the phone, and Mike fell silent. "I never realized how many people cared about me. Where were you when I REALLY FUCKING NEEDED YOU?" Earl was screaming now and the somehow smell of corruption seemed to increase with it.

"Manning?" Mike said cautiously, and the cursed man punched another button, putting the call on speaker before beginning to laugh.

"In the flesh," he said. "Although maybe not for much longer, as it seems to be sliding off my bones even as we speak." He grinned at Sharon as though sharing a private joke and she felt her stomach begin to turn over. She clenched her jaw and willed herself not to throw up. Beside her, Parker rubbed his cheek vigorously where he had scraped it against the wire mesh and chanted to himself softly. It sounded like he might be praying.

"Where's Officer Dupont?" came the voice from the

cell phone.

"Officer Dupont? Who's Officer — "

" — Where is she, Manning?"

"Oh, you mean *Sharon* Dupont? The sweet little piece of ass we have in common? I spent time with her too, you know, although she's probably never mentioned that little tidbit to you. Of course, our time together came before she got all high and mighty, before she started toting a badge and a gun to work. Still, I find it interesting to note that all the places you've been, I've been, too, and long before you. If you get my drift. Isn't that something, Chief? You and me, we're practically one and the same, carnally speaking." He winked at Sharon and she stared back, horrified.

"I'm going to ask you one more time. Where is she, Manning?"

"As it so happens, she's right here with me. Care to have a word?"

"You're damn right I want to speak with her. Now."

"Well, that's just too goddamn bad, Chief; sometimes we don't get what we want in this world. Didn't your mama teach you anything?"

"I'm warning you, Manning, you harm one hair on Officer Dupont's head and I'll — "

" — you'll what, smart-guy? Hunt me down and kill me? Too late for that, wouldn't you say? Now, I'd like nothing better than to continue this delightful discussion, but time's a-wastin', as my dear departed granny used to say, and I'm not getting any younger. Or any older, for that matter. Because I'm DEAD. See ya on the other side, Mikey-boy."

Manning punched clumsily at the END button to

disconnect the call and tossed the phone back down on the seat.

He swiveled his head and glared into the back seat. "Now, where were we?"

41

Except the call wasn't disconnected. Manning must have missed the button on the touchscreen when he tried to terminate the connection, and now Mike listened, frantic with fear, as the rapidly dissembling revenant taunted Sharon. "Honestly, sweetheart, that fucking loser's dumb as a stump. Why the hell'd you even bother leaving Paskagankee in the first place if you were just going to come right back and get tangled up with an idiot like him when you could have stayed with me and saved yourself all that trouble?"

His voice seemed to be thickening and he had begun slurring his words as if drunk. That frightened Mike more than the threats and taunting. Sharon didn't respond, or if she did, Mike didn't hear her answer. He tried to control his escalating panic and confusion. Was Manning at the hospital, and if so, how had he managed to snatch Sharon without anyone else in the building sounding an alarm? It was simply impossible to conceive of any scenario in which the foul-smelling, skeletal bag of bones Mike had tangled with in the basement of this house just a few hours ago could have gotten into Mercy Hospital without a dozen separate 911 calls being placed within seconds.

Then through the earpiece of his phone came the unmistakable sound of a police cruiser's engine revving. The sound was deep and throaty and powerful, and Mike heard Manning exclaim, "Yeah, baby," and the picture began to come into focus. Sharon wasn't at Mercy Hospital at all; she likely wasn't even in Orono. Mike knew she would never have walked away and left their prisoner/witness unguarded, so she must have convinced another Paskagankee cop to make the drive to Orono, and then hopped into her cruiser and headed north, anxious to get back to where the action was. Somewhere along the way, she had crossed paths with Manning.

Mike cursed, angry at himself. He, of all people, should have expected this. It simply was not in Sharon Dupont's nature to sit on the sidelines with an investigation beckoning. It was that need to be involved which had made her simultaneously such a good cop and such a frustrating girlfriend.

When she had been a girlfriend.

He tamped down on his fear—it wasn't easy to do—and ran a quick timeline through his head. Undoubtedly Sharon had placed the call to whoever she badgered into taking her place almost immediately upon arriving at the hospital. Given a few minutes to convince someone to come, and then the time it would take that officer to drive there, Mike determined Sharon was likely either already back in Paskagankee or close to it.

He clamped his hand over the mouthpiece of his cell phone. He certainly didn't want to alert Manning to the fact his every word was being monitored, although as quickly as the revenant seemed to be coming apart, Mike wondered if it would even matter to him if he knew he could be heard.

Mike thought hard. Interrogating Raven Tahoma would have to wait. With the information he had gotten from Don Running Bear's widow, there didn't seem to be a pressing need to speak with her, anyway, at least not right away. Finding Sharon and Earl Manning was now the clear priority.

Pete Kendall walked out the front door of the house and broke into a trot when he spotted Mike. "Hey, boss, I've got a question for ya."

Mike shook his head and raised a finger to his lips in the universal "Be quiet" gesture, and Kendall stopped in his tracks. "What is it?" he said softly, obviously puzzled.

"I've got a lead I need to check out. Can you handle things here?"

"Of course, but where are you heading?"

"I need to take a quick drive toward Orono. There's been a possible Manning sighting." All Kendall knew—indeed, all *anyone* on the Paskagankee Police Department besides Sharon knew—was that lifelong Paskagankee resident and longtime minor troublemaker Earl Manning had been implicated in the murder of the victim whose throat had nearly been ripped out in the basement of this home. Any explanation involving sacred Navajo ceremonial stones and reanimated corpses would have to wait. It would take up too much precious time and likely wouldn't be believed, anyway.

Mike continued, "I don't want to pull anyone off the crime scene investigation here for what is probably a wild goose chase, so I'm going to drive out there myself. I'll be back as quickly as I can."

He gave his second-in-command a long once-over and nodded, satisfied by what he saw. Despite being under thirty years of age and one of the younger officers on the force, Kendall was a solid cop and a good investigator. "The Staties I called should be here soon. Make sure nobody touches the body until the evidence techs do their thing."

Kendall nodded, staring inquisitively at the cell phone in Mike's hand, still with the mouthpiece covered up. "Of course. Are you okay, Chief?"

Now it was Mike's turn to nod. He was getting impatient. If he had any chance of catching up to Manning, he had to leave now. Should have left three minutes ago, in fact. "I'm fine," he said, "but I can't afford to hang out here any longer. I'll be back as soon as I can."

He turned on his heel and slid behind the wheel of his cruiser, wondering whether his statement contained any truth at all. "An unstoppable killer," was how Kai Running Bear had described Earl Manning. If Mike managed to catch up to him, what were the odds he would survive?

He pushed those thoughts to the back of his mind as he fired up his cruiser and backed quickly down the driveway. The car hit the pavement and he spun the wheel in his hand and shifted into Drive and goosed the engine, taking one look back toward the beaten-down house with a dead body lying in the basement. Pete Kendall stared back at him, a look of bewildered concern on his face.

42

Manning hit the gas and Sharon felt the G-forces pushing her into the back of the bench seat. Next to her, Brett Parker had screwed his eyes tightly shut, an expression of distaste on his face, as if wishing he could extricate himself from this situation through sheer force of will. Sharon knew how he felt.

The car weaved along the road and she prayed they would not encounter anyone traveling in the opposite direction. If that happened, the odds of surviving the inevitable head-on collision would be practically nil, both for them and for the unwitting victim driving the other car.

Where the hell did he think he was going? Parker had said Manning was holding out hope that the billionaire could use his contacts and his money to reverse the damage that had been done to him somehow. But Parker Software's base of operations was about as far away as it could be and still be on this continent—Seattle, Washington. Did he really think he was going to drive all the way across the country?

She didn't have to wait long to find out. Manning slammed on the brakes and wrenched the wheel to the right and this time she was ready for it; she had no desire to revisit her close encounter a few moments ago with the wire mesh separating the front seat from the back of the cruiser. Sharon lowered her shoulder and twisted sideways, taking the brunt of her collision with her shoulder and back.

Parker wasn't so lucky. His eyes flew open but he was helpless to prevent himself from being thrown directly into the mesh again, and this time a gash ripped open on his cheek and he screamed in pain and fear and probably frustration, too.

Manning didn't seem to notice. His head lolled on his shoulder and he punched the accelerator again and steered the car like a missile into a gap in the thick forest that seemed much too small to accommodate the still fast-moving cruiser. Branches scraped the molded steel of the car's body, sounding almost exactly like Parker's screams. The car bounced and jolted along the narrow trail until finally it lurched to a stop in a cloud of dust.

They were parked in a fire lane. Sharon was intimately familiar with the system of trails surrounding Paskagankee from her days as a teenaged addict and alcoholic, having taken advantage of their solitude many times in her unending quest to get high or drunk. It was a trail just like this one she had been drinking on with her friends that night all those years ago when she had slept with Earl Manning in exchange for his free beer. Hell, maybe it had been this exact one. She wasn't sure, they all looked the same.

The memory of that awful night came rushing back and Sharon had to force herself out of the past and back to the present. Fixating on long-ago memories of the victim she had once been were counterproductive and, at the moment, dangerous. If she were to stand even the remotest chance of getting out of this seemingly impossible situation, she would need to keep her wits about her.

The front door of the cruiser opened and Manning stepped out, disappearing from view through the side window as he dropped straight down, crumpling in a heap on the forest floor. Then he reappeared, hanging onto the side of the car for balance, grinning like a Halloween Jack O'Lantern. He pulled the rear door open and Sharon thought about jumping him; leaping out of the back seat kicking and punching and trying to put him down that way. With his balance rapidly deteriorating, it seemed like something she might be able to pull off.

But there was one glaring hole in that potential plan: It would be impossible to kill Earl Manning, impossible even to injure him, meaning even if she were able to knock him down and escape, Brett Parker would still be at his mercy. The billionaire was at the moment slumped down in the back seat of the cruiser staring steadfastly out the window in the opposite direction and seemed to be in no condition to make a mad dash anywhere. Sharon knew she couldn't live with his death on her conscience if she managed to escape and Manning took out his anger on the civilian she left behind.

And then the moment was gone anyway, as Manning reached into the car and dragged her out by the collar of her uniform shirt, then kicked the door closed. Despite his increasing issues with bodily coordination his grip was still strong and sure, and Sharon felt herself propelled through the air, landing in a heap a few feet from the car.

She hit the ground and rolled, climbing immediately to her knees, only to look up and see Manning looming over her. He swayed and rocked like he was being pushed by a high wind but he locked eyes with her, and Sharon knew things were about to get immeasurably worse, at least for her. "Let's share the front seat," he said in a low growl.

Rising slowly, Sharon brushed twigs and pine needles off her uniform, thinking hard, knowing there must be a way out of this seemingly hopeless situation, but not having a clue what it might be. The forest had gone silent, the insects and birds and small animals in the woods seemingly waiting to see what would happen next.

How did you fight an opponent who could not be harmed? Sharon thought about what she had told Parker, who had abandoned his inspection of the forest and now watched the drama developing outside the cruiser with a kind of detached resignation. "Stay calm and wait for a break," she had told him, but that was total bullshit. There was no break coming.

Manning wrapped a bony arm around Sharon's waist and steered her toward the driver's side door. He was acting simultaneously threatening and bizarrely chivalrous. The stench was overwhelming, it rolled off his ruined body in waves, and she felt hot, acidy bile work its way up her gullet. She clamped her jaw and swallowed hard and avoided puking all over her captor, at least for now.

Manning bent down at the cruiser's front door and his tattered shirt billowed open. Sharon could see clearly the gaping hole in the center of his chest where his heart had once resided and where Josh Parmalee, Parker's security guy, had shot him. The skin was ripped and puckered and greyish-green, splinters of shattered rib bone thrusting obscenely through the hole when he moved.

And this time Sharon couldn't help it. She gagged and coughed and then vomited, spewing chunks of her partially digested lunch and greenish-yellow stomach acid all over Manning's filthy jeans and threadbare shoes. Normally the puke smell was among the worst things Sharon could imagine, but right now she savored it, inhaling it like a starving man might breathe in the aroma of a grilled steak. The smell was disgusting, but far better than the alternative, a temporary respite from the odor of death and corruption enveloping Earl Manning like a noxious cloud.

Manning either didn't notice the vomit or didn't care. He tossed Sharon into the cruiser, expending barely more effort than a flick of his wrist, and she crashed down across the molded plastic center console between the two front seats, her knee smashing the onboard mobile data computer, cracking the screen and knocking the unit to the floor, breaking it right off its stand. Her body slid along the cloth seats, her momentum stopped only by the passenger door when she impacted it with the crown of her head.

Manning followed immediately behind, his body

dropping onto Sharon's, driving her hip into the console, causing her to cry out in pain. "Shut up," Manning grunted, fumbling with her belt buckle with his left hand while slapping his right hand over her mouth. Sharon had the absurd thought that the guy sure hadn't improved much as a lover over the years.

She kicked and bucked, trying to throw him off, wondering whether he would even react if she was lucky enough to catch him in the groin with her knee. Her heavy boot sole connected with his shin with a satisfying *crack* and he grunted, whether in pain or annoyance Sharon could not tell.

But either way it didn't stop him. He continued fumbling with her belt and finally Sharon heard the buckle give way and then felt her uniform slacks unzip and she knew she was seconds away from being raped, and not *just* raped, but raped and violated by a dead husk, a lifeless shell of a former human being, and she would be raped while staring helplessly up at the steering wheel of her own police cruiser, at the steering wheel and the dashboard and the goddamned box containing the sacred stone that was at the heart of this whole impossible misadventure, tucked neatly and safely into the corner where the dashboard and the windshield intersected at the far left side of the vehicle. She would be raped, and there was nothing she could—

—wait a second.

Wait just a goddamned second.

The box.

She tried desperately to force her panicked mind to think clearly, knowing a clear head likely represented her only chance for living beyond the next few hideous minutes, and just like that a plan sprang to life in her mind. It took shape as if by magic, and it was a damned unlikely plan at that, one which she had no way of knowing would even work.

But that didn't matter, because right now, with a dead man yanking her pants down and his cold bony hands scraping her skin and the threat of the worst experience of her life staring her straight in the eyes, followed by an agonizing death—Sharon knew if Earl Manning raped her right now she would never survive, nor would she want to—this plan represented hope. It represented the possibility of survival and the end of this nightmare, and whether it could really work or not was almost irrelevant, because it was all Sharon had to hold on to, and she clung to her hastily devised plan for all she was worth.

She knew exactly what she had to do, and knew she would get only one try. She stopped struggling, stopped resisting, let her arms and legs go limp. She needed to convince the dead shell that once was Earl Manning that she had given up hope, and Sharon figured that shouldn't be too difficult to pull off, because she damned near had.

For a long couple of seconds the frenzy of activity stopped entirely. Manning clearly had not expected this development and seemed suddenly unsure of how to proceed. Sharon panted, gasping for breath, winded from her struggle. She forced herself to lie still while the dead weight atop her body shifted. Manning wasn't panting or breathing heavily—wasn't breathing at all, in fact—and for one awful moment as Sharon contemplated that fact she thought she was going to puke again, which of course would mean choking to death on her own vomit, with Manning's skeletal hand clamped over her mouth.

But she didn't puke, and the feeling of nausea began to pass, and Manning began to move once again. He hadn't said a word since ordering Sharon to shut up, but she could sense he believed he had beaten her down and broken her resistance, that it would now be clear sailing because she had resigned herself to her pending fate. Sharon wondered how anyone could be so deluded as to believe any woman would ever stop fighting against an attack like the one Earl Manning was perpetrating. His current status as a cold, unbreathing corpse made the situation worse, but it would barely have been more palatable had blood been pumping through his veins.

Manning's cold left hand scratched her thighs as he struggled to slide her pants down her legs, and Sharon eased her knees together. The horrifying fact was that in order for her plan to stand any chance of working, she needed to allow him to proceed. In a force of will greater than any she had ever exerted, she allowed the monster to ease her uniform pants over her hips and knees and down to her ankles. She prayed he would not yet reach for the waistband of her panties. If that happened, the iron will she was somehow exerting would break and she knew she would not be able to stop herself from struggling.

Her only hope was that it wouldn't get that far.

It didn't. Manning placed a hand on either side of Sharon's prone form, pushing against the stained cloth of the cruiser's bench seat, raising his upper body off hers. His cracked lips parted in a hideous smile of triumph and he said, "That's more like it," in a gravelly rumble as he reached for his own belt buckle.

And that was when Sharon made her move. Manning hadn't given her the perfect opening—it was barely an opening at all—but she had no idea whether she would get another. So she took it. She thrust her right hand at the center of his chest as if to throw a punch, but instead of making a fist, Sharon clustered the tips of her fingers together as tightly as she could, forming them into a point, turning her arm into something like a makeshift arrow.

Her hand tore through the remains of Manning's shirt like it wasn't even there and plunged deep into the dead man's chest. Her knuckle scraped a fragment of thin, unyielding mass, probably a rib bone. Sharon felt the vomit coming again and tried to close her mind off to the sheer horror and insanity of her situation, failing this time, and again showering Manning with puke, just seconds after he had removed his hand from her mouth.

Her stomach acid and digestive juices splattered off Manning and rained down on her and she ignored it. She pivoted her wrist and wrapped her slim fingers around the rib bone, praying she could maintain her grip. Then she clamped her left hand around her right wrist and yanked upward, propelling the emaciated corpse directly into the passenger side door and closed window. Manning's head struck the glass with a hollow-sounding *thunk* and then bounced off.

He let out a surprised "uhhh," and the force of his momentum caused him to roll partially off Sharon, the left side of his upper body tumbling into the cruiser's foot well, his hip jammed against the mobile data computer's metal mounting brace.

Sharon yanked her hand out of Manning's chest, ignoring the dry sucking sound that followed, amazed that even during this moment of extreme stress she had the presence of mind to think, *I'm going to have to wash that hand with a belt sander.* Then she shoved him hard against the brace, struggling, no match for his immense strength as he began moving to regain his position. All she needed was to keep him incapacitated for a couple of seconds and she began to fear she would not be able to manage even that.

The revenant brought his hands together under his chest and pushed, beginning to pivot his body to face Sharon.

NO!

In desperation she lifted herself up off the seat and snaked her hand behind him, reaching for what she had seen Manning slip under the waistband of his saggy jeans a few minutes ago—her Glock 9 mm service pistol.

Sweat poured off her in a tidal wave and her slick fingers scraped the butt of her gun and she grabbed desperately for it. For a split-second she had her weapon in her grasp and then the gun slipped away as Manning continued turning. He twisted slightly farther and Sharon knew it was now or never, and she shoved the revenant against the brace one last time and stretched farther than she would have thought possible.

Her fingers wrapped around the butt of her gun and she pulled again, and Manning twisted again, but this time Sharon was ready for it and she maintained her grip with a strength born of desperation, yanking hard, and then the weapon was free. She clutched it fiercely, taking strength from its mass and deadly power, but of course it *wouldn't* be deadly because Earl Manning could not be killed.

One thing at a time.

Sharon reached out with her right hand and placed it over her left, hanging on to the Glock in a two-handed grip that had less to do with aiming accuracy than her fear the weapon might slip out of her sweaty palm and tumble to the floor when she needed it most, and if that happened all would be lost.

Manning pushed himself up and twisted his skeletal body and grinned as Sharon jammed the gun in his face, shoving it between his eyes. "Something about me you apparently don't know," he said, as somewhere in the back of her mind Sharon heard Parker panting and moaning in the back seat in abject terror. She had almost forgotten he was there, but now that she heard him she knew exactly how he felt.

She said nothing to Manning, simply concentrated on keeping her hands steady. Her stress and her fear and especially her skyrocketing adrenaline levels caused the Glock to jitter and jump like she had drunk two dozen cups of coffee. Manning continued, "You can pull the trigger on that thing till you're blue in the face—welcome to my world if that happens—and all you'll do is add a few holes where there weren't any before. This reanimated corpse gig is a major drag, but it does have one advantage. I can't be killed, you stupid bitch, because I'm *already dead!*"

And just like that, a sense of calm descended over Sharon. This was it. Her desperate plan would either work or it would not, and if it didn't, she wouldn't live much longer than a few more seconds, anyway. Instead of making her more frantic, that thought had the opposite effect. This nightmare was about to end, one way or the other. Her hands stopped shaking and the Glock steadied against Manning's forehead and she stopped panting and began to breathe normally for the first time in what felt like a century.

Then she lifted the pistol away from Earl Manning, banking on his arrogance about the knowledge that he could not be stopped with the weapon to prevent him from simply snatching the gun out of her hand. He was certainly strong enough to do exactly that if he thought of it quickly enough.

His horrifying grin began to falter and his eyes narrowed as Sharon twisted slightly to the left. She forced herself back in the passenger seat to get a better angle, sinking into a position that was a crude parody of an invitation, legs spread, pants around her ankles. She curled her finger around the trigger and locked her elbows, taking careful aim on her target. She would get only one chance.

Suddenly her plan seemed to dawn on Manning. Sharon squeezed the trigger just as her captor unleashed a bellow of fear, whipping his dead hand toward the weapon. The Glock roared, the sound incredibly loud inside the closed cabin of the cruiser, and fire belched from the end of the barrel just as the back of Manning's hand impacted the gun, knocking it from her grasp and sending it tumbling to the floor, exactly as she had feared.

But he was too late. The wooden box tucked safely into the corner of the dashboard exploded, and so did the windshield, and so did Earl Manning's heart. The box disintegrated into a thousand wooden matchsticks and the heart flopped onto the dashboard, torn apart by the 9 mm slug, as shards of safety glass pelted it, falling like glittering raindrops.

Sharon's ears were ringing and she could just barely make out the sound of Brett Parker screaming behind her and the sound of Earl Manning screaming next to her, muffled and far away, as if someone had stuffed several pounds of cotton batting into her ear canals.

She ignored the screaming and sat up, focusing on Manning's shattered heart, lying on the dashboard of the cruiser like some kind of hideous Halloween display. It beat once, struggled to beat again, and then managed a third. And then it simply stopped beating and lay still.

Sharon swiveled her head, turning her hopeful gaze at Manning. Her heart sank. He was still looming over her. He stared at the unmoving muscle on the dashboard, eyes wide and fearful, but still alive.

Or undead.

Or whatever the hell he was.

Her plan hadn't worked. Mike had said whoever controlled the box containing the heart controlled Manning, so she figured it stood to reason that if she could destroy the heart she would destroy whatever bizarre curse had been placed on Manning allowing him to maintain this strange state, halfway between living and dead.

It made perfect sense. It should have worked.

But it hadn't worked. And Manning seemed to reach the same conclusion as she did, and at exactly the same time. He nodded in satisfaction and turned to look at her, and the grin which had disappeared at this unexpected development returned with a vengeance, leering and horrible.

"Nice try, sweetheart, I wasn't expecting that," he said, or at least Sharon assumed that's what he said, since the ringing in her ears hadn't even begun to diminish. "Now, where were we, do you remember?"

He pulled his legs into the foot well and lifted himself up onto his knees and faced Sharon's prone body, reaching for her breasts with both hands and she knew she was about to die. She hoped it would be quick and wondered how much pain would be involved and thought about Mike, about the hurt in his eyes when she had broken it off with him and about how humiliating it would be when her body was discovered with her pants down around her ankles.

She squeezed her eyes shut, waiting for the end, wishing she could grab the Glock and put a bullet in her brain and cheat Manning out of his fun.

And she waited.

And nothing happened.

She opened her eyes to see Manning's body disintegrating soundlessly in front of her, just inches from her face. His skin, which had been grey and paper-thin already, began to shrivel, stretching over his bones like it was being shrink-wrapped right before her eyes. His mouth opened and closed like a fish out of water and no sound came out, but his teeth *did* come out, a few more blackened stumps falling out of his mouth each time he opened it.

The shrinking skin pulled his lips back over his now-toothless gums, revealing a hideous grimace, and his thinning hair began dropping out of his head in great clumps. Soon his skeletal bones began breaking through his skin, his forehead splitting down the middle and his skull taking its place. His eyelids disappeared and a milky caul covered his lifeless eyes in an instant and he swayed above Sharon as she watched, horrified.

Then he dropped, falling on top of her one last time.

And she screamed, her voice joining Brett Parker's in a chorus of horror and disbelief.

43

Mike stomped on the accelerator, the cruiser's engine wailing as he rocketed out Route 24 toward Orono. If Sharon had, in fact, returned to Paskagankee from Mercy Hospital as he believed, there was only one route she would have taken, and this was it. For the hundredth time, he glanced at his cell phone, willing more information out of it, and for the hundredth time he was disappointed as it sat, noiseless, in his hand.

He had no sooner backed out of the driveway at the Max Acton murder scene than Sharon's cell had gone dead. Either Manning had discovered that it was still on and had switched it off, or the battery had picked the worst possible time to quit, or maybe someone or something had fallen on the damned thing and broken it. What had happened didn't really matter. The frustrating fact was Mike now had no connection to Sharon and she was obviously in big trouble.

"Dammit," he muttered and forced the accelerator a little closer to the floor. The road between Paskagankee and Orono was a single winding, twisting lane in each direction that had been built eighty years ago during the Great Depression by the Army Corps of Engineers, and at the time of its construction had been more than sufficient to handle the slower speeds of 1930's vehicles and the minimal traffic between the two communities.

But now, the county highway was a death trap in waiting for those foolish enough to drive it at the higher speeds of which modern vehicles were capable. Practically every year saw at least one serious car accident along this road, often involving area teens, often sending them to the hospital, occasionally sending them to the morgue.

So, despite his stint of barely more than one year as chief of the Paskagankee Police Department, Mike was intimately familiar with the dangers of Route 24, known to locals also as Mountain Home Road. He knew he was pushing his luck by increasing his speed. He just couldn't help himself. Sharon was in trouble and she needed him and he was damned if he was going to allow the shitty driving conditions on this eighty year old glorified cow path to slow him down.

A voice in his head whispered that she was already dead and he tried to ignore it. *Manning was about to attack her at least fifteen minutes ago. She's dead,* the voice insisted.

He refused to heed the voice, so it changed tactics. *And even if by some miracle she's still alive, he's unstoppable, remember? What can you possibly do to save her?* And he ignored that, too.

The awful fact was that there was *nothing* he could do, but he refused to abandon Sharon when she needed him most. She had tossed him aside—why wouldn't she, really? She was young and beautiful and had a bright future ahead of her, and he was old and guilt-ridden, with a mediocre past and a murky future—but he still loved her. He knew he would always love her.

And he would not let her down, even if that meant he would die, too. *Especially* if that meant he would die, too.

The trees flashed by, so many trees, it sometimes seemed trees were all that existed in this remote area, and then out of the corner of his eyes as the cruiser flew past, he glimpsed a splash of color and movement. It was off to the right along one of the fire roads that dotted the area, which weren't really roads at all, but rather narrow firefighting passageways hacked into the forest. He saw the flash for a split-second and then it was gone.

Mike slammed on the brakes. Black smoke rose up out of the cruiser's rear wheel wells as the vehicle fishtailed down the ancient pavement, Mike funneling all his concentration into keeping the damned car on the road. It finally ground to a stop and Mike jammed the transmission into reverse and dropped his foot onto the accelerator and then he was moving again, backing toward the fire road, traveling more slowly than he had been, but not by much.

When he reached the spot where he believed he had glimpsed the flash of movement, Mike hit the brakes again. The cruiser shuddered to a stop and he looked down the trail and there she was. Sharon was filthy and bedraggled, trudging through the forest with her head down, moving like a person in her seventies rather than her twenties, but it was definitely her and she was alive!

Walking next to her was Brett Parker, who looked equally filthy and just as bedraggled, but who was quite clearly alive as well. The pair hadn't noticed the cruiser yet, they were still a good sixty feet from the road—Mike had no idea how he had even seen them—and his first thought was, *where's Manning?* Just a few minutes ago the revenant had been taunting Mike, clearly in control of the situation. Now he was nowhere to be seen. Could this be some kind of a trap?

But Manning would have no way of knowing Mike would show up here, and given his rapidly deteriorating mental state, probably wouldn't care, anyway. Whatever was going on, it seemed obvious Earl Manning was not a part of it. Mike gave a short blast on his siren to let Sharon and Parker know he was here, then opened the door and stepped out to meet them.

At the sound of the siren, Sharon shoved Parker to the ground next to her and stepped in front of him, dropping to one knee and adopting a two-handed shooter's stance. Mike ducked instinctively behind the cruiser and shouted, "Whoa, it's me, Chief McMahon! Hold your fire!"

Silence reigned and after a couple of tense seconds, Mike lifted his head over the hood of the car. Sharon remained in a crouch, but she had lifted the gun over her head, its barrel pointed toward the sky. Even from this distance, Mike could see her hands shaking. He stood and walked slowly around the front of the vehicle, holstering his weapon. "It's just me," he called. "Are you alright?"

Sharon and Parker nodded at the same time, although neither spoke. She rose and bent in a crouch, hands on her knees, still holding her gun, as Parker stood and brushed off his pants. Given the state of his clothing, it seemed like wasted effort.

Mike moved forward, still cautious and confused, still concerned about a possible trap. "Where's Manning?" he asked.

Sharon lifted her head to look at Mike and her face looked lined and haggard, like she had aged fifteen years since he had last seen her and not slept a wink in any of that time.

"Earl's gone," she said.

44

The cruiser bounced along the fire lane, occasionally threatening to bottom out on the rough terrain, until finally Sharon's vehicle came into view. Mike was amazed at how deep into the forest Manning had managed to drive it without smashing into a tree and killing his passengers.

Parker was stretched out in the back seat of the police car with his eyes closed. He claimed he was fine, that he didn't need medical attention, but his complexion was chalk-white and Mike was more than a little concerned about the possibility of the billionaire suffering a heart attack or a stroke. He had called for an ambulance and for backup before entering the woods—both of which were now on the way—but didn't dare leave Parker and Sharon alone on the side of the road and knew he couldn't afford to wait for the arrival of backup before ensuring that Earl

Manning, the supposedly unstoppable monster, had somehow actually been stopped.

"Where is he?" Mike said softly.

"Front seat," Sharon answered. Her hands seemed to have mostly stopped shaking and her color, which had been nearly as white as Parker's just a few minutes ago, was slowly returning.

"And he's dead?" Mike was dubious. Don Running Bear's widow had been adamant that there was no way to stop him once he had gained control of the sacred stone.

"He was *already* dead, remember? What I said was that he's gone."

Mike stared at Sharon quizzically; still so relieved to have found her alive and more or less unharmed that he was having trouble concentrating on the matter at hand. Finally he shrugged and opened the car door to step outside and investigate. He didn't understand, but he and Sharon had been through so much together over the past year, he trusted her implicitly. If she said Manning was gone, then Manning was gone. "Stay here with Mr. Parker and I'll be right back."

"The hell I will," Sharon snapped and opened her door as well. "Parker will be fine. I'm coming with you."

Mike leaned back into the car and peeked into the back seat. "You'll be all right?"

Parker nodded and waved his hand as if shooing them away.

"Okay," Mike said. "This should only take a couple of minutes, anyway, and then we'll get back out to the road and wait for the EMT's." He turned away and began walking toward Sharon's cruiser, wedged into the Paskagankee forest with both doors on the left side of the vehicle hanging open.

Sharon fell into step beside him and he said, "I'll send a full investigative team out in a little bit, although it will probably have to be after the State guys arrive. But before I do anything else I need to see this for myself." He stopped and looked straight into her laser-blue eyes. They were beautiful as ever. "How did you stop him?"

She took a deep, shuddering breath. She seemed to be recovering, but whatever had gone down out here in this secluded section of the great north woods forest was still weighing heavily on her. "I think it will be easier to explain after you've looked inside the car."

"Fair enough," Mike answered, and leaned into the cruiser, grabbing the roof over the door for support. What he saw took his breath away. A pile of loosely connected bones lay in the foot well of the cruiser's passenger side, covered with the filthy, tattered remnants of what had once been Earl Manning's clothing. Mike recognized the clothes from his altercation with Manning earlier in the day. They looked as though they had been dragged through a sewer—smelled like it, too.

A grinning skull lay on the bench seat, facing him. Its teeth were gone, scattered around the floor of the cruiser. The sagging skin which had covered Manning's face— another feature Mike recalled from his fight with the revenant—was nowhere to be seen. The skull looked as though the person it belonged to had been dead for weeks, not minutes.

Mike stood and looked over the roof at Sharon, who had moved to the other side of the vehicle. "This makes an explanation *easier*?"

"I don't know if there *is* any logical explanation,"

Sharon said. "All I can tell you is what happened, although everything went down so fast, it's kind of a blur."

"Give it a try."

"Okay. You know about the history I had with Earl when I was a teenager, right?"

"You told me, yes."

"Well, apparently he was anxious to relive the not-so-good old days, because after he drove into the woods, he hauled my ass into the front seat and tried to rape me."

"*What?* The guy was a walking corpse, an undead shell of a human being, and he was worried about having sex?"

"I always heard that's all you guys ever think about. I guess it's the case even after death." Sharon flashed a crooked grin and Mike could see how hard she was trying to keep herself together, and his admiration for her increased. He wouldn't have thought it possible. "Or maybe somewhere deep down he realized he was never going to get out of the mess he was in, with or without Brett Parker, so he figured he might as well enjoy one last roll in the hay, I don't know."

Mike stared at her, horrified, and she continued. "Anyway, after he threw me onto the front seat and fell on top of me, I looked up and spotted the wooden box containing his heart and the sacred Navajo stone. He had placed it on the dashboard, for safekeeping I guess. I shoved him hard and grabbed for my gun, which he had jammed into the waistband of his jeans after taking it away from me. I knew I couldn't stop him by shooting *him,* but I figured maybe if I blasted his heart I could somehow break the mystical connection that was keeping him alive. Or dead. Or whatever he was."

"What made you think that would work?"

"I had no idea whether it would work or not, but I knew shooting *him* wouldn't accomplish anything, except to piss him off even more than he already was. I guess at that point I figured I had nothing to lose. I took the shot and got lucky."

Mike leaned down and looked back into the cruiser. On the dashboard, covered by a blizzard of automobile safety glass, was a shriveled grey lump of muscle tissue that he knew immediately was Earl Manning's heart. The lump had been torn almost in half by Sharon's 9mm slug. He blew out a breath and felt suddenly very cold.

"The stone's on the floor under the brake pedal," Sharon said. "I assume you'll want to bag it as evidence, but *I'm* not going to touch it. It's powerful and it's dangerous and I'll be happy if I never see it again. It's cursed. Literally."

Mike fell to his knees and rummaged around on the floor until locating the stone. He kept his eyes on Manning's remains, just a few feet away, not entirely convinced the revenant couldn't somehow come back to life. But the pile of bones remained motionless and dead.

Mike hefted the stone and stood, examining it closely. It was greyish and smooth and perfectly round. He had half-expected to feel some kind of power emanating from it, but it felt no different than any other rock, just an inanimate lump. But he knew looks could be deceiving.

Sharon backed away instinctively, despite the fact she was on the other side of the vehicle. "Keep that thing away from me," she said, her voice thin and shrill.

"This is evidence," Mike said, "and beyond that, it's Navajo property and should be returned to its rightful owners, eventually. It's too bad it was destroyed when you fired into the box."

"What are you talking about?"

He tossed the stone onto the ground without speaking. It landed to the left of the cruiser and rolled to a stop on the forest floor a few feet away. Mike drew his weapon and took careful aim, moving deliberately, determined not to miss. He fired a single shot and the stone disintegrated, pebble-sized chunks flying in all directions, dust rising into the air.

"Like I said," he told Sharon, who was staring at him with a look of disbelief on her pretty features. "It's too bad the stone was destroyed. Now, let's get back out to the road. The ambulance will be along any second and we need to get Parker to the hospital. You should be checked out too, and I want to cordon off this area until we can begin the official investigation."

Sharon shook her head and Mike knew exactly what she was going to say before she opened her mouth. "I'm not going to the hospital. I'm fine. I'll stay here and help you."

"You know the procedure," he answered. "You were physically attacked and then involved in a shooting, and—"

Sharon glared at him, her blue eyes flashing. "I said I'm fine."

"I'm sorry, Officer Dupont, but you know the rules. You need to be examined by a doctor. It's important, and I'm not going to bend on that. You're going."

She kicked at the dirt and turned toward Mike's cruiser, muttering under her breath. "Oh, and one more thing, before I forget," Mike said. "I'll need to relieve you of your weapon pending an official review of the circumstances of the shooting. You'll be assigned to desk duty until the review is complete."

Without a word, Sharon retraced her steps, unsnapped her holster, and handed Mike her Glock, her lips compressed into a thin white line, fury evident on her face. Then she stomped back to his cruiser, arms folded, and slumped into the front passenger seat. She stared straight out the windshield, refusing to meet his gaze as he slid into the seat next to her.

45

The Katahdin Diner was typically busy this time of the morning, and today was no exception. Waitresses scurried from the kitchen to the dining room and back again, slinging food, coffee and barbs with the customers in equal measure. Mike sipped his coffee and watched as Sharon entered the restaurant, scoping out the dining room, searching for him. It was a rare day off for both of them; the entire department had been working practically around the clock wrapping up the dual investigations of Max Acton's murder and Officer Dupont's shooting of Earl Manning.

Sharon finally spotted him in the corner and weaved her way through the crowded diner to his table. She was dressed down in faded jeans and a University of Maine Black Bears sweatshirt, but Mike decided if she was trying to blend in with the rural crowd she was doing a damned lousy job of it. *She could wear a potato sack and look gorgeous,* he thought. Her short pixie hairstyle framed her pretty face as sat, nodding hello, working hard to keep her face neutral.

He had taken the liberty of ordering breakfast for her—a toasted bagel with cream cheese and coffee—and waited for her to complain about his presumption. To his surprise she said nothing, instead sitting and taking a sip of coffee before biting delicately into the bagel.

Mike could see curiosity was killing her. They were no longer dating and she had been placed on desk duty, so there was no reason for him to have called. He was amused and wanted to drag out the suspense just a bit longer. So he brought up the weather—it was unseasonably cool, even for northern Maine. Then they discussed the fortunes of the Red Sox, currently suffering through a horrific mid-season slump.

Finally she could stand it no longer. "So," she began, and waved her bagel in a circular motion at him.

He shook his head. "So . . . ?"

"So, I know you didn't call me here just to talk baseball, boss. What are we doing here? It's our day off, remember?"

"Ah, our day off. Well, I thought you might appreciate me getting you up to speed on things."

"Up to speed? What do I need to get up to speed on? I'm a desk jockey, remember? Do we need to order more toner for the copier?"

He tried, unsuccessfully, to keep from smiling. "Your statement's not entirely accurate. You *were* a desk jockey. My investigation's complete and as of now you are officially reinstated to active duty. Welcome back." Mike picked Sharon's weapon up off the diner's vinyl seat next to him and slid it across the table. "I'd have a little ceremony, but I don't want to freak out any of these happy diners by waving a gun around in the air."

Sharon stared at her weapon for a moment before picking it up with a smile of her own and placing it on *her* seat. "I almost wish I was wearing my uniform so I could put this baby on my hip where it belongs. But what gives? It's only been a few days. When you said 'investigation,' I pictured a weeks-long process."

"Ah, that." Mike waved his hand like he was shooing away a mosquito. "That was just for show. My main goal was to get you to a doctor, make sure you were telling the truth about being okay. Fighting with a dead guy is kind of uncharted territory, you know, in case you weren't aware of it."

"Oh, I'm aware of it, all right. It's not something I'm likely to forget any time soon."

"That's what I figured. The investigation into the shooting was going to be a formality right from the get-go. There was a witness to the whole thing, after all. Besides, how the hell do I write up the circumstances of *that* confrontation? No one outside of you, me and Brett Parker — who's already out of the hospital and going to be fine, by the way — would believe it if I told the truth."

"Good point. But won't that also be the case with the ME's report? What is Dr. Affeldt going to have to say about the fully decomposed skeleton of Earl Manning lying in a pile in the front seat of my cruiser — the skeleton of a dead man with none of my bullets lodged in him?"

Mike sipped his coffee and smiled. "You know, after

the incident last fall with Professor Dye and Chief Court, I think our friendly neighborhood medical examiner has decided to follow the path of least resistance. The poor old guy has now been confronted with medical impossibilities twice in less than a year, and I don't think he has the energy to do much more than rubber-stamp an autopsy report. His findings won't be available for some time yet, but I'm betting when they're published, Mr. Manning will have died from a single gunshot wound following an attack on Officer Sharon Dupont in the front seat of her police cruiser."

"You won't be able to fool Manheim the Maneater, though. That reporter's going to smell the supernatural connection from a mile away."

"She already has. She called me last night requesting an interview. 'Work with me and we'll get out the real story,' she said."

Sharon laughed at Mike's falsetto imitation of the reporter's voice. "What are you going to do?"

"Ignore her, what else can I do? She's already going to make a fortune off one tell-all Paskagankee book, I'll be damned if I'm going to give her the chance to write another."

"Think she'll give up that easily?"

Mike shrugged. "I hope so, but I doubt it. In any case, the crew from Hollywood is due next week to begin filming location stuff for the movie based on her book about last fall's murder spree, so I'm hoping she'll be too busy hob-nobbing with the glitterati to worry about badgering me."

"She'll never leave you alone," Sharon muttered.

"What do you mean?"

"Come on, I've seen the way she looks at you. She'd like nothing better than to sink her man-eating teeth into you."

"Is that right? Well, as much fun as that sounds, I'm hoping she'll soon get the message that this broken-down old cop is off the market."

"And how are you going to convince her of that?"

Mike ignored the question, instead glancing down at the floor next to his chair. "Would you look at that. I dropped my napkin." He eased down to one knee.

Sharon looked down. "I don't—"

Out of his pocket Mike pulled a gold band, topped by a glittering diamond.

"—see any—" Sharon froze, her confusion evident.

"I know I'm not any great prize," he said. "Most of my future is behind me and you've barely scratched the surface of yours. And I swore after Kate left me that I'd never get married again. But that was before I met you. And now I can't imagine living a fuller life than one with you as its centerpiece, or an emptier life than one without you. I love you, Sharon, and I need you, and I always will. Would you do me the great honor of becoming my wife?"

The tears spilled down her cheeks and Mike sensed diners all over the restaurant turning in their seats to watch the drama unfold. The clatter of silverware on porcelain and coffee mugs on Formica came to an abrupt halt and the buzz of conversation died away.

Sharon nodded. "Yes," she whispered after an eternity, and the diner erupted in applause as Mike slid the ring onto her finger, then pulled her to her feet and engulfed her in a bear hug.

He wiped her tears away and took a deep breath,

blowing out forcefully. "I don't think I've ever been so nervous," he said. "Fighting a murderous dead guy was nothing compared to that."

They settled back into their seats as the applause died away. He noticed a strange look on Sharon's face. "What's bothering you? Second thoughts already?"

"Never. But what about our jobs? The whole reason we had to stop seeing each other is that you're my supervisor. The Town Council will really freak if we get married. They'll never allow it; you'll lose your job for sure."

"I've already considered that. It's a non-issue."

"What do you mean?"

"I mean my last official act as Chief of the Paskagankee, Maine Police Department was to reinstate you to active status. I've already submitted my resignation to the council, effective noon today." He looked at his watch. "Or in about ten minutes, according to Timex."

Sharon stared, her mouth agape. "What if I had said no?"

"Then I suppose I would have been heartbroken as well as unemployed."

"But . . . who's going be chief?"

"That's up to the Town Council, but I've recommended Pete Kendall. The guy's an outstanding cop for such a young officer—he's a lot like you in that sense—and he'll make a wonderful chief if he gets the chance. But that's out of my hands."

"And what are you going to do for work?"

"I don't know. I figure I'll watch TV all day in my underwear and live off the hard work of my wife." Sharon kicked his shin under the table and he grinned. "Okay,

okay, I'll get off my lazy ass and seek gainful employment. There must be a security firm in the area that could use a moderately successful ex-cop on their roster."

"Moderately successful? I don't think you're giving yourself enough credit. But good luck finding a security firm way out here in the middle of nowhere."

"Yeah, well, we'll figure something out. That's an issue for another day. I came to the conclusion pretty quickly that you're a hell of a lot more important to me than any job, especially one where people sometimes shoot at me or lock me in freezers and leave me there to die. But right now, I think we need to celebrate."

"Agreed. What did you have in mind?"

"Why don't we go back to your place? I'm sure we can think of something."

Sharon smiled. "But it's barely past breakfast."

"Even better. That gives us all day."

REVENANT is the second entry in Allan Leverone's series of supernatural suspense novels set in the isolated little town of Paskagankee, Maine. The first in the series is titled PASKAGANKEE, and is available in ebook format.

About the author

Allan Leverone is a 2012 Derringer Award winner for excellence in short mystery fiction and a 2011 Pushcart Prize nominee. He is the author of the Amazon bestselling thriller, THE LONELY MILE As well as the thrillers, FINAL VECTOR and PASKAGANKEE. He has authored three horror novellas: DARKNESS FALLS, HEARTLESS and THE BECOMING. Allan lives in Londonderry, NH with his wife, three children, one beautiful granddaughter and a cat who has used up eight lives. Connect with Allan on Facebook, Twitter, @AllanLeverone and at AllanLeverone.com.